PULLED TO YOU

MIRANDA VALENTINE

To anyone who has ever struggled to find healthy ways to cope with their anxiety.

And to those who have encouraged and loved me through my own struggles.

While the overall tone of this book is lighthearted, *Pulled to You* contains discussions of anxiety, OCD, body-focused repetitive disorders, loss of a parent, and grief. It's an adult book, with adult language, conversations, and situations.

Take care of yourselves.

Love,
Miranda

ADA'S PRIVATE ANXIETY THOUGHTS

(SERIOUSLY...NO ONE WILL EVER SEE THESE.)

May 15, 2019

I've been thinking a lot about the first time I pulled. (Just a warning–I have a lot on my mind tonight, blog. And I'm also sadder than usual, so sorry, you're going to have to deal with it.)

Dad had been gone for two weeks when *it* happened. Do you ever have one of those moments where you just don't feel...human? Well, I do. It happens less now, but during those first couple of months without him, feeling empty was my normal state. I was basically a living, breathing lump. I couldn't eat, I couldn't sleep, and I could only feel one emotion. (Hint: it wasn't happiness.)

When *it* happened, I had been sitting in my bed staring at the wall, per usual. It was all I had the energy to do. And it's not like Mom or Amry tried to pull (ha, look, a pun) me out of it. They were fellow sad lumps. I missed him so much. *We* missed him so much. Before then, I didn't know pain like that could exist.

It all started with the simple act of combing my fingers

through my hair. The first time I was just trying to get my bangs out of my eyes. The second time it felt good– like that little massage they give you when you get your hair washed before having it cut. So I kept doing it. It was relaxing, and I didn't want to stop.

One detail I don't remember is exactly how this action led to pulling that first strand out of my scalp. All I can recall is what I felt when it came free. It was like a small shock—uncomfortable, but not painful. This may sound weird, but for some reason it brought what I can only describe as a sense of relief. That small bit of relief is why I did what I did next.

I went back for more.

I grabbed another strand between my fingers and pulled, then quickly studied the root before I dropped it onto the floor. Then I pulled another. And another. And another.

Long story short, I haven't stopped pulling since. Even as the pain of losing Dad became less and less heavy. Even as I went back to school and other things that were supposed to be "normal." Even as my life moved on, I pulled. Even as Amry and Mom found out. Even as I went from doctor, to therapist, to medication, I pulled. Even as my hair became thinner and thinner. Even as my friends began to notice, I pulled.

If someone were reading this right now (and they're not, see: the title of this blog), they'd probably have a lot of questions for me. Maybe they would feel sorry for me, or just wonder what's wrong with me. If someone were reading this right now, I'd tell them that I'm working on it. I don't know if I will ever get better. I don't know if this lingering anxiety will ever leave me alone, but I'm going to move forward with the hope that it will.

And if it doesn't, I hope I'll still be okay. Maybe it's

something I just have to accept and learn to live with. That idea sounds like a step in the right direction, but the problem is, I don't know how to do that. I don't know how to convince myself that it's *okay* to do that.

Side note: this blog is helping me work through some things, but please don't tell Amry I said that. She doesn't always need to know when she's right.

CHAPTER 1

I just love sugar.

Put that on my headstone when I die one day. *Here lies Amry Phillips–she really messed with a good molten lava cake.*

Well, any dessert really. The aforementioned just happens to be what I'm lucky enough to behold as the server plops the plate onto the white tablecloth in front of me. Chocolate oozes out around the lit candle that is standing in the middle of it. I'm about to stick my finger into the dollop of whipped cream when Matt pulls the plate away from me and situates it in the middle of the table between us. He grins and digs a fork into it and offers me the bite. There's no whipped cream on it but I accept it anyway.

"Happy Anniversary, Am," he says before carefully choosing his own bite. I narrow my eyes at him when he takes half of the whipped cream for himself. If I wasn't the perfect level of tipsy at the moment, I might chastise him for it. Instead, I tip what is left of my red wine into my mouth and go in with my own fork.

"Somehow I both can and can't believe that we've been together for ten years," I tell him as the server shows up to refill my glass. Matt holds his own glass out for more. I can see that he's also pleasantly tipsy just by looking into his face, and it's not because his eyes are bloodshot or glazed over.

It's because he's tinged pink and smiling dopily. As much as I love him, Matt is one of the most uptight people I've ever known. His features are usually arranged in such an obvious expression of seriousness that I'm fairly certain he'll never develop a single wrinkle thanks to his lack of emotion. I told him that once, and he asked why it was a bad thing.

"There's no one else I would rather be with," he replies, uncharacteristically winking in my direction through a pale eyelash.

Equally out of character, he's also been constantly touching me all evening—crossing the space between us to rub my arm or slide his foot up and down my leg beneath the booth. For any other couple this would be totally normal. For Matt and I, PDA, or touching each other at all really, occurs more and more sporadically, so there are no complaints from me. I wouldn't say I'm *starved* for affection, but I *am* gobbling it up faster than the cake in front of me.

Will this be the night he finally asks me to move in with him?

I gulp my wine faster and smile at him over the rim of the glass. He grins back and suddenly the situation feels eerily similar to our first date, which consisted of flirting across the table at our local Texas Roadhouse and eating at lightning speed because we both secretly wanted to fast forward to the inevitable makeout session in his 1998 Chevy Lumina.

Except now we're at a restaurant that is at least three

times more expensive than Texas Roadhouse (Though, dare I say the free bread didn't even compare?), and we're hopefully gearing up for sex in the luxury apartment that he pays way too much for. It's certainly an upgrade though —the Lumina always smelled like old cheddar for some reason.

Our server brings the check and Matt rudely slaps his AmEx into her palm without peeking at the total. She looks taken aback and I overcompensate for his rudeness by thanking her profusely and raving about the meal. She scuttles away, most likely in a hurry to get us out of the restaurant before we can ask for more wine.

I would like to say we simply look like a young couple out having a good time. The truth is, Matt is probably drinking too much for the same reason I am. We both want a buffer for the progressing awkwardness in our relationship. I need the liquid courage to feel out where he is on the timeline of living together, and getting engaged. He needs the liquid courage to keep avoiding the subject.

Somehow though, it seems the liquid courage has decided to manifest in the form of liquid lust instead.

Matt slides out of the booth, standing and holding a hand out to me. "Ready to get out of here?"

"Yes, please." I look up into his face, working overtime to give him my best *take me home and ravish me* eyes.

The Uber meets us at the corner. Matt opens the door for me and I climb in first and exchange a quick hello with the driver. Matt scoots in after me, choosing to sit in the middle so our bodies are pressed together. He places a hand on my thigh. I can feel the warmth of his palm through my silk skirt.

"I like this a lot." He runs a finger over the hem of the skirt then slowly slides his hand beneath it to knead at the bare skin. I cast a nervous glance at our driver before letting myself relax and enjoy the feeling of being desired —the *relief* of knowing that he still desires me. More often than not lately, I haven't been so sure.

"Thanks. You look nice too." I lean my head into his shoulder and reach up to straighten his shirt collar.

"It's nice to see you dressed up for once."

It's a backhanded compliment if I've ever heard one. My mood plummets along with the words as they fall out of his mouth. Self-consciousness punches a hole through my trusty wine haze. I pull my head off his shoulder and push his hand off of me, then turn to gaze out of the window.

"Oh come on, Am. You know I didn't mean it like that."

"Then how exactly did you mean it?" My focus remains glued to the surrounding Orlando traffic.

"It's just nice to see you put some effort in. That hasn't happened much since your dad…"

"DON'T, Matt." I clench my fist around my purse strap and succumb to my transition into wine-drunk sadness. We sit in silence for several minutes.

He eventually tries to change the subject. "Have you had any luck getting that Google review removed?"

"Nope," I reply shortly. I *definitely* don't want to talk about that right now either.

The Uber stops in front of his apartment building and we clamber out onto the sidewalk. I stand with my arms crossed and consider going home. He had to bring Dad up. Not only that, he managed to use my grief to insult me. And I can't even say it's the first time he's made me feel bad about my appearance over the past two years.

Yet, I still love him. I keep reminding myself that every relationship goes through phases. This phase in particular just royally sucks. Eventually we'll be back to normal ol' Matt and Amry. *Mamry*, as Casey tried so hard to coin us back in high school. I fought hard to prevent that from catching on–it just sounds too much like "mammary."

Matt places a hand on my elbow and guides me toward the entrance. "I'm sorry, Am. I shouldn't have said that. Please, let's go up. I don't want to end the night here."

Remaining committed to the silent treatment, I let him coerce me through the door and into the empty waiting elevator. I slump into the wall and wait for the doors to close. Once they do, he moves to stand in front of me, placing his hands on either side of me. I have no choice but to look him in his blue eyes.

"Please forgive me." He kisses me on the forehead. "You really do look beautiful."

The warmth of his body seeps into mine, instantly recharging my desire. That was almost too easy for him, and it's not fair. How's a girl supposed to resist?

His hand moves down to my waist and slides around to my backside. I relax beneath him and he presses his mouth to mine, hungrily parting my lips with his tongue. Then it's just '98 Chevy Lumina levels of making out and roaming hands as we continue up to his floor.

I mentally waggle a finger at myself. *Now Amry, you know how Matt can be. Grow up and take it with a grain of salt.*

The elevator doors open with a sharp ping, startling us both. Matt peels himself away from me and grabs my hand to yank me into the hallway behind him. We drunkenly stumble in the direction of his apartment door, narrowly avoiding death by face plant and giggling like teenagers. This dynamic is such a breath of fresh air. I could jump for joy.

We're fine. We're totally fine! I allow myself to do a little celebratory spin as Matt struggles to unlock the door. He gives me a funny look and I lean in to help him slide the key into the lock. Then we're back at it.

My shirt is somehow off before the door closes behind us. He tosses it somewhere behind me before removing his own, then his lips are back on mine before they move down to my neck, to my collarbone, to my…

When did my bra come off?

He turns me around and guides me toward the bedroom with his hands on my shoulders. His apartment is as sterile as ever—full of basic yet expensive furniture and sparkling with cleanliness, thanks to the maid he insisted on hiring, which I think he did strictly because he can afford it. He pulls the clip from my hair as we maneuver around his Pottery Barn sofa. The sudden swish of hair on my shoulders sends a shiver through my body.

"I've always loved your hair." Matt buries his face in my mass of waves and breathes deeply. My own breath catches in my throat. I can't remember the last time I felt chemistry like this between us. Does he feel the same way? Sometimes I miss him when we're in the same room. Does he understand that too?

Again, *phases*, Amry. *We'll make it through this phase.*

I swat the unwelcome negativity away and turn back to face him as we reach the bed. He pushes my skirt down, struggling to get it over my hips. I return the favor by undoing his belt and assisting his jeans down his thighs, taking a second to appreciate the familiarity of his body.

"It's been too long, Amry." His voice is throaty. He cradles my face and pulls it to his. I take a moment to search his features, smiling at the freckles that are a long-time weakness of mine. A lock of strawberry blond hair is stuck to his forehead and I feather it back.

Then tears are blurring my vision. I look down so he

doesn't notice. *Get it together, this is a good night! Only good thoughts are allowed from here.*

In fact, let's view this as a whole new beginning; a refresh of a high school romance that is far too solidified to just give up on. We're basically a Lifetime movie storyline. (Not one of the creepy stalker ones, though.) Who cares if this is the first time in ages we've had spontaneous, passionate sex? Let alone, sex at all for three months? We've been together since we were sophomores in high school. Things change. We're not supposed to be hopping around like feral rabbits. *Right?*

My sloshy brain resumes control and I turn Matt so his back is to the perfectly made bed. I plant my hands on his chest and shove him backwards onto the crisp, white comforter. He laughs and props up on his elbows as I crawl on top of him, and we're quickly lost in our longing again.

I remove my panties and slide to the side so he can remove his boxers. It's official; I've never been so ready for sex in my life. And one quick glance below his waist tells me that we're on the same page. He grins and reaches out for me.

He pushes me down onto the comforter and I go willingly, letting him take control, ready to submit to the fervent fate that awaits me. Only, the comforter suddenly isn't there. *Nothing* is there. I'm straight up falling—plummeting to the hard floor below. I'm a human anchor, and in less than a second I'm on the cool, wood floor. Every last bit of breath whooshes out of my body, and I want to be angry. But my emotions take a hard turn and I'm laughing instead.

"Oh shit, are you ok?" Matt's head pops over the edge of the bed, followed by his legs as he tries to stand up.

The pain kicks in and my laughter subsides quickly. I make a mental note of the areas that will most likely be bruised come tomorrow. Matt bends down to lend me a hand but I wave it away. "Just give me a second." Groaning, I roll over onto my side and plant a hand to push myself up.

Being naked makes this so much more humiliating.

Dust bunnies under the bed come into focus as my vision readjusts. "You may want to have your maid clean under…"

Something else catches my eye and my train of thought goes out the window.

A blue, lacy something. A blue, lacy something that Matt's girlfriend, AKA: Amry, AKA: I, would never wear. Because lace is just an invitation for nipple irritation. True story.

I suddenly can't hear. Blood is rushing into my ears. Goosebumps are invading my arms and legs. Every hair that I shaved off of my body a mere two hours ago is growing back. My Spidey senses are tingling. My *betrayal* senses are tingling.

"Am, are you sure you're ok?" Matt's voice is distant through the rushing sound. I ignore him, reaching into the abyss to pluck the bra from its likely accidental hiding spot. And yes, it is a bra. For a moment I hoped it would be, I don't know, maybe a blue, lacy tie or something? I can feel my intestines icing over. Pure adrenaline comes from nowhere, flooding my veins.

Pushing up to my knees, I hold the bra out to Matt. A white tag with the size 34B shines in the soft white lighting of his room. I cover my own D-cup chest and pale, ample stomach with my free arm.

"What is this?" My voice shakes. Matt's pupils dilate the second he lays eyes on the thing. And I know that this is it. This is the thing that is about to ruin it all—about to ruin us. He might not be saying anything, but his eyes are giving everything away.

My intestines thaw abruptly and I feel like I'm being stabbed in the stomach with thousands of tiny icicles. I stand all the way up, tossing the bra on the bed and searching for something, anything, to cover myself with. Matt grabs his boxers from the floor and pulls them on over the area that appears to be rapidly softening. His freckles have disappeared into a now beet-red face. My head pounds and my thoughts can't keep up.

He's cheated on me.

But maybe there's another explanation?

He had sex with someone else.

But maybe he didn't?

There's no way. He loves you.

You love him.

No, he's definitely hooking up with another woman.

But—

He's been with another woman.

You love him!

Jumping to conclusions has never been a talent of mine. Even now, when the clues couldn't be more obvious, I can't make a decision about how I should feel. Matt gently grabs my arm, and it's only then that I realize I've been pacing around the bed, changing direction in synchronicity with my internal discourse. We make eye contact and he attempts to pull me into a hug but I freeze in place. He may as well be trying to connect with a statue.

"Let go of me." My throat is becoming more and more constricted.

"Amry, can we plea—"

"Let GO of me!" I yank my arm just as he releases it, which causes me to stumble backwards and trip over my panties.

I snatch them up and wiggle them on, followed by my skirt, which I yank over my chest to keep covered until I can find the rest of my clothes. Matt's now the one pacing, searching for words. For a smart guy, he is really struggling to spit something out.

What is happening? What the fuck?

Matt has been in my life for ten years. Did he really cheat on me? *Could* he really cheat on me? I back out of the bedroom just as the tears begin to roll. I become more and more sober as I gather my remaining clothes. The pounding in my ears is replaced by a high-pitched ringing.

I have to get out of here.

"Can we just talk about this?" Matt's voice breaks the silence. He stumbles around behind me as I rip throw pillows off of the couch to search for my missing purse. Cushions fly in every direction and he has to duck to avoid being hit in the face.

The purse appears and I grab it. Unfortunately for me, the zipper is undone and my things fly out of it and ping-pong across the living room floor. Almost blinded by tears at this point, I drop to the rug and begin to feel around for at least my phone, wallet, and keys. Matt approaches me like he wants to help and I hold a hand up to halt him.

After what seems like an eternity, I've found everything. I catapult to my feet and make a beeline to the door, collecting my shoes from the polished entryway in my hurry. I reach for the doorknob and my hand falls just short of it as I'm pulled backwards.

He's behind me, his arms around my waist. His lips are on my ear. "Please, Amry."

The feeling of him against me now is nauseating. I shake free of his hold, refusing to look over my shoulder and into his panicked face. Refusing to waste any more of my breath to formulate something to say to him. I'm out the door before he can say anything else, already requesting an Uber as I dodge the tenants waiting at the elevator and push into the stairwell.

MATT GERALDS

I really am sorry, Am!

Can you really blame me though?

It's been so hard to connect with you lately.

CHAPTER 2

"LIAR!" I throw my half-eaten bag of Doritos at the TV, mimicking Reese Witherspoon's action with her box of chocolates on the other side of the screen. Chips float through the air and land on my media stand and rug like orange snowflakes.

I've had *Legally Blonde* on repeat for over 24 hours, mainly so I can rewind to the parts where Elle is mourning her breakup with Warner. That way she and I can mourn together. It's also been a fun experiment to see which foods are the most fun to throw across the room. There's still a smear of guacamole in the middle of the screen, which has inspired another new game where I eat an Oreo every time the strip of avocado appears beneath an actor's nose.

The obvious winner of the throwing contest though— marshmallows. They make a nice little *slap slap slap* when they hit the screen.

My phone lights up beside me on the couch. I glare down at it out of the corner of my eye and watch uninterestedly as another text comes in. I'm officially up to 50 missed calls and 118 ignored texts between Sloan, Mom, and Ada. Considering I haven't actually told anyone what happened, I can only assume Matt made contact with the three of them to have some way to check in on me. Face ID unlocks my phone and I'm able to read Sloan's newest message:

SLOAN PINNER

COME ON, AMRY! ANSWER THE PHONE.

I know I'm being a baby, but I can't bring myself to interact with anyone right now. I pick the phone up and attempt a reply to Sloan, then delete it two words in. She immediately sends another message:

SLOAN PINNER

Dammit, Am. You know I can see when you're typing, right?

My mind wanders back to the TV, where Elle is now being annoyingly optimistic. It makes me lose interest. I find the remote on the floor beside a stray Dorito and use it to switch the TV off. Silence floods my apartment and I begin to think of all the reasons I should get up and get my life together. Unfortunately, none of them are good enough. Not even work, or, related to work, that *godforsaken* Google review.

So I go in for another Oreo instead.

I've just twisted the cookie in half when there are three loud beats on my door. My heart jumps into my throat and I drop the cream-covered side of the Oreo into my lap. I pick it up and slide it into my mouth anyway, chewing as quietly as possible.

If I don't make any noise, maybe whoever it is will go away.

The pounding starts again. Sitting up, I turn to look at the door over my shoulder and try to muster up courage to go look through the peephole. The hinges look like they're barely holding up. Should I call maintenance for that? More pertinent to the present, should I call 911?

"AMRY, I KNOW YOU'RE IN THERE!" Sloan's voice wafts clearly through the door. "Open up or I'm using my key!"

Ugh, why did I give her a key? I hurl the remaining half of the Oreo at the door and pry myself out of my depression nest. I refuse to give her the satisfaction of using her key to bust in on me. I slink toward the door.

"You have until the count of three!" Sloan continues knocking. "One, TWO—"

I twist the deadbolt and fling the door open. Sloan is standing on my welcome mat, one hand still raised into a fist, the other fumbling to find her spare key. It's Saturday but she's dressed in black slacks and a white blouse; business casual from head to toe. Which has always kind of been her thing for some reason.

To my surprise, a little of the weight lifts from my chest at the sight of her. I thought I didn't want to see anyone, but a girl can't deny the comfort of having one of her best friends around.

"Finally, I was getting worried!" Her nose crinkles as she looks from me, to the apartment behind me, then back to me. "You look like shit."

"Thanks," I deadpan, stepping aside as she forces her way around me. Heat creeps up my neck. I don't know what I'm more embarrassed about—the state of the apartment or the state of myself.

"Amry, what the actual hell have you been doing in here?" She flits around the living room, picking up food wrappers and empty water bottles only to drop them back to their starting places. "WHY is there so much food on the floor? Is that GUACAMOLE?"

She rushes over to the TV. Doritos crunch beneath her practical mules. I trail behind like a puppy who just got in trouble for pissing on the rug.

"If I knew I was going to have company I would have straightened the place up a little." I shrug at her.

Her mouth remains in a flat line. She drops her keys onto the media stand and moves closer to place her hands on my upper arms. Sloan isn't a very affectionate person so I'm surprised at the gesture, assuming that she's going in for a hug. I relax and prepare to happily collapse against her chest. Instead, she shakes me, which is more on brand. My brain rattles around in my skull.

"I will NOT let you do this to yourself." She reaches up to pluck a crumb from my hair then points behind me. "To the bathroom, now."

"What, why?"

"You're getting a shower and then you're coming out with me."

"But I don't wa–"

"To the bathroom!" She uses her boardroom voice. I jump into gear and truck it. I hate when she goes corporate on me. It's scary.

Sloan starts the shower while I get undressed. I'm still in the same clothes I left Matt's in, so pulling them off is almost a welcome relief. Sloan turns her back while I climb in. My body immediately relaxes beneath the warm water and I almost hate that she knew this would make me feel better. I'm still going to put up a slight fight. "Sloan, I seriously don't feel like going anywhere. Do I have to?"

"We're just going to IKEA and then I'll bring you back. You were supposed to go with me today, remember? You need to get out. You need someone to talk to." Her voice comes from the doorway. "I'll go find you something to wear."

"Something comfortable!" I argue. "And I want ice cream!"

"Deal." I hear her walk into my bedroom. I pull a piece of stuck marshmallow off my arm and reach for the shampoo.

Sloan is in the unique situation of knowing both Matt and I, even though she really only has a friendship with me. She's a sales executive at Matt's software company; we hit it off at his office holiday party a few years ago. And thank god for that, because she's basically the only real friend I've made in Orlando.

She's not like the other close friends I have in my life. I tend to attract bubbly extroverts who pull me out of my shell. While Sloan is an extrovert, she's also a force to be reckoned with. What she wants, she gets. I think I needed someone like her when we met. She supports me, yet challenges me. She boosts my confidence and makes me feel capable. Just like Matt always has.

Or, rather, how he used to.

"How is this?" Sloan returns and I peek around the shower curtain. She holds up a pair of black leggings and a UCF tshirt. I give her a thumbs up and return back to my conditioner.

"I still don't want to go," I grumble through the steam.

"Too bad."

She passes me a clean towel as I step out of the shower and waits in the living room while I get dressed and brush my teeth. I can hear her shoving trash into a plastic bag and cursing under her breath. I skip brushing my hair and throw it up into a wet bun instead.

"Why aren't you begging me for details right now?" I ask, stepping out of the bathroom.

"Oh, that's coming. Just not in this apartment." She tosses the half-full bag of trash onto my coffee table. "No offense, but the sadness is so thick in here I can't breathe."

"You're telling me..."

Sloan retrieves my phone from the couch and passes it to me along with my purse. I slip my Converse on and she makes me exit through the door in front of her. I can feel her eyes on the back of my neck, boring two little holes, just waiting for me to try and make a run for it. She's lucky in this scenario, however, because I only run for very selective reasons, and my current energy levels won't power any of them.

She ushers me through the breezeway and down the stairs to ground level. The sun burns my eyes. I want to return to my lair. Have I always been such a pushover? I couldn't be complying any more willingly if she was holding a gun to my back.

Her blue Mini Cooper sits in the nearest parking spot, holding all the energy of a big white van that I'm about to be shoved into. The only thing preventing my neighbors from calling 911 to report an abduction is the fact that I don't have a bag over my head. Come to think of it, I'm surprised she didn't consider that. Maybe she has one stowed in her back pocket, ready to be used only if I put up a good fight.

Which I won't, because as much as I don't want to be outside, I really do need her. I need the relief of telling someone all the gory details of mine and Matt's failed anniversary evening. I'm not dumb enough to believe it's going to end in anything other than a breakup, and the sooner I say it out loud, the better.

"How much do you know?" I ask as Sloan steers us out of the apartment parking lot.

"Not much." She glances over at me before putting her sunglasses on. "But I sense Matt did something shitty."

"You sense correctly..." And then the whole story pours out of my mouth.

She listens attentively, only chiming in with the occasional gasp or grunt of disapproval. I finish rambling as we come to a red light. Sloan picks up her phone to send a text and places it back in the center console. It chimes with a reply not even ten seconds later, followed by at least five more notifications.

"Sorry, work stuff." She silences the phone and places it in her lap. "I hate that this is happening, Amry. Do you have any idea who the bra belongs to?"

It's not the question I was expecting. I was waiting for something more along the lines of *You know you deserve better than this, right?* However, this is Sloan. And *Direct* is her middle name. *Facts* is her second middle name. The light changes and we move forward.

"I have no idea." I slump back into my seat and a thought hits me. "Do you think it's someone you work with?"

Her grip on the steering wheel tightens and her knuckles turn white. She sits up a little straighter and clears her throat a couple of times. Her mouth falls open and sticks there; nothing comes out. She looks like a stunned owl.

"*Sloan.*" I twist in my seat to stare at her. "What aren't you telling me?"

We're turning into the IKEA lot and she whips into the first available space, slamming the car into park. She twists to face me and removes her sunglasses to look me in the eyes. I can see her visibly relax as her normal composure filters back over her body.

"I've never mentioned this because I honestly didn't think it was an issue," she begins. "You know the coffee counter on the first floor of our office building?"

"Yes." I've noticed it the few times I've visited Matt. If I worked in that stuffy building, the convenience of coffee is the only thing that would get me out of bed in the morning.

"There's a barista that works the mid-day shift–Angie. Word around the office is that her and Matt are quite…flirty."

"That makes no sense." I wrinkle my forehead. "Matt doesn't flirt! And I don't say that because I'm his girlfriend. Well, *I was* his girlfriend. Well, I technically still am. Whatever! Matt doesn't flirt. He's just not capable of it as a person. He's too…boring."

What the heck. Ada has been calling Matt boring for years. I've spent so much time trying to convince her otherwise, sometimes even to the point of tears. And now here I am, realizing that it's actually true. I press my fingers to my temples. I want to scream, but that would probably crack the windows in Sloan's tiny car. Then I would have to add paying for glass replacement to my current list of stresses.

Have I ever really known him?

"Don't shoot the messenger." Sloan raises her hands in surrender. "It's only what I've heard. Should I give Angie a good talking to?"

"No." I take a deep breath and open the car door. I'm in immediate need of fresh air. "If the bra is hers, she probably doesn't even know that Matt has a girlfriend."

"Everyone at work knows about you, Amry." We climb out of the car and meet at the back. "You think too highly of people."

"I'm giving her the benefit of the doubt, ok? This is on him, not her. If it even is her!"

We enter the store with a pack of other shoppers. I wait off to the side while Sloan grabs a cart, attempting to arrange my face into something other than a scowl, which proves to be impossible. *A barista? Matt flirting? That STUPID BLUE BRA. Ten years of my life!*

"Move it." Sloan pulls the cart up beside me and sets off at a quick stride. "I have stuff to buy."

I follow behind, partly relieved to be out and about with my friend, partly thinking about the previously promised ice cream that will come after shopping.

For the next few minutes, we fly through the various showroom displays, conversation turning primarily to opinions on decor. It *is* a nice distraction, I can't argue about that. Sloan has been trying to decorate her townhouse for as long as I've known her, yet she never seems to make any progress. Her spare bedroom is dedicated to all of the things she buys, but is too busy to actually do anything with because of her job.

"I expected you to be sad, but I'm surprised you don't seem a little more...I don't know...angry? I would be so angry." Returning to the lingering subject at hand, Sloan picks up a burgundy throw pillow and punches it, then slams it into her cart with surprising force. A passing elderly couple eyes her nervously. They pick up their pace to skirt around us. I give them an apologetic smile but Sloan doesn't even notice.

"Don't get me wrong. I am." I cross my arms and fall into step behind her as she moves down the aisle. "But more than that, I'm just kind of exhausted."

We wander into the mirror section and Sloan stops to check her reflection, ruffling her blunt, brown bangs with her fingers. She removes a pink lipstick from her purse and applies it carefully. I stop myself from stepping beside her to check my own appearance. She always looks like she's about to close a multi-million dollar deal. Seeing the comparison of my leggings, unbrushed hair, and dark under-eye circles won't make me feel any better about my current state of affairs.

"Are you going to forgive him? Because he doesn't deserve you. I've been telling you this for months." Drill Sergeant Sloan has officially entered the building. We move from the mirrors and find ourselves amongst lamps and lighting of every imaginable shape and size. Sloan removes her phone from her back pocket and takes a few photos of various fixtures before responding to a text.

"I know, I know." I switch one of the lamps on and off. "Things have been...strange. I've always been willing to overlook the issues because I love him, Sloan. I love him so much. But what if that's not enough anymore?"

She nods, thinking.

"Did he text you, by the way?" I ask. "How did you know to kidnap me—I mean, come to my rescue?"

"He did." She holds two fake plants up for my opinion and I point to the cactus on the left. "He was worried about you."

For the first time, I wonder if it's weird for her to know so much about the personal life of one of her co-workers. Does she pass his office at work and politely wave, all while thinking about how mediocre I've said he can be in bed?

I hope so.

"How chivalrous of him. You know what would be fun?" I give her an evil smile. "You should give him the cold shoulder for the foreseeable future."

"That was already a given." She tosses the cactus into her cart with a clang and I cringe. "I'm excellent at the cold shoulder approach."

"Wha ha ha!" My villainous laugh receives an eyeroll. "Is it almost time to go get ice cream so I can get back to my self-loathing?"

"Yes," she purposely bumps my hip with her cart. "But

first you have to help me pick out some curtains for my bedroom."

I want to ask her what happened to the other five sets of curtains I helped her pick out, but refrain. Instead I wrap my arm around her shoulders and pull her close as we walk, which she pretends to hate but I know she secretly loves.

May 20, 2019 1:34 PM
From: matthewgeralds@casanasoft.net
To: amry_edits@tmail.com
Subject: Meeting Request

What: Matt & Amry Inevitably Breakup
When: Wed, May 22, 2019 7:00 PM - 8:00 PM EST
Where: Matt's Apartment

Accept? YES NO

May 20, 2019 1:40 PM
From: amry_edits@tmail.com
To: matthewgeralds@casanasoft.net
Subject: Re: Meeting Request

Amry Phillips has accepted your meeting request. Click HERE to cancel this meeting.

CHAPTER 3

"He sent you a MEETING REQUEST to discuss breaking up?!" Ada's voice comes through the speaker at such a high pitch I have to turn the volume down.

I toss the phone back onto my bed and hoist my suitcase up beside it. It takes every bit of energy I have. I may or may not have spent another day and a half as a recluse —this time in bed. My beige comforter is scattered with empty water bottles and processed food wrappers, some of which fall to the floor as I fold the suitcase open. It's similar to the scene from my living room a few days ago, except there's much less catapulted food.

"That's...sadly what I said." I wince as my toe connects with an empty glass on the floor. "And don't forget it was set for a one-hour duration. The most 'Matt' action of our entire relationship."

The sound of pots and pans filters through the phone and I know that Mom is cooking dinner. I can visualize her, in the cotton pajamas she always puts on as soon as she walks through the door from work, prepping Friday night spaghetti and garlic bread while Ada sits at the kitchen island. The idea of familiarity is comforting, and it hits me that I'm really looking forward to going home for the weekend.

"Well." Ada swallows a gulp of what I know is blue raspberry-flavored sparkling water. "I've always told you that Matt has a permanent stick stuck up his a—"

"ADA!" Mom's voice pipes in for the first time. "Don't finish that sentence, please."

A snort escapes my nose. I cross my room to the closet, kicking random objects out of the way. Surprisingly, most of my clothes are on hangers rather than the floor. Probably because I haven't rummaged through them to get dressed the past few days. I grab a few items and toss them over my shoulder for packing.

"Are you feeling a little better today?" Mom's voice is closer to the speaker now and I know she's joined Ada at the bar.

It's a loaded question. I haven't booked any new editing clients in a month, thanks to a scathing Google review from someone who has chosen to remain anonymous. My boyfriend that I've been with for a decade and I broke up in the most unexpected way. It's only been a week since what will forever be deemed "The Blue Bra Fiasco." Am I feeling better?

I sure as hell am not.

"Yeah, I guess." Mom usually means well so it's worth the lie. Plus I kept her up until 2 AM crying over the phone after I left Matt's apartment on Wednesday night. I'm sure it wasn't easy for her to teach a class full of third graders the next day.

"Look on the bright side," she continues. "You're only twenty-six so you still have plenty of time to date and find a soulmate before your child-bearing years are over."

Andddd there's the part of her that doesn't mean so well.

"Oh, PLEASE." Ada takes over again. "Are we in the year 1912?"

I know her and Mom are staring each other down now; Mom's feigned innocence matching Ada's perfected 17-year-old scowl. I silently hope that Ada backs down and doesn't start an actual argument. Mom tends to get easily offended by Ada's angst, which always surprises me, considering she has already raised one teenage daughter.

But then I remember the nine-year age difference between Ada and I. Mom had a lot of time to lose her touch. Not to mention, Dad is no longer around, and that doesn't help the frequent tension between the two of them. He was always the voice of reason; the calm in a heated conversation.

"What should we do this weekend?" I change the subject to be safe. "I'm looking forward to coming home for a couple of days."

The oven opens and closes in the background, followed by what sounds like typing. Is Ada doing homework? Or maybe, just maybe, she decided to listen to me and try blogging. I want to ask but also don't want to embarrass her. The blog is definitely not something Mom would know about.

"Hello? Are y'all ignoring me now? First I go through a breakup and now my other two favorite people in the world—"

"Oh, shut up." Ada giggles and the typing sound ceases. "Maybe we can go to the arts market tomorrow morning? We could stuff our faces with food truck snacks and buy some shit at the booths."

Mom sighs loudly over the noise of cooking prep. The thought of the arts market immediately perks me up a little. It was always one of my favorite things to do when I still lived at home in Jacksonville.

"You had me at food trucks." I toss my clothes into the suitcase and zip it, then carry it to my bedroom doorway. Along the way I take a quick look in the mirror and it makes me cringe enough to consider freshening up before I leave. Then I remember that I'll just be sitting in my car for two hours. Who is going to see me?

"Are you sure you don't want to wait until the morning to drive up?" Mom's voice echoes from her position at the stove. "It will be dark by the time you get here. I worry about you driving at night."

"I'm beyond positive."

I can't spend another night by myself right now. Sloan is out of town and I've watched a season and a half of *90 Day Fiancé* in less than 48 hours. I'm behind on the work I do have and I don't even know what motivation is anymore. I need a change of scenery and the two people I love more than anything to bring me back to reality before I can further crash and burn.

"She can see when she drives at night, unlike you Mom." Ada sounds proud of her joke but no one laughs. I'll take Mom's side on this one. Besides, she is the reason I'll have homemade spaghetti waiting in the microwave when I arrive.

"Alright, I'm heading out in ten minutes." I pull my suitcase into the living room and search the beige, carpeted floor for my favorite sandals. "Enjoy your dinner. See you in a couple of hours!"

"Ok, love you!" they respond in perfect unison.

I end the call and shove my phone into my back pocket before moving over to my cluttered desk. My work bag sits open on the chair and I load my charger and planner into it. Waking my laptop, I bend over to type a brief email I meant to send earlier in the day, then add it to the bag and close it up. I will inevitably have to do some work this weekend after slacking off. Deadlines are still ahead, but that could change in an instant if my time is managed too poorly.

Which I can't risk in the slightest. A second bad *Amry Edits* review is the worst thing that could happen right now. All of my free time has already been devoted to playing detective and trying to figure out who left the first one. I know all of my clients extremely well, and there are no clues as to which one of them it could be.

Uneducated excuse for an editor. She couldn't even proofread her way out of a children's book.

That's all it says. The words have been circling in my brain for weeks.

Now they've been joined by *Matt never loved you. You're going to die alone.*

Shaking my head, I sling the bag over my shoulder.

I've been a freelance editor for almost five years now. I know, I know—a lot of people assume that "freelance" is just a fancy word for "struggling." But I've gotten pretty lucky, and I try not to take that for granted.

Matt and I had started college together at UCF right after high school. He thrived in his computer science program, just like we all knew he would. I, on the other hand, despised college. I changed my major twice— English Lit to Elementary Education to Marketing. None of them felt right, and after my third semester, I didn't go back.

Mom was cool with my decision and didn't question me too much. Dad, however, being the excessive worrier that he was, didn't leave me alone for weeks. He texted or called every single day. At first he just wanted to make sure that I was positive about my decision. Then he wanted to know what my backup plan was. When I didn't have a solid answer for that, he started throwing out alternatives. I know this sounds overwhelming, but if you had known Dad, you would understand. He was the most gentle persuader I've ever known, and probably will ever know. It came from a place of love. I know that now more than ever.

I spent a year working various retail jobs while trying to figure myself out. I knew that I loved two things—books and the English language. A lot of research led me to the possibility of being an editor and it was the first thing that truly struck my fancy. Without a degree, no one was going to hire me to do it in this day and age. So, I went to my marketing genius dad.

Eight months later I had a fancy website, growing social media presence, and enough editing work to quit retail. I found my niche in the indie author community. I know it probably wouldn't have happened without Dad's help, and I remind myself every day to acknowledge that privilege.

I do a quick scan of the apartment to make sure all lights and appliances are off. My worn leather couch is covered in at least ten blankets and all of the throw pillows are on the floor. The kitchen counters are packed with dishes that I bribed myself into washing, but avoided putting away. On the upside, I did clean up the *Legally Blonde* food chaos. The place could be worse. To be fair, it's never immaculate. I take after Mom in that regard.

The Florida humidity envelops me as soon as I step out into the breezeway, key in hand to lock up. My building sits beside a lake, and the gentle wind coming off the water keeps me from breaking too much of a sweat as I descend the single flight of stairs with my bags. The sun is setting and the sky is clear. I appreciate the golden hue that coats everything as I walk to my car. It's like living in an Instagram filter.

I love being beside the water. I love the quiet. I love the fresher air on the outskirts of the city. Matt can keep his stuffy, eighth-floor "luxury" apartment downtown. I'll stay here where my apartment is just as nice and save exorbitant amounts of cash on rent. Which will be even more important if I can't put the review to rest and get my hands on some new manuscripts.

Ugh, Matt.

A combination of anger and sadness flares within me at the thought of him. I slam the hatchback of my Rav-4 a little too aggressively. It's only been two days since seeing him, and the newness of everything still burns fresh. Strangely though, I've only cried twice—once after finding the bra, and once more after the actual breakup on Wednesday evening.

Sulked in bed? Yes. Avoided responsibilities? Yes. Cursed our entire relationship? Yes. But cried? Not a tear. Maybe the Blue Bra Fiasco tears were the last few I had left after so much time grieving Dad. Maybe it's just a screaming sign that Matt and I were long past our expiration date.

I do miss him though. Tough times or not, I wish this hadn't happened. I wish I was heading to his apartment for a sleepover right now.

I start my car and carefully exit the parking lot, turning right onto the highway. I'm heading to my favorite local coffee shop for a road trip latte. Then I remember that they don't have a drive-thru and my appearance is currently, for a lack of a better word, frightening. Also, possibly, concerning. So I change lanes and opt for the closest Starbucks instead.

The barista passes my iced caramel latte with an extra

shot through the window with a genuine smile. My own smile subconsciously fades as I make eye contact with her. I thank her and swiftly exit the line, my brain now in a different place and time.

"I'm sorry about the barista, Am. She was just always so nice to me. A friendship developed, and the rest—well, that was all an accident."

"Oh, don't refer to her as 'the barista.' That's gross... She may have slept with my boyfriend but she's more than just her job title."

"Can we have this conversation without you finding some way to work feminism in?"

"No promises."

"We're really breaking up aren't we?"

Matt's entire demeanor had softened with that question, and for a brief moment I wanted to move closer to him and hold him.

"I think we are. I mean...yes, it's time. Do you disagree?"

"No—I agree. I just had to hear you say it out loud to accept it myself."

The conversation hadn't even lasted the full scheduled hour. Thirty minutes after my arrival we were standing in the hallway outside of his front door, me holding a reusable grocery bag containing the few items I had been allowed to keep at his magazine-perfect apartment. We hugged one final time, and he was back inside before the elevator doors fully closed to take me downstairs.

My heavy thoughts fill the car. Where is Sloan to shake it out of me when I need her? I take a big gulp of the latte (too much caramel syrup) and choose a Spotify playlist. Most of the Friday afternoon traffic has cleared and I'm able to merge onto I-4 East with relative ease.

"I hope you don't feel like this was all for nothing."

"A part of me wants to. But, I couldn't if I tried."

How does someone who was your best friend for so long come to feel so far away?

My car picks up speed and I force myself to look ahead. I know one peek into the rearview mirror will give me a glimpse of the picture-perfect setting sun. But it will also give me a glimpse of downtown Orlando, where Matt is in his apartment, possibly in the company of a woman who isn't me. It's time to keep moving forward and start figuring out who I am without Matt Geralds.

May 24, 2019 5:37 PM
From: amry_edits@tmail.com
To: from_adams_to_suarez@tmail.com
Subject: Minus One (Possibly "Replaced" One)

Hey Casey,
I was going to text you about this, but then I remembered that you have this personalized wedding email for a reason. You're always so organized...teach me your ways.
Long story short, Matt will not be accompanying me to your wedding next month. I'll fill you in on the gory details after you're married and things have calmed down. I'm going to try to find another friend or someone to come with me, but if I haven't by the end of the weekend I'll let you know for seating chart purposes.
I'm sorry! Please let me know if any of this is a problem. Miss you!
Love you (Even more than your soon-to-be husband), Amry

May 24, 2019 8:03 PM
From: from_adams_to_suarez@tmail.com
To: amry_edits@tmail.com
Subject: **Re:** Minus One (Possibly "Replaced" One)

Amry,

I'm trying super hard not to jump to conclusions here. I hope you're okay! I'm here to talk whenever you're ready—whether that's before or after the wedding.

No worries about your possible guest swap. Bring anyone you'd like! I appreciate you giving me an update. No rush on getting me a final answer. We're flexible.

Love you (And will hurt Matt if I need to),
Casey

CHAPTER 4

The smell of brewing coffee enters my nostrils, and for a moment, I think I'm dreaming. Millions of people wake up to this smell every day, but I'm not one of them. I don't make my own coffee. Blame it on my millennial age bracket and the wildly convenient availability of over-priced lattes in our country.

I turn over, hoping to drift back into a deeper sleep when I get the prickly feeling that I'm not alone. Through my delirium I can feel a presence near my bare feet; the warmth of a body radiating at close distance. I can also smell...perfume? Is that Marc Jacob's *Daisy*?

Oh my God, someone is in my house.

I sit up in a full panic, wide awake in a matter of two seconds. I'm staring at a vintage coffee table covered in various candles and a half-eaten bowl of spaghetti. The rug under my feet is much softer than my apartment's carpet. Through my parted thighs I can see the fabric of Mom's velvet, emerald green couch.

Dad always hated this couch.

That's right...I'm home.

"There she is!" A voice comes from my left, followed by a giggle when I jump completely out of my skin.

I turn to face the source and find myself looking into eyes so much like my own—deep brown and crinkled with a smile. Except, unlike mine, Ada's eyelids are covered in a layer of exceptionally done eyeshadow. Today it's purple, and the color makes her eyes look almost golden. The makeup perfectly matches the silk hair scarf that is folded into a triangle and tied bandana-style in her hair.

"Why are you on the couch, loser?" She drops down next to me and tilts her head onto my shoulder. I wrap my arms around her, appreciating the soft, cool feel of her hair scarf on my cheek. My mind wanders to what is underneath said scarf, but the thoughts flee as Ada pulls away from me.

My laptop is on the floor by my feet. I bend over to retrieve it. A quick swipe over the mouse pad shows that it's dead. "Y'all were both asleep when I got here last night. I sat down to do some work and apparently passed out myself."

Ada stands and offers her hand to me. I clasp it and she pulls me up. As always, I feel like I tower over her five-foot frame, even though I'm slightly over average height at best. Ada inherited Mom's small, yet curvy physique. I got Dad's sturdy build, but also some of Mom's shape to even things out.

I head toward the kitchen, beckoned by the coffee that I'm grateful wasn't just a dream. I have to step over a couple pairs of Mom's shoes and clear a stack of third grade worksheets from one of the bar stools, but it all feels like second nature. Ada pours two cups of coffee and sets one down in front of me before turning to the refrigerator.

"We have oat milk, heavy cream, or hazelnut creamer." She glances at me questioningly over her shoulder.

"Hit me with the heavy cream." Black coffee with a splash of cream—it was always Dad's combo of choice. The corner of Ada's mouth turns up and I know she remembers too. She pours some into each of our mugs and places the carton back on its shelf.

I'm mid-sip when two arms wrap around me from behind. Mom's breath tickles my cheek and the smell of her signature soap swirls around me. She squeezes me twice before letting go and joining Ada on the other side of the kitchen island.

"I tried to wait up for you last night, but it was such a long week. I was exhausted." She smiles and leans over to prop her elbows on the counter top. Her wavy, auburn hair is loose and it falls forward into her face. She shakes her head to flip it back behind her shoulders.

It's the one feature that all three of us have in common —Mom's is free flowing and speckled with silver, mine's tied messily on top of my head, and Ada's sits underneath her scarf. Ada watches Mom's hair fall perfectly into place and reaches up to adjust her scarf before knotting her hands in front of her on the island. She notices my gaze and gives me a tight-lipped smile.

"It's alright." I wrap my fingers around my mug and lean into the cold, metal back of the barstool. "I had some work to get done anyway."

Ada comes around the island and climbs onto the stool next to me. Mom fetches her own coffee and adds some oat milk to it. For a couple of minutes we all sit in comfortable silence, sipping from our mugs and slowly waking up together. Well, at least I'm slowly waking up. The two of them are dressed and ready for the day.

Despite the serenity of the moment, there's the absence of a fourth person that I know we all still feel—that we'll probably always feel. The past couple of years have been hard, but we've grown through it. Just like any other family, we'll always have differences and disagreements to work through. Regardless, Mom and Ada are my people. Some people have mothers and sisters who would be all over them with a million questions immediately after a breakup. Mine will wait for me to talk—for the most part. In some cases they won't be able to help themselves.

"So what are we looking for at the arts market today?"

Mom's question breaks the silence and leads the way into thirty minutes of incessant chattering. Mom talks about how all of her students are advancing to fourth grade and how proud she is of them. Ada dramatically insists that the last two weeks of eleventh grade will never end. I give them a brief synopsis of the latest book I'm editing. (A young-adult romantic fantasy, not much less dramatic than Ada's teenage complaints.) The pot of coffee slowly empties, and conversely we are filled with caffeine and the importance of being together.

Ada jumps off the stool, gathering our mugs and carrying them to the sink where she fills them with water. I take note of her typical black ensemble—today it's a cropped black tshirt, paired with ripped black jeans and a sleek black belt.

When she was 12, her and I curled up on the couch and watched *Funny Face* together. She became enamored with Audrey Hepburn's clothes, particularly the all-black turtleneck outfit she wore while dancing. I've rarely seen Ada in anything other than black since then.

"You look stylish as usual, Ada." And I mean it. Between her makeup and carefully styled wardrobe, she always looks like she should be running with an artsy crowd in New York or L.A. Not a public high school in Jacksonville, Florida. She even sews some of her clothes herself. What teenager does that?

"Thanks!" Ada's response is brief, but I can tell by the blush in her cheeks that she loves the compliment. She wipes her hands on the dish towel, then reaches up to adjust her scarf again. It's not so much an adjustment as a quick touch, like she just needs to be sure that it's still there. I don't even think she realizes that she does it at this point.

Mom sighs and also turns to look at Ada's outfit. "Every day I hope to see her in some color, and every day it's the same dark clothing."

Four years ago Mom was convinced Ada's clothing choices would be a month-long phase. Now she has run out of ways to convince her daughter to leave that phase behind, so she turns to sarcasm and feigned disappointment instead. She doesn't understand that her attitude toward the matter only makes Ada more determined to wear what she wants. As an observer of their conversations on the subject, I can always sense the tension.

And honestly, I think Ada's clothes make her happier than most things in life.

"Well, luckily she looks perfect in everything," I say in a joking tone for the sake of them both.

Mom doesn't take the hint. "I'm not saying she looks bad, I'm just saying she would look better if—"

Ada stalks out of the kitchen before Mom can finish her sentence.

"I swear, I can't say anything anymore." Mom pierces me with an expectant look and I know she wants me to agree with her.

"She's gotta be her own person, Mom." I pat her hand as I slide off of the stool. "Remember, you and Dad raised us that way. Terrible, terrible parents."

She gives me a half smile and I walk back to the living room to gather my things. I plug my laptop in to charge and unlock my phone. Casey's email notification is displayed on the screen and I read it with a sigh of relief. That's one less thing to worry about for now.

"I'm gonna shower." I leave Mom in the kitchen and push my suitcase down the hallway. The first door on the right is closed tightly. I pause in front of it and press my palm against the barrier that all three of us can't bring ourselves to pass. Dad's office sits on the other side, dusty and untouched. "Love you, miss you," I whisper before pulling my hand away.

The guest room is just across the hall. It used to be my room, but Mom and Dad updated it after they realized I wasn't going to move back home anytime soon. Besides Ada's, it's the cleanest room in the house, with nothing but necessary furniture and a couple of basic paintings on the white walls. I won't lie, it's peaceful—but I still prefer to pretend the walls are purple and covered in boy band posters.

A shared bathroom connects my room to Ada's. I start the shower before peeking my head into her room. It's pristine. The photos on the walls and the stack of textbooks on the desk are the only signs of teenage existence. Her sewing machine sits in the corner next to an IKEA rack of black clothing that I can only assume are works in progress.

She's sitting on the edge of her bed, scrolling through her phone with one hand and twirling her hair around the index finger of the other. She sees me and quickly releases the hair. Her face flushes and she forces a smile.

"Nosey much?" She tries to joke, but it's obvious she's afraid I'm going to say something. I can see it in her eyes. And I do want to ask her about it, but decide not to. Besides, twirling and pulling are two different things.

Plus, I think she's been doing better lately.

———

THE SUN TWINKLES off the St. Johns River as we drive over one of Jacksonville's many bridges. Mom takes the first exit on the other side and quickly finds street parking. She forces us to lather on sunscreen because we have skin the color of uncooked chicken. It fries pretty similarly too.

We gather our purses and reusable shopping bags and walk to the overpass where the market happens every Saturday morning. Ada's scarf flutters in the breeze. Mom's hair billows out behind her and I can smell her shampoo. It's a short walk, but I'm sweating in my jeans by the time we hit the first booth. May in Florida is basically July.

Mom is immediately drawn to an artist selling colorful cat statues and Ada shoots me a horrified look. The guest room and Ada's room are exempt, but every other space in Mom's house is decked out in true "maximalist" style; thrifted and vintage bits and bobs cover every surface. I have no idea where she is going to find room for a lime green cat holding a ukulele, but I trust she already has a predetermined spot in mind. She pays for two and the artist thanks her profusely.

"If you find anything today, it's my treat." She tucks the cats into her bag and falls into step beside us. We leisurely make our way down the first row of booths. Ada finds a table of handmade jewelry and chooses a silver ring with a turquoise lighting bolt. I find a windchime crafted with various crystals that create rainbow patterns in the sun. We take our time, perusing every display until we find ourselves standing in front of the food trucks. Ada and I exchange a glance because we know this is where the real fun begins.

I pull my wallet from its pocket, waving it at Mom and

Ada before heading into the cluster of trucks. "Snacks are on me, ladies."

Several trucks are crammed into one small area, but somehow every distinct smell holds its power. We walk from truck to truck, reviewing the menus as we go so we can make our final choices. Ada chooses tofu tacos. Mom sticks with a classic pulled pork sandwich. I finally decide on a sushi burrito. I pay for three bottles of water at the last truck and we meander to the small, outdoor amphitheater to find a place to sit. An independent dance team is finishing their set and we wait for them to take a bow. Ada claps voraciously and then tears open her first taco eagerly.

"Oh no!" She drops the taco back onto the tinfoil and pulls her phone out of her purse. "I forgot to take a picture for my Insta story!"

She tries to shape the half-eaten tortilla into a photo-worthy position. She snaps a few photos and promptly deletes them all. "Oh well, there will be other food, I guess."

"Here, take a picture of this instead." Mom crosses her eyes and shoves her sandwich into her mouth. Ada laughs and snaps the picture, then taps around on her screen before turning it back for us to see. She has added a GIF of Cookie Monster to the photo and posted it to her story.

"You have no shame," I say to Mom and narrow my eyes at Ada. "Don't you dare take a picture of me eating this sushi."

"I won't, but only if you let me have a bite of it." She holds her hand out.

I slap the burrito into it, which leads to all of us sampling each other's food. When I have another bite of my burrito, it's completely amplified against the background of Mom's tangy pork and the spice of Ada's tacos.

Crumpling up the empty tin foil, I toss it into my

reusable bag and retrieve my phone. There are two work emails, which I quickly respond to. There's also an email from Google, telling me for the millionth time that they're looking into the possibility of removing the review. I sigh and drop my phone onto the seat beside me. A kid that can't be any older than twelve is finishing a saxophone solo on the stage. He nervously waves to the spectators as he bows and stumbles away.

My phone vibrates loudly. Ada and I both peer down at it. She picks it up and stares at the screen before passing it to me.

"Why the hell is Matt Venmoing you six hundred dollars?"

I snatch the phone from her and check the notification before elbowing her gently. "Why the hell are you such a busybody?"

"When the hell did you both start cussing so much?" Mom leans forward in her seat to look back and forth between the two of us.

Ada sticks her tongue out at me and crosses her legs. I cross my fingers, wishing for the Venmo subject to be forgotten. but they're both still staring at me. Mom crosses her legs to match Ada's. Now I'm in the hot seat. There's no recovering from this.

"It's for his half of the hotel in Savannah. We were going to spend the week before Casey's wedding there, remember?"

"No," Ada responds at the same time that Mom says "Oh, yes!"

"Well we *were* planning to," I say to Ada before addressing Mom. "And I was going to totally cancel and only go for the night of the wedding, but I can't get a refund from the hotel. Matt agreed to give me his half since I paid for it all up front."

"How decent of him." Ada's tone drips with sarcasm.

"So are you going to go by yourself?" Mom asks.

"I'm not planning to. I texted Sloan last night to see if she wants to come make a week of it with me but I haven't heard back from her yet. She's in Dallas for work."

Mom stands up to stretch and checks to make sure her peasant-style dress is covering her butt. "I'm sure she will say yes! If not, I know you'll figure something else out. I'll help if you need me to." She tucks her cats back under her arm and Ada grimaces at the sight of them again.

"I can't believe she bought those hideous things," Ada whispers to me as we stand, shielding her mouth with her hand.

"She told me she got them specifically for your bedroom," I say through a smirk. Ada pushes me and I bump into Mom's shoulder. She gives us her best stern teacher face, but it doesn't have the same affect on me as it once did.

"I'll just move them to the guest room then. To the nightstand. So they're the first things you see when you wake up in the morning." Ada takes the final jab.

We make our way to the market exit. The sun punches me in the face again as we leave the shade of the overpass. We all fumble for our sunglasses and slide them on at the exact same time, like we're Charlie's Angels.

The interior of the car is stifling. Heat radiates from the leather seats, making me thankful that I'm wearing jeans and not shorts. Mom turns the AC up as high as it will go and we all click our seatbelts into place, careful not to burn ourselves on the metal buckles.

My phone vibrates again just as Mom is merging back onto I-95. It's a text from Sloan. If I didn't know better, I'd say she heard us talking about her.

SLOAN PINNER

> I'm so sry, I have a conference in Denver that week. I really wish I could. Thx for inviting me though! How did your "meeting" with Matt go?

I sigh, locking the screen and making a mental note to text her later. "Looks like Sloan can't go."

No one responds. Mom keeps glancing at Ada in the rearview mirror. I want to turn around to take a look too, but refrain. Ada struggles when she's stagnant—sitting in the car, studying, watching TV—if she has a free hand or two, they're probably in her hair, feeling and searching and eventually pulling.

"ADA!" Mom's voice is much angrier than I know she means for it to be. "Stop...NOW."

Ada doesn't respond, but I can still feel the hurt and embarrassment pouring from her. The anxiety floods the interior of the car. I flip my visor mirror down and pretend to check my face, but take a quick peek at her in the backseat instead. She's staring out the window, arms crossed, mouth in a tight line.

I know Mom wants to help her daughter. I only wish she could somehow do it in a gentler way. It's one thing to bring attention to Ada's disorder when it's just the three of us, but she handles it the same way in front of everyone—even strangers.

This type of silence isn't comfortable. I return to my phone screen for a distraction, re-reading Sloan's text and trying to figure out what to do about this trip that is supposed to happen in two weeks. The only other friend I would want to invite is the one who's getting married.

Curse being an introvert!

We're turning into our neighborhood when it hits me. I swivel around in my seat.

"Hey Ada. What are the chances *you* would want to go to Savannah with me in a couple of weeks?"

May 25, 2019 7:48 PM
From: amry_edits@tmail.com
To: from_adams_to_suarez@tmail.com
Subject: Re: Minus One (Possibly "Replaced" One)

Hey Case,
Ada is going to come with me! We're gonna have a nice little sister week in Savannah and then she'll be my wedding date.
So you'll have one less alcohol drinker, but every-thing else should even out. Can't wait to party with you and Ed!
Just three weeks to go. I'm sure you're pumped!
(But also stressed.)
Love you (Still more than Ed),
Amry

May 25, 2019 9:03 PM
From: from_adams_to_suarez@tmail.com
To: amry_edits@tmail.com
Subject: Re: Minus One (Possibly "Replaced" One)

Whoo hoo! I love that girl. I'm excited to see her—
and you of course!
Also, don't think I've already forgotten that you
have a lot of stuff to catch me up on. Sorry I've
been so unavailable. Am I a terrible friend?
Love you (And Ed says you're wrong),
Casey

ADA'S PRIVATE ANXIETY THOUGHTS

(SERIOUSLY...NO ONE WILL EVER SEE THESE.)

May 26, 2019

I'M GOING TO SAVANNAH WITH AMRY!

I didn't think I was going to have anything to look forward to this summer. But now I get to go somewhere new—with my sister, and, even better, without Mom. It's not very far...Georgia is just a quick drive from Jacksonville. But I've heard cool things about Savannah. We're leaving the weekend after school lets out!

I would say I'm 60% excited, 40% nervous. Amry said there will be a pool at the hotel, and we might go to Tybee Island one day. The thought of swimming always makes me worry. People expect me to take my scarf off and get my hair wet. It's hard to explain why I can't, and I always feel left out when this happens. If my friends don't notice the bald spots when my hair is dry, they will definitely notice when my hair is wet.

I guess it will be different with Amry, though. She understands. And she's nice about it, unlike Mom. She won't pressure me to do anything I don't want to.

It's called trichotillomania, by the way. Or trich for short. Not that I ever say the name out loud. It leaves a bad taste in my mouth.

I have constant urges to pull my hair out. Dr. Reilly says it's an obsessive compulsive disorder that developed as a result of my anxiety and depression. It was triggered by Dad's death, when I was looking for ways to distract myself and make myself feel better. Dr. Reilly also says I shouldn't feel guilty for not being able to control it. I've tried to stop...trust me on that. Who would do this to themselves on purpose?

All of the important people in my life know about it at this point, but it doesn't make it any easier. A lot of them still don't understand. Everyone treats me differently, which is weird because deep down, I still feel like me. It's especially hard to explain to new people, so I haven't made a new friend in a couple of years now.

And FORGET about dating.

Mom told me I take after Dad when it comes to my anxious nature. She says he was dealing with it before they met, and continued to deal with it for their entire marriage. He never tried to get help for it. His heart attack was stress-induced.

That's why I want to try to do everything I can to live my life. I'll take the medicine. I'll go to my weekly sessions with Dr. Reilly. I'll make my clothes, and practice my makeup, and do fun things with my friends. I'll even continue to write, and soon it will be time to think about college!

I know there will be stuff to work through along the way, but I want to be as happy as possible. I want to try harder—for Dad.

And I'll start with this trip.

Wow...this post really took a turn. Sorry about that. Tomorrow is Monday, which means school. I guess I better get some sleep.

Until next time!

CHAPTER 5

"Thanks, have a good one!" The teenage girl behind the register returns my credit card and receipt to me with a friendly grin.

Ada grabs our smoothies from the counter and gives her a shy smile. She hands mine over and we push through the front door to walk the few steps to my car. I climb in and sit my drink in the cup holder long enough to search for a good playlist.

"Road trip! Road trip! Road trip!" Ada chants and takes a giant slurp of her blueberry concoction. Almost immediately, she slaps her hand to her forehead. "Ugh, brain freeze."

"Sucks to be you," I say, taking a more responsible sip of my plain strawberry smoothie.

It's been two weeks since I asked Ada to come to Savannah with me, which means it's been almost three weeks since Matt and I split. Generally, that doesn't seem like a very long period of time to me. Yet, I feel like a lot has happened.

I've caught up on work, making sure to get ahead so I

don't have to do anything other than respond to emails this week. I've cleaned my apartment. (It may or may not already be in a state of disarray again.) The nightmare review still looms, but I did manage to sign a new client.

I've seen Sloan twice, and she's now fully caught up on the final demise of Matt and I. She's already begging to set me up with other people. I told her I couldn't be less interested.

Trust me, I've toyed with the idea of finding a rebound, but it just doesn't appeal to me. Yet, anyway.

Speaking of Matt, I also gathered his stuff from around my apartment and returned it to him. There's no point in having to relive a different memory every time I find something else of his. The only bump in the road was —I couldn't talk myself into personally delivering it.

So...I FedExed it. I believe it was the healthiest decision, and he texted me to say thank you. Yes, I toughened up and unblocked his number. Slow progress is still progress!

Checking behind me, I put the car in reverse. "We couldn't even get out of Jacksonville before our first snack stop," I joke.

"It's the pre-road trip, road trip snack. Plus, I didn't have breakfast and it's practically lunch time," Ada replies.

Neither did I, now that I think about it. I was too focused on making sure I was fully packed and running somewhat on time. I succeeded at the latter, but I'm not so sure about the former. We'll see when I open my suitcase in Savannah.

I've never been to Savannah, despite growing up within an easy driving distance. When I was a kid, most of our family vacations were beach vacations. Which seems kind of funny now, considering we've always lived roughly five miles from the beach. The majority of our getaways also happened before Ada came along, so her excitement is most of the fun for me. It more than makes up for Matt not being with me.

A red light stops us and I glance over at Ada. Her sandals are on the floorboard and her bare feet are resting on my dash, tapping along to the music. She's wearing a black cotton romper that hits mid-calf. Her scarf is yellow today, and her makeup is more minimal than I've seen it in a while.

"I can't waste good makeup on sitting in the car!" she had said when Mom made a remark.

I look down at my gym shorts and Young the Giant band tee that I've had since 2012. I pull the waist of the shorts up to cover more of my stomach. Is it normal to be jealous of your younger sister's fashion sense?

"Do we have to listen to your old music the whole way?" Ada asks, leaning back into the headrest.

My mouth drops open. "Did I not just catch you vibing with the music?"

"Don't say 'vibe!' It's so dumb!" She laughs and presses the "skip" button on the dash.

"Listen to whatever you want." I pass my phone to her. "I'll just be over here, catching allll the good VIBES regardless of what you play."

She chooses a pop-y song that I've never heard before and sings along. Badly. Sometimes I forget how large our age difference is. I'm not far from thirty and she still has a year of high school left. I can't even remember what I was like at seventeen. All I know is Casey was my best friend, Matt was my boyfriend, and nothing else mattered.

Now, Matt is part of my history. But I do have Casey. And we're still best friends—just in a more adult way where we can't stay in touch 24/7 and we live in different cities. I'm in Orlando and she's in Jacksonville, yet we love each other just as dearly.

Traffic thins as we exit the outer limits of Jax and I set my cruise control. There are no clouds in the sky. I-95 stretches as far as we can see. The inside of the car becomes warmer and warmer as we drive along beneath the strengthening sun. I kick the AC up a notch.

A Spice Girls song comes over the speakers and we smile at each other. It's something we can both appreciate. *Wannabe* defines my so-called "prime." I can't help but laugh out loud as I comprehend that Ada probably considers it a classic. I do love when things stretch across generations. Even something as simple as the Spice Girls.

"What are you laughing at?" Ada turns the volume down.

"Just using humor to cope with the fact that I actually am getting old."

"You're not!" Ada skips to the next song. "I was just kidding when I said that about your music." She's genuinely concerned she hurt my feelings. Another thing about Ada— she loves to pick and be sarcastic, but she's also terrified of hurting someone she loves. I've decided it's because she is so sensitive herself.

"Oh no, it wasn't that." I reach over and playfully punch her thigh. "It's all good."

We're approaching the Georgia state line. Ada rushes to unlock her phone and films an Instagram story as we pass through. She captures a video of the welcome sign just in time, turning the screen to show me. I glance at it and return my gaze to the road.

"I never thought I'd be so excited to go to Georgia of all places." She posts the story and sits her phone on the center console.

A lack of family vacations as a kid is one thing, but Ada

has also been particularly hermit-like since Dad died and trich has taken over her life. Her and Mom come to Orlando to stay with me sometimes. We go to Disney and do the typical touristy Florida things. Outside of that, Ada has turned down multiple trips with friends. She's dropped out of drama club. She has developed a fear of anyone she doesn't already know and love.

And of some people she loves dearly, too.

I know Mom doesn't do it on purpose, but she contributes heavily to Ada's anxieties. She thinks she's being sneaky by constantly watching and waiting to catch Ada in the middle of a pulling session. She thinks she's helping.

But I know Ada feels smothered. I would too. Ada has so much to give, yet is too afraid to give it. Not everyone gets to see the funny, creative, and caring parts of her that I get to see. That may be what I hate the most.

"Maybe you'll meet a cute Georgia boy," I joke.

"It's a 'no' from me. But maybe *you'll* meet a cute Georgia boy!" She pulls her legs down from the dash and stretches them out onto the floorboard.

I turn the music back up and we ride without conversation for a few more miles. Eventually we cross over the still, brown waters of the Ogeechee River. The sun disappears behind a stray cloud, giving us a momentary break from its overzealous rays.

"You know…" I pick my empty cup up and shake it. "My smoothie is long gone."

"That means it's time for a gas station junk food run." Ada points to a sign as we drive past. "Looks like there are a couple on the next exit."

———

ONE HOUR later we're entering Savannah's city limits. My GPS leads us to a large bridge that spans across the Savannah River. We catch a glimpse of our hotel on one side, and the historic district on the other. A couple of boats cruise along, leaving white trails in their wakes. Ada's nose is pressed against the glass as she takes it all in.

She turns her face to me. "Our hotel looks so nice from here! I can't wait to see inside."

Matt and I saved for months to be able to afford this hotel. We loved the location for its proximity to the historic district, but also the distance the river provides for breaks from the tourist action. According to my research, Savannah is extremely walkable, and the hotel has a free water taxi for transportation across the river. The plan is to park my car and not touch it again for a week, unless we decide to drive to Tybee Island one day.

"We're treating ourselves this week," I say, confident in my decision to still take this vacation. "By the way, do you have your half of the money for the hotel?"

I try to keep a straight face. She whips her head around, eyes wide. Unable to commit to the charade, I crack and let out a high-pitched laugh.

"I'm just messing with you. So, so gullible."

She rolls her eyes and flicks me on the arm before turning back to stare out of the window. I reach the end of the bridge and take a right. A couple of minutes later we're in the hotel parking lot, where I claim the first available spot and shut the engine off.

Ada immediately starts gathering our empty snack trash and discarding it into a plastic bag. She ties it neatly and places it on the back floorboard. We climb out of the car and head to the trunk for our luggage. I take a peek at the time before slipping my phone into my backpack.

3:17 PM. Just in time for early check-in.

Heat radiates off of the pavement as we trek to the entrance. The humidity here is just as relentless as it is at home. Automatic doors slide open as we approach and air conditioning floods out.

The lobby is covered in shiny white tile. Our sandals smack against it, creating a slight echo as we walk to the front desk. We pass seating areas full of lush, burgundy couches and chairs. Hotel patrons lounge around with coffee and books. A small fountain serves as the lobby's focal point. Water trickles down in a zen rhythm. Floor-to-ceiling windows fill the room with airy, natural light. Ada looks around in admiration. I feel at home already.

"Checkin' in?" A middle-aged woman with kind eyes and a heavy Southern accent glances up from her computer. I pass her my credit card and I.D. A few minutes later she hands me two room keys and two small bags containing giant chocolate chip cookies. I give them to Ada so I can put my wallet away.

"Enjoy your stay, and please let us know if you need anything!" The woman smiles and we thank her before taking a left down the nearest hallway to a pair of elevators. The doors open almost immediately and we drag our stuff in. Ada presses the button for the ninth floor and we rise rapidly.

"These cookies are WARM!" Ada says excitedly, breaking a piece off of one and shoving it into her mouth. "Are you going to eat yours?"

I rescue my cookie from her. "What do you think?"

"*Wishful* thinking…" She polishes off her final crumb and shoves the crumpled bag into her pocket. The elevator doors swish open. I find the envelope containing the room keys and entrust one of them to Ada as we walk down the hallway.

"Guard this with your life," I joke. We come to a halt in front of 904. "Here we go!"

We rush in and discard our luggage in the first available corner. A squishy king-sized bed covered in a down comforter sits in the middle of the room, enclosed by oak nightstands on each side. A flat screen TV hangs on the light gray wall across from the bed, and two red arm chairs sit on either side of the window. Ada runs over and flings the curtains apart.

My eyes land on the Savannah River before looking further to see a narrow, cobblestone road and a row of old, charming buildings. Groups of people wander up and down the street, popping in and out of the buildings along the way. From this distance, it all looks so small. I want to be one of those people taking a leisurely stroll beside the water.

"Is that River Street?" Ada asks. "We're going to go there, right?"

"Of course, all the time!" I point at the small boat house on our side of the river. "We'll catch the water taxi there, and it'll take us over to the historic district whenever we want."

"This is amazing!" Ada pushes off of the glass and rolls across the bed before bolting up to run into the bathroom. "Oh my God, Amry! There's a TV in this mirror!"

I follow her to the bathroom to investigate. Sure enough, there is a TV *inside* the mirror. A hotel welcome message plays on repeat. "I never knew that watching TV while on the toilet was something I needed in my life, but I think it's a new requirement." I reach over to change the channel a couple of times before switching it off.

We wander back to the main room and sink into the chairs on either side of the window. It's all so beautiful. In an alternate universe, Matt would be sitting in Ada's place.

Him and I would have entered together and checked out all of the details, just like me and Ada.

I reach into my pocket to pull out the cookie and take a nibble, chewing slowly. Matt probably would have given me his cookie. He was never one for sweets. Maybe he would have surprised me and seduced me on the big, fluffy bed. Or maybe he would have pulled out his laptop and immediately responded to work emails. Yeah, that seems more realistic.

Why do I still miss him then?

I finish the cookie and return my attention to Ada. She smiles and tucks her legs beneath her on the chair. Her genuine excitement brings me back to reality and the current situation.

Screw Matt. Ada needs this. We both need this time away, for our own reasons.

"What are we doing first?" Ada asks.

"Let's start with a shower and change of clothes." I toss the empty cookie bag at her. "Then dinner and a stroll on River Street?"

She wads the bag up tighter and shoots it at the trash can across the room. It lands perfectly in the center. "Sounds great!" She stands and stretches, then takes off across the room to grab her bag. "Dibs on the first shower!"

————

Exiting from one of the hotel's side doors, we follow a path down to the boat house. The worst heat of the day is gone, replaced by a steady breeze from the river. Orange and pink skies surround us on every side, serving as the perfect backdrop for the buildings of River Street. The smells of water and algae grow more potent as we draw closer to the dock.

Ada walks in front of me. The breeze ruffles her black maxi dress around her ankles. I have to hold my own sundress down tightly to avoid flashing innocent bystanders. Ada's hair flows behind her, shiny and glowing red in the evening light. The length escaping her scarf appears healthy and full, just like Mom's. Just like my own, which the wind is currently attempting to pry from its trademark bun.

"You have to keep an eye on her this week, Amry. She will pull when she thinks you're not looking," Mom whispered her concerns to me while Ada rolled her suitcase to the car earlier today.

I know she's right. But I want to be smarter about how I choose to handle things. I want to help Ada keep her hands away from her hair without nagging and ruining her vacation. We'll keep busy this week, and I'm hopeful that will work in her favor.

It was me who first discovered Ada was balding. She had been sitting on the couch, zoned out in front of *Never Been Kissed*. Dad had only been gone for a few days, and during that initial period I was with Mom and Ada more than I was in Orlando. We were all struggling terribly.

I had walked up behind her and wrapped her in a hug before standing to ruffle her hair. That's when I noticed. I panicked. Ada panicked. Mom panicked.

I don't think she fathomed that her actions could cause such a strong reaction from us, or cause the balding in the first place. And so began a seemingly endless journey to get Ada the help she needed—the help she still needs. I understand what it feels like to be stressed, but I guess I don't understand what it feels like to have that level of anxiety. It breaks my heart for my little sister who is still so far away from the worst stresses in life.

We join the line of people waiting for the next taxi. Ada holds up her phone and motions for me to come closer. "First pic of the trip!"

She snaps a photo then opens her gallery to show me. It's the first picture we've taken together in a while, and golden hour has done us justice. Ada's eyeshadow matches the setting sun. My natural face looks bare next to hers, but I love seeing our similar sister features side-by-side. "You'll have to send me that one."

"Don't worry, I'll send you an entire album at the end of the week."

A boat docks and those aboard exit. Our group begins boarding slowly. Ada and I are the last to step on, but we still find seats right away amongst the small group. A captain in a white uniform goes over a quick list of safety precautions, then we're sailing in the direction of River Street.

"What's for dinner?" Ada turns sideways in her seat to take videos for her Instagram story as we chug along.

My stomach growls at the mention of dinner. After snacking all day, a real, substantial meal sounds amazing. "Seafood? It always screams vacation to me."

"Works for me!" She balances her phone on her thigh and reaches up to check the security of her scarf.

Another boat passes and everyone waves. I can hear the dull sound of cars passing over the bridge in the distance. Voices from the shore float across the river as we draw closer. Smells from the various restaurants join the voices. My mouth waters in time with the symphony of my stomach. We reach the dock with a gentle bump, and the captain secures us before we line up to disembark. He smiles and wishes everyone a good evening, offering a hand to assist people off the boat as needed.

"Don't forget, the last taxi back to the hotel departs at midnight!" He winks at Ada and I.

We take a set of slimy stairs up to street level and immediately get absorbed by the heavy crowds. I grab Ada's elbow to make sure she doesn't get swept away. She hooks her arm through mine and we veer right, treading carefully to adjust to the unevenness of the cobblestones. "It should be just a couple minutes walk this way," I say.

We pass by a variety of shops—homemade candy, ice cream, coffee, souvenirs, and more. I make a mental list of the ones I would like to visit. Ada is doing the same, silently mouthing the names of the stores. People of every age, shape, size, and color are out enjoying their evenings. Some smile when I make eye contact, and others hurriedly shove their way past.

There are always two types of people.

I stop us in front of a red brick building covered in ivy. The sounds of conversation escape through the front door and the windows on the upper floors glow yellow with light. We locate the hostess stand on the sidewalk. A teenage boy adds my name off to his list and grabs two menus. "Table for two! Follow me."

He weaves Ada and I through the crowded dining room and pulls chairs out for us at a cozy table in the corner. He places the menus on the table, which has a checkered cloth and holds a single faux candle, before advising that our server will be with us soon. He departs and we drop onto our seats to dive into the menu.

I'm reviewing the drinks when our server—a short, plump woman with fantastic purple hair—appears with two glasses of water. She plunks them down on the table in front of us and reaches for the cat-eye spectacles hanging on a chain around her neck. "Hey there, I'm Susie! I'll be helping y'all out tonight." She perches the spectacles on her nose. "Can I get ya started with a drink?"

"Too many choices!" I quickly read the remaining options. "I'll go with the rum runner."

"Good pick!" Susie jots my order on her pad and glances at my I.D. before turning to Ada. "And for you, beautiful?"

Ada's cheeks flush at the compliment. "Just water for me, thank you."

"You sure, honey? I could whip you up something yummy, with no alcohol. Virgin strawberry daiquiri, maybe?"

Ada ponders this, then nods enthusiastically. "Yes, please!"

Susie bustles away and returns with our drinks within three minutes. She takes our food orders and drops two straws on the table. Then she's gone again.

We taste our drinks at the same time and voice our approval. Ada offers me a sip and I accept but don't recip-rocate. "I'm not trying to get arrested."

Slurping away, we take in the surroundings of the restaurant. Families, couples, groups of friends, and even a bachelorette party enjoy their meals. Susie and the other servers move at lightning speed, never dropping a single beverage or plate of food. I sink into the familiar relaxation that only occurs with just the right amount of alcohol. One drink will be enough for me tonight.

"How closely has Mom told you to watch me this week?" Ada stirs her straw in circles around her glass.

I pull my attention away from the bustle of the restau-rant to focus on her. "Nothing gets past you, huh?"

She laughs quietly. "I'm used to it. She asks the same of anyone who is sometimes responsible for me"

"I'm not just anyone." I take another sip. "I'm your sister and I told her that she doesn't need to worry."

"I wish she could learn to trust me sometimes." Ada trails a finger through the condensation on her water glass. "Or at least trust that I'm trying my best."

I reach across the table to place my hand on top of hers. "She means well. We both know she doesn't always handle things in the best way. Trust me, I'm the only person who knows that just as much, if not more, than you."

"Dad knew." Ada stares past me.

"You're right, he did." He had balanced Mom out so well.

"I know it's because she loves me," Ada recognizes. "And I know you understand. I remember the things she would say about your weight when you were a teenager. Words from a place of love can still hurt."

Instinctively, I smooth my dress over my stomach. Sometimes I wonder if I would still be insecure if Mom had never made me aware of the fact that I was over-weight. As a kid, the size of your waist isn't something you think about until you're told to. Sure, the occasional remark from a classmate would have also done the job. But when your Mom comments on the fit of your jeans every morning before school, that's what makes you feel the worst. Not just emotionally, either. You begin to feel like you, yourself, your body—are bad.

I don't completely feel that way anymore, but as a result, my confidence is a work in progress.

"I know, Ada." I finish off my drink and take a sip of water. "I promise, things will get better between you two. She will realize that you can still be an independent person, regardless of what you're struggling with. As you get older, it will get easier."

"I sure hope—" Ada is interrupted as Susie arrives with our food.

She sets our plates down in front of us and refills our water glasses. "Is there anything else I can get for you girls?"

"No, thank you!" Ada and I say in unison, eyeing our food.

Once Susie is gone, I unwrap my silverware. "If you ever want me to talk to Mom, I will. For now, know that we're going to have a great week. I'll always have your back without making you feel bad or embarrassed."

"Thanks, Am." Her face relaxes.

"Now let's fricken' eat!"

I shove my spoon into a steaming bowl of seafood bisque. Ada takes a bite of her fried fish sandwich and wipes tartar sauce from the corners of her mouth. We swap food and keep the conversation light as we polish off every last bite of our first meal in Savannah.

AMRY

We're getting ready to go to bed! Had a great drive and first day. All is well.

MOM

Good. Thank you for the update. Miss you two, and love you lots! Send pics pls.

ADA'S PRIVATE ANXIETY THOUGHTS

(SERIOUSLY…NO ONE WILL EVER SEE THESE.)

June 8, 2019

We're here! It's a dream!

We just got back from dinner. I'm sitting in bed while writing this, eating a homemade peanut butter cup that I bought from Savannah Candy Kitchen on the way back to the water taxi. It tastes like heaven. (The peanut butter cup, not the boat.)

The hotel is sooo nice—the nicest place I've ever been, probably. Everything is so perfect, I almost feel out of place. It's like being in a movie. What did I do to deserve this? I have the best sister.

Speaking of Amry, I'm worried about her. She seems sad. I know it has to be because of her breakup with Matt, but she hasn't talked about it much. And I don't think she's sad because she misses him, but because she feels…lost, maybe? She will most likely never openly talk to me about it, and that's ok. I'm just her loser younger sister. I wish she would though.

It won't hurt for me to be the one worried about her for once.

In the car, she joked with me about finding a cute Georgia boy this week. I, however, was serious when I said she's the one who needs to find a cute boy. Ok, well a cute MAN. You know what I mean.

Dinner was good and the waitress even made me a virgin drink! (I can't wait until I'm 21.) Am and I talked about Mom. I'm glad to have someone who understands my relationship with her. Mom's "help" rarely actually helps. I could probably try harder to not be so sensitive all the time, but it all feels like too much. Life feels like too much. I know all teenagers must deal with this, but I wish I was an adult already. I want to figure myself out.

Tomorrow is our city trolley tour. I can't wait to explore more of Savannah! Amry is also on the hunt for a particular coffee shop for tomorrow morning. They apparently have something called a churro muffin? Churros and muffins are yummy individually, so there's no way a combination of the two could be bad. Can't wait to confirm that hypothesis.

I'm gonna sign off so I can post to Instagram and go to sleep. Much, much more to come this week!

CHAPTER 6

Bright and early the next day, we're back on the water taxi. Last night's coolness still lingers in the air as we dock and make our way up River Street for the second time. It's 8:00 AM, and everything seems quiet compared to the previous evening. Only a handful of people wander up and down the sidewalk, coffees in hand, enjoying the peace of the morning.

"How far is it?" Ada asks. "And more importantly, do you know where we're going?"

I open Google Maps and type in the address. "I'm working on it, I'm working on it." The directions load and I turn to the right, looking at Ada over my shoulder. "It's a ten minute walk. We're looking for Broughton Street."

"Churro muffins, here we come." Ada jogs a few steps to catch up to me.

The map leads us to a steep, wide alley between two buildings. Paved in large river rocks instead of cobblestone, it appears to have a dead end. Halfway up, I notice two sets of curving, narrow stairs that lead to the level of the main streets.

"Oooh, I read about these online," Ada says, skipping to the base of the steps on the left. "People call them the Stairs of Death."

"That's...dramatic." I join her and stare down at the first step. It doesn't even look deep enough to hold my foot. The space between the railing and wall is barely large enough for one person to go up or down at a time. "But I think I see why."

Ada begins her ascension, continuing her lesson as she rises higher and higher. "They're basically as old as Savannah itself. Tourists apparently fall down, and up, them all the time."

"Look at you, doing research." I steady myself on the first step, clutching desperately to the rusty railing. I watch as Ada's Converse sneakers disappear above the top stair and wish I had chosen my own Converse over the sandals I'm currently wearing.

Her head pops back over the ledge. "Come on slow-poke. It's not that bad!"

I remind myself to find an alternative route if I ingest any alcohol. Savannah has open container laws, so it's likely a good majority of its visitors have a drink on them at all times. I can only imagine the accidents that drunk frat bros and tipsy vacationers have had on these stairs.

One step at a time, Amry. One step at a time.

Eventually joining Ada at the top, I release the breath I've been holding the whole climb. My shorts have worked their way into my nether regions and I do a little dance to maneuver everything back into place. After taking a look around, I'm relieved to see that we're on mostly-flat terrain.

"Ok, screw those stairs. This way." The map updates and we head to the Bay Street traffic light. Ada presses the crosswalk button and straightens her black denim mini skirt. It's more crowded in this area, with people milling about searching for Sunday breakfast amongst the countless food options. The light changes and we cross the street. I read the chalkboard menu in front of one of the restaurants on the other side.

Chicken and waffles...yum!

But that's not what this morning is about. Today we're after a churro muffin and latte from a little shop I've been excited to visit. Ada may have done the research on Savannah's history, but I've done the digging on the food scene. And I'm happy to announce, it's bountiful.

We follow the map onto Whitaker Street, past several parking garages nestled between centuries-old buildings that have been renovated into houses, cafes, boutiques, and even hotels. The modern establishments and presence of ourselves and others are the only things that keep me grounded in the present day. I glance over at Ada and she is also looking around appreciatively.

"Hey, there it is!" She points ahead. Right on the corner of the next street sits the cafe. Its sign hangs over the entrance, swaying slightly in the morning breeze. Bistro tables decorate the sidewalk. Ada pauses to snap a picture as we draw closer.

We step inside and merge into the line of patrons waiting for their Sunday morning caffeine. Three baristas dart around behind the counter, going back and forth between the cooler and giant, silver espresso machine. Pastries and other breakfast sweets are artfully displayed in a case next to the register. My eye is drawn to the coveted churro muffins right away.

Would it be wrong to press my face against the glass?

"Breakfast is my treat this morning," Ada tells me, looking up at the coffee menu. "I think I'm going to have a vanilla latte."

"Thanks, sugar mama." I wink at her. "I'll have a lavender one—iced of course."

We step up to the register and a young, red-haired barista greets us with a grin. "Good morning! What would y'all like today?"

"Can we please have one hot vanilla latte, one iced lavender latte, and two of the churro muffins?" Ada orders so quietly I can barely hear her. She looks everywhere but the barista's face, avoiding eye contact. Her cheeks are bright red from the simple interaction. Her demeanor around strangers never ceases to surprise me. It's a shock compared to the vibrancy she exudes with Mom and I.

"You bet." The barista takes Ada's cash and counts her change, then motions to the end of the counter. "You can pick up your order down there. Have a good day!"

Ada stumbles as she moves away from the register. She does a double take to make sure the girl didn't see, then aggressively shoves the change into her purse. Something about the interaction has thrown her off balance. To the untrained eye, it looks like she's just standing there. I know all of her coping mechanisms though.

More than once, she tightens the knot on her scarf. When her hands are at her sides, she picks her cuticles. Her knee jiggles at the pace of a jackhammer, like she's physically trying to shake off whatever is making her mind run a million miles a second. I gently rub my hand across her upper back.

"Breathe, Ada," I whisper.

When our order is ready we take everything out to one of the tables on the sidewalk. Ada releases a giant breath only when the door closes behind us.

"She's really pretty," Ada says.

"YEAH, she is," I respond, admiring my muffin.

"Not the fricken' muffin. The girl at the cash register."

"Oh, sure, her too."

Pretty baristas are common...just ask Matt.

Stop it, Amry.

I hang my purse on one of the chairs and place my food on the table. Ada adds hers and slides it all into an aesthetically pleasing layout. "Don't touch anything, I'm going to grab some napkins. Then I need a picture before we eat!" She scuttles away, good as new. Like she wasn't just having a meltdown in the middle of a crowded coffee shop. There's no denying that she's resilient.

Sinking into my chair, I try to follow orders. The cinnamon sugar on top of my muffin glints in the sun, looking oh so enticing. Condensation is already running down the side of my latte, thanks to the humidity. I take a quick photo and text it to Sloan. She replies with the drooling face emoji.

With the way Ada has it all arranged, it could be in a commercial. Everything is so appetizing. How am I supposed to follow her instructions?

One bite won't ruin the picture, right?

Half of the muffin is shoved in my mouth when a shadow falls over me. "Just one bite, I swear!" I choke on the baked good. And MY GOD, it is *good*.

"Amry?" The voice isn't Ada's.

I crane my neck to look up. Who the heck? The sun is directly behind their head, casting a shadow over their face and illuminating a halo of curls. Two brown, toned arms flank either side of a long torso. One arm is completely covered in tattoos. A mountain beneath a sunset decorates their bicep. Artfully drawn trees, birds, and other animals wrap around their forearm. Various plants and flowers fill in the gaps.

The figure stoops and a face replaces my view of the ink.

"Amry Phillips?" asks a pair of incredibly inviting lips.

Prying my eyes from the beautiful mouth, I swallow my hunk of muffin with a painful gulp and examine the other facial features. Hazel eyes and a toothy grin? Familiar— very familiar. I *do* know this person. But how? I'm preparing to apologize when he speaks a third time.

"It's Jace... Jace Adams. Casey's cousin?" Realization smacks me in my cinnamon sugar-coated face.

Jace Adams?

"Oh my God, Jace!" My voice is absurdly high. "I'm so sorry, I didn't recognize you! Well, I did. But I didn't! If you know what I mean."

"Phew! It is you!" He leans down and wraps me in a solid hug, squeezing so hard my butt lifts off the chair. "I was beginning to worry I had the wrong person. That would have been embarrassing."

He pulls away and takes the clean scent of Ivory soap with him, along with some of the sugar from my face that is stuck to the shoulder of his shirt. I swipe my hand across my chin and wobble to my feet, surprised when I only reach his shoulder. Last time I saw him we were virtually the same height. When WAS the last time I saw him? Casey's graduation party? He was a year behind her and I in school.

"I didn't recognize you!" The words are out before I can stop them. "I don't mean that in a bad way, it's just been so long and I've never seen you on social media, so I knew you were alive and a—"

"No offense taken." He holds his hands up and projects a laugh that blasts me back to 2010. "I live out of state now and don't really use Facebook or anything."

"Seems like you came for a vacation before the wedding, too. Can you believe Casey is getting married?" I ask.

His brown curls keep flopping into his eyes. I follow his movement each time he reaches up to smooth them back into place. His flexing muscles are flames, and I am a moth.

It's like I've never seen a man in my life or something.

"Well, she and Ed have nothing on you and Matt, but I'm so happy for them!" His eyes slide to the second latte and muffin. "Speaking of Matt, where is he?"

I wasn't anticipating broaching this subject for at least a few more days. But that's okay. I can do this. I can say it out loud. No worries at all. "Matt is...not here. He's, he's...not coming. We broke up."

Jace's eyebrows raise ever so slightly.

"Oh, ok. Wow—" He sticks his hands in his pockets, seeming nervous all of a sudden. "Not gonna lie, I'm shocked. I'm so sorry, Am."

He sounds comfortable using my nickname again. Like we just hung out yesterday. There are some things time can't touch.

"It's ok. It was for the best." A beat of silence passes between us.

"Will you be at the rehearsal dinner?" He changes the subject and pauses briefly before asking another question. "Maybe… I'll run into you again before then, though?"

My mouth quirks at the corner, a response to the question I was, perhaps, secretly crossing my fingers for. I bend down to retrieve my phone from my purse and pass it to him. "Put your number in. We'll grab a drink one night and catch up on the past eight years." His long fingers move gracefully over the keyboard.

"Cool, I'll wait for your text!" He hugs me again. This time my face smashes into his hard chest. I don't hate it. Breaking the connection, he puts his hands on my shoulders to hold me at arm's length. "It is really

73

awesome to see you! That muffin looks great by the way."

"See you soon, Jace." I reach out to give him a fist bump, internally cringing at my decision as it's happening. With a final grin, he walks away, turning over his shoulder one last time to wink at me. I stare after him. He's the same, yet different, from his height, to his hair, to his—

"Who is that, and why are you staring at his butt?" Ada appears at my elbow, a stack of napkins in her hand. She moves around me, sighing as she sits down. "Looks like I'm taking my picture with one giant bite missing out of your muffin."

"That was Jace Adams, Casey's cousin," I reply, watching until he turns the corner.

"Never heard of him." She turns my plate to hide the missing half of the muffin. "Was he wearing plaid shorts?"

"Yeah, I believe he was." I smile at the memory of a younger, nerdier Jace in his signature clothing item.

"Nice, very early 2000's vintage." Ada blows on her latte to cool it before taking a slurp.

Vintage? Fucking hell.

——————

THE TROLLEY FOLLOWS its route around Chippewa Square, narrowly avoiding cars parked on both sides of the street. Ada and I exchange nervous glances with the other passengers. I'm not sure what's more interesting–the tour itself, or the rush of not taking out someone's side-view mirror.

"Do we have any movie buffs on board?" the driver asks over his headset. Almost everyone raises their hands.

"Can anyone tell me what incredibly famous movie scene was filmed in this exact square?" We all stay silent, waiting for someone else to gather the courage to speak first.

"I'll give you a hint—it involves a bench and a box of choco-"

"Forrest Gump!" an older man shouts from the back seat.

"You got it!" The driver gives a thumbs-up over his shoulder. "And that isn't the only major film that has been shot right here in beautiful Savannah…"

We exit the square, picking up speed on our way to the next area of the tour. Wind rushes through the open trolley windows; a welcome relief from the rising temperatures of the June day. Large oak trees and various lush, flowering plants line both sides of the road. Spanish moss drifts lazily from tree limbs, adding to the old Southern charm that the colonial-style homes and buildings already exude.

"I just love the VIBES of Savannah." I lean over and whisper to Ada. She twists her ankle around and kicks me in the shin.

"If you look to the right…" The driver's voice comes back over the speaker. "You'll see Poetter Hall, one of the many historic buildings in Savannah that has been reno-vated by our own Savannah College of Art and Design."

Ada sits taller in her seat, ears perked. "There's an arts college here?" she whispers. "I wonder if they have a fashion design program."

The hope in her voice is music to my ears. "That could be perfect for you!"

"Yeah…maybe." She opens the internet browser on her phone and searches for the Savannah College of Art and Design website, then bookmarks it.

I drain the last of the water in my bottle. "Should we get off at the next stop for something to drink?"

As if he heard me, the driver brings the trolley to a

slow halt. "This stop gives you access to Madison Square, shopping, restaurants, and more!" I drop a tip in his jar before clambering down the steps. He tilts his hat in thanks, then rings the bell and drives away.

Crossing the street, we step into the shade of Madison Square. Brick walkways stretch in every direction, leading to bench-filled corners where people sit to eat lunch and read. In the center of the square, a man throws a frisbee for his Golden Retriever. It soars through the air and lands at our feet. Ada bends down to pick it up, then places it in the dog's mouth. It wags its tail and trots away happily.

I consult Google Maps for the hundredth time. "There's an outdoor bar just a couple of blocks away."

We walk through the square to exit on the opposite side, passing a charming bookstore along the way. A tabby cat stares at us from the roof and hisses as we walk by. Its pale orange fur is the same color as Matt's hair.

What is Matt up to right now? I check the time: 11:55. It's Sunday, but he's probably still at the office. Or maybe…he's with her. Maybe they're spending the weekend doing all of the things he never wanted to do with me. Like driving to the beach in St. Pete for the day, then coming back home to have a movie marathon and snuggle while we nap on the couch. Maybe he *wants* to do these things with her. Like he did at the beginning of our relationship. But did he even *want* to do it then?

Did he ever love me at all?

How much longer until I feel the relief of not loving him anymore?

STOP, Amry. These are the exact thoughts we're trying to avoid this week. I've been derailed by a cat, of all things.

"What's wrong?" Ada asks. "You're breathing super heavy. And walking VERY fast."

"Huh?" I stop in the middle of the sidewalk. I'm a

solid five steps in front of Ada and she hustles to catch up to me.

"It's like you zoned out or something." She stares up at me, concerned.

"I'm fine," I lie. "It's just, that cat. Stupid orange color. And Matt. Oh my god, Matt and cat. That rhymes. No love. The cat probably hates me too. I'm so thirsty."

Her brow furrows. "I think the heat is getting to you."

"No, it's not that. It's…nevermind." I start walking again, making sure to keep pace with Ada.

"Do you wish he were here?" she asks timidly. "Matt, I mean."

"No. Well, a different version of him, yes. Or rather, I wish that he and I both as our past selves were here. Does that make sense?"

Ada thinks about this. "Kinda…so things weren't okay before he cheated, then?"

"We were younger than you when we started dating," I tell her, shaking my head. "People change a lot in ten years."

"Who do you think changed the most?"

"Him." My answer is abrupt. "100% him." I think about his growing obsession with work; his increasing lack of time for fun or spontaneity. His lack of time for me, that only worsened after Dad died, when I needed him more than ever.

But you changed too.

My brain serves the counter-argument I've been avoiding. After Dad died, I made less time for Matt on my end as well. I was angsty and sad all the time—and often still am. Can I really blame Matt for not fighting for me? I barely wanted to fight for myself.

"That's a lie," I admit with a sigh. "I changed too."

The corners of Ada's mouth turn up slightly, and she

links her arm through mine. She doesn't say anything else, but she doesn't have to. I'm a different person than I was before Dad died. Other than Mom, who could understand that better than Ada? Maybe I just wanted someone to be there for me in the same way *I* was there for Mom and Ada. Someone to be the "strong one," to carry the burden for me and tell me it's going to be okay.

Matt wasn't built for that. I never should have expected him to be.

"Anyway…" Gripping tighter to Ada's arm, I change the subject. "There's no one I would rather be here with now than you."

"Cheesy, but I believe you." She momentarily rests her head on my shoulder.

We finally find ourselves in front of the outdoor bar. Ada orders a strawberry lemonade. It looks so refreshing that I order the same, but with the addition of a little vodka.

"To a week in Savannah!" I proclaim. We toast with the plastic cups and continue to meander.

"That guy from the coffee shop—what's his deal?" Ada fishes a whole strawberry out of her drink and pops it into her mouth.

"What guy?" I chew on my straw. "Oh, you mean Jace? What about him?"

"Do you think he's cute?" Her voice is filled with the innocence of someone who has never had their heart broken.

"Ma'am, we are *not* going there." I elbow her in the shoulder. "It's way too soon for me to think about stuff like that."

The joke is on me though, when I'm still thinking about Ada's question thirty minutes later as we wander in and out of shop after shop. She has a bag of new silk scarves in tow. I haven't been able to focus on buying anything.

Do I think JACE is CUTE? Ada shoots me a funny look and I realize I've scoffed out loud.

Objectively, yes. He's turned out to be quite...*breathtaking* actually. Anyone attracted to men would agree, though. Who wouldn't think floppy hair and a giant, pearly white smile were cute?

Not to mention, his new and improved adult physique, but I digress.

He could also have a partner for all I know.

STOP IT, AMRY.

This blast from the past has me feeling strange. Darn you, Ada!

We walk to the nearest trolley stop, ready to rest our feet for a while.

"I'm sorry about this morning, by the way. In the coffee shop," Ada says. "I just felt, like, panicky all of a sudden...I feel stupid."

"There's nothing to be sorry for." I grab her free hand and swing our arms between us. "The important thing is you pushed through. However, if I ever hear you call yourself stupid again, I'll kick your ass."

CHAPTER 7

We arrive back at the hotel around 4:30 PM, disheveled and slightly sunburnt from the day. Well, I'm disheveled. Ada's makeup looks as fresh as it did when she first applied it this morning. Sorcery of some kind, I'm sure.

"Should we go to the pool?" Ada's question catches me off guard. She usually avoids swimming like the plague.

"Are you sure?" I ask. Our room's air conditioning wraps me in a hug as we enter. I want to sprawl out on the bed and cuddle with the chilliness.

"Yeah, it's hot as hell." Mom isn't here to reprimand her for cussing. And I'm certainly not going to, because that would just be hypocritical.

"The pool sounds great." I flip my suitcase open and rummage around for a swimsuit. Ada has unpacked all of her clothes and placed them in the dresser and closet. Opening the top drawer, she pulls a black two-piece from a neatly folded stack before retrieving a beach bag from the closet.

"How did you even think to bring a beach bag?" I ask.

"I don't know." She shrugs. "I thought it seemed obvious. We can share if you want."

Ada and I have the same organizational dynamic that Mom and Dad always had together. Realizing that we're carbon copies of them is comforting and depressing at the same time.

We find the pool on the ground floor. It sits in the middle of a massive concrete patio that has been bleached white by the sun. Long rows of deck chairs line three sides of the water and a few palm trees grow from the ground in random spots. An outdoor bar sits near the entrance and the bartender waves at us as we enter. "Let me know if there's anything I can get you!"

"Where should we sit?" I scan the chairs. At this time of day there are only a few people swimming and sunning, leaving us with plenty of choices.

"Let's go back there." Ada points to a couple of shade-covered chairs in the far left corner.

The wonderfully clear water sparkles invitingly. I consider jumping in immediately, wishing I didn't have to take my clothes and shoes off first. We walk past a teenage girl with a cute, blonde bob. She's tanning, covered in oil and wearing a purple bikini. She pulls her attention away from her Nintendo Switch and glances up at us as we walk past.

"Oh, shit. Oh no, oh no," Ada says under her breath, speed walking the remaining distance to our chairs.

"What?" I sit my towel down before pulling my shirt over my head. "Do you know her?"

Ada gathers her scarf-free hair and ties it in a low bun. "Yeah, that's Gemma Adams. She goes to Hamilton—we're in the same grade."

"Adams?" I try to remember the names of Casey's younger cousins with no luck. I look over at Gemma and she's looking back. We make eye contact and she quickly returns to her game. "I'm sure she's here for the wedding too."

"Is Casey related to *everyone* in Jacksonville?" Ada jokes.

"She does have a big family. Her dad has four brothers. Well...had. One of them died a long time ago." I pull my shorts off and drop them to the ground with my shirt. "Is she mean or something?"

"Maybe?" Ada pauses, handing me the sunblock as she thinks. "Maybe not? I don't know. I've never really talked to her."

"You're in the same grade at the same school and you've never interacted with her?"

"It's a big school, Amry!" She's becoming flustered.

Time for a change of subject.

"Hey, rate my cannon ball!"

Adjusting my boobs so that they're better covered by my burnt orange one-piece, I check to make sure no one is in the deep end of the pool. I take off at a slow jog, speeding up as the pavement begins to burn the soles of my feet. Reaching the edge of the pool, I tuck my knees up as far as they'll go and worship the delightfully crisp water as I sink to the concrete bottom where I use my legs to rocket back to the surface.

"Are you sure you're twenty-six?" Ada asks as I emerge, wiping away the streams of water running down my face. I swim to the edge, giving her the middle finger as I get closer.

"I give that an eight out of ten on the cannonball scale!" a male voice shouts from somewhere behind me. I whip around, squinting into the bright sun. Standing tall and thin next to Gemma's chair is Jace. They both wave at me.

Twice in one day?

"Long time, no see," I say, shielding my eyes with a hand as I swim to the shallow end of the pool.

"Small world, huh?" He squats to look me in the face. "Are you staying here too?"

"My sister and I are." I tilt my head in Ada's direction.

"Ah, so you're here with your sister. I thought you may have brought a date." He gives Ada a wave that she skeptically returns.

He stands and gestures to the blonde girl. "This is my cousin, Gemma. So, Casey's cousin too. Gemma, this is Amry—"

"I thought that was you!" Laying her game aside, Gemma slides off her chair and sits to dangle her legs in the water. "You used to come to family dinners with Casey when I was little. And I recognize Ada from school."

Her voice is deeper than I expected it to be. She has one of those smiles that reach all the way to her eyes, which are the same blue as Casey's. Combined with her hair and height, she looks almost exactly like Casey did when we were teenagers. Maybe that's why I immediately like her.

"Hey Ada!" I yell across the water. "Come here!"

She tightens her scarf before standing to move quickly across the hot pavement.

"This is Jace. And Gemma, who I think you probably know. They're Casey's cousins."

Ada shakes Jace's outreached hand before facing Gemma. "Yeah, you go to Hamilton." Her voice starts out quiet and grows louder as she continues. "I've seen you around, but I don't think we've ever really had any classes together."

"We actually had English together sophomore year," Gemma corrects. "I remember because that's when I started paying attention to your clothes. You have killer style." Gemma pulls a pair of sunglasses from the top of her head and slides them on.

"Really?" Ada swells with pride. "Thank you so much. I didn't think anyone at school noticed."

I look up at Jace. He grins when our eyes connect. I allow myself to do a quick scan of his body, noticing that his swim trunks are also plaid. He's thin, but also toned and strong. His hair is tucked behind his ears, revealing a small gold hoop in his right lobe.

How cute is he?

"I was about to get a drink." Jace uses his thumb to point to the bar behind him. "Amry, wanna come with?"

"I'll have a glass of Moscato!" Gemma tells him.

"In your dreams," he replies. She jokingly pokes her bottom lip out, making Ada and I laugh.

"A drink sounds great." I paddle my way to the pool steps and climb out. Jace meets me at the exit. Feeling more naked than I actually am, I reach back to pull my swimsuit down securely over my cheeks. Jace's eyes roam down to my chest, then return to my face just as quickly.

"I love your bathing suit." Gemma says to Ada as we retreat.

"Thank you...I actually made it."Ada sounds proud.

"No way, that's sick. I wish I could sew!"

"So what game are you playing?"

———

"It was *under his bed*?" Jace stares at me incredulously.

I polish off my third banana daiquiri and sit the empty glass on the ground beside my chair. "Indeed, it was."

"What the hell?" Jace leans on his elbow and downs his last sip as well. "Is it bad that all I can think about is HOW she could possibly forget her bra of all things?"

"Maybe she did it on purpose?" I theorize. "Not necessarily for me to find—I'm not even sure she knew about me. But I think she thought it would be sexy for him to find it randomly."

"Hm, interesting hypothesis." Jace retrieves two more daiquiris from the approaching bartender's tray and passes one to me. "Still, I hate it for you, Am."

My heart warms at his use of my nickname for the second time today.

"This is seriously my last drink." I eat the pineapple chunk garnish and toss the rind into an empty glass. "I'm sorry, I don't even know why I'm telling you all of this."

"I'm happy to listen." Jace looks me in the eye. "But I am shocked... In my mind the two of you have always been a single unit."

"Honestly, I've decided it's for the best. I'm not sure we would have had the guts to end things otherwise. At least... I think so. I don't know. Everything is confusing."

I sit up from my lounging position. Jace does the same and we find ourselves face to face, knees touching. It's golden hour and his brown skin glows. There's a small smear of daiquiri on his upper lip. Would it be embarrassing if I wiped it away?

Chill, Amry.

"Your hair is so much longer than it used to be." I'm dying to touch it. "You kept it so short back in the day."

"It took me a while to embrace the curls, but I love them now."

"You look really good. I mean...your hair looks really good." I shove my straw into my mouth.

"You look really good too." He reaches out to touch my knee but pulls away at the last second. I look across the pool to check on Ada and Gemma. They're in the exact same spot we left them, chatting and dipping in and out of the water. Ada's scarf and hair remain dry.

Jace and I have let them be, engrossed in our own rum-tipsy conversation. He's told me about his new life in Nashville, where he works in upper management for a cell phone company. He's single, and spends his free time traveling and hiking national and state parks, which explains the tattoo theme on his right arm.

"Amry." Jace's tone is more serious now. "I was really sorry to hear about your dad."

I've been avoiding the subject. Since Dad has been gone, I've depended on the expectation that everyone I interact with already knows he's dead. And if they don't, then I don't know that person well enough for them to need to hear otherwise. It's still too difficult to talk about, and bringing it up in conversation feels wrong.

"Thanks, Jace." My nose burns and the pressure of tears builds behind my eyes. Will I ever be able to speak about him without breaking down? "We really miss him."

"I know." Jace adds his empty glass to our collection. "I wish I could tell you it gets easier. In some ways, sure. But in most, it doesn't."

Remembrance dawns on me—the uncle Casey lost was Jace's dad. The passing of time and my own grief have made me forget that Jace also lost his parents—plural, as in both of them. I can remember seeing them at the famous Adams family dinners like it was yesterday.

Jace's dad was always funny. He was tall and thin, just like Jace, and had a dad joke ready for every occasion. His naturally pink face would turn red when people laughed at his jokes. His mom was the epitome of beauty. Casey and I were obsessed with her clothes, perfume, and signature cherry red nails. She was a journalist. I would flip through Dad's Sunday papers just to read her articles.

They died in a car accident when Jace was thirteen. His grandparents on both sides were essentially best friends, and he lived back and forth between their homes after that. Jace always used to joke about how lucky he was to be raised by an entire extended family. But now I know from experience that humor is often just a way to deflect from what you're actually feeling. Like me, he probably still lies down at night and replays his final moments of interaction with those he lost.

Letting myself reach out to him, I place my hand on his forearm and squeeze supportively. He covers my hand with his and squeezes back. Joined by our shared loss, we sit in silence for several minutes.

"What do you miss most about your dad?" Jace's voice is quiet, sincere.

Dad's face flashes into the forefront of my mind. I can still remember every detail of his face—his scratchy facial hair that Mom hated. His brown eyes, exactly like mine and Ada's. The scar on his left cheek from the only fight he'd ever been in. (Between classes his senior year of high school. Someone had thrown a Science book at his best friend.)

"Everything." It's almost impossible to choose. "He used to call me at the same time at the end of each week, just to chat. Sometimes I still expect my phone to ring at four o'clock on Fridays."

"I know that must have been special to you." Jace's hazel eyes, full of genuine concern, never leave my face.

"How about you?" I ask.

"They've been gone for half of my life," he ponders, looking into the distance. "It seems like more memories fade each year. But there is something my mom used to tell me every single day. That I know I'll never forget."

"What did she tell you?"

He looks me in the face again. "*Lespwa fè viv.*"

"What does that mean?" I question, smiling at the look of peace that has crossed over his face.

"It's a Haitian proverb," he explains. "It means 'hope makes one live.' "

It could be a trick of the setting sun, but I'm pretty sure we both have tears in our eyes.

An unanticipated splash of cold water brings us both back to the present, soaking Jace's tank top and the towel I'm wrapped in. I look over to see that Gemma and Ada have made their way to our side of the pool. Ada is holding a bucket. The second we notice them, they swim off through the waist-deep water.

"Oh, no you didn't! We'll get you for that!" Jace sways a bit as he stands, then falls back onto his chair. "What I meant to say is, we'll get you back at another time in the future where we haven't had four daiquiris each."

"Here here!" I raise my mostly empty glass into the air.

AMRY

It was nice chatting today. So good to see you!

This is Amry, btw. In case you didn't know

JACE ADAMS

Who's Amry?

Sorry, dumb joke. Had a great time at the pool for sure. See you tmrw, maybe?

ADA'S PRIVATE ANXIETY THOUGHTS

(SERIOUSLY...NO ONE WILL EVER SEE THESE.)

June 9, 2019

Hello again from Savannah!

It's the end of our second day! I just finished showering and now I'm sitting in bed writing this. Amry went downstairs to pick up the pizza we ordered. We were both too exhausted to get ready and go out again.

Today was full of ups and downs, but mostly ups. The trolley tour was fun, even though to be honest, I had already researched most of the things we learned. I did like being able to see the places and put a "face" to them. Plus, I had no idea Savannah has an arts college! When I get home, I'm going to look into their programs and admission requirements. My GPA is really good, but my extracurriculars leave a lot to be desired considering I dropped out of everything. I've been thinking it may be fun to re-join the drama club, but as a costume designer instead of an actor. We'll see.

I'm still embarrassed about what happened at the coffee shop today. Every time I have an episode like that, I overthink it later. Have you ever felt panicky for no good reason? Like something triggers your fight or flight mode, and you feel like you either have to run away or break down where you stand?

I've talked to Dr. Reilly about this before. He said that my normal reaction to anxiety is to pull, so when I'm in a situation where I can't pull, like in a public place or around other people, I shut down. It makes sense. But I hate that it makes sense. Mom tells me all the time to try and control my emotions, but it's not that simple. I've tried. I feel like I'm in a never ending cycle. My anxiety triggers my trich, but in return my trich triggers MORE anxiety.

My sessions with Dr. Reilly do help. I just hope that we'll eventually find a medication that works, and I'll be able to remain pull-free for more than a couple weeks at a time. Like I mentioned last post—maybe my goal to "live" more will help with this process too.

Moving on...I think I made a new friend today. When I saw Gemma at the pool, I was freaked about seeing someone from school. I'm on vacation and I want to be free of my normal worries. I wasn't lying when I told Amry I've never really talked to Gemma. I've only seen her in the halls, and she's a super talented lacrosse player so everyone knows her name. She's pretty popular.

I'm intimidated by girls. I'm intimidated by most people, but girls especially. Maybe it's because my hair loss has stolen a lot of my self-confidence. Maybe it's because I'm jealous. Maybe it's because most of my friends stopped talking to me the moment I tried to explain my disorder to them. Monica and Elliot are the only close friends I have left. Is it bad that I don't really blame the others who left, though? Maybe we're just not mature enough for these things yet.

But I also wouldn't do what Addison did to me. One

day she was my best friend. The next she was behind me in the library, snatching my scarf from my head and running away with it.

"I told you she's bald now." She had laughed as she ran. Most others in the room had laughed along with her. I pulled all of my new growth out later that night.

I keep getting off subject. All of that is to say, Gemma is cool. Super cool. I had a good time with her. She likes video games and she wants to be an engineer. I'm jealous of her ability to tan, and she seems like she could be best friends with anyone. I'm not sure if she knows about my trich. A lot of kids at school do, but if she's one of them, she didn't say anything.

New topic: I talked to Amry about Matt today. I had no idea they were in a bad place before he cheated on her. Am has always been good at hiding her true feelings—a little too good if you ask me. This has really been an issue since Dad died. I think she feels like she shouldn't add any more potential stress to our lives than necessary. Who knows? Maybe she talks to Mom more than me. Maybe she thinks I'm just too young to care. But, I do.

Amry obviously had fun with Jace today as well. No wishful thinking from me though. If Am says it's too soon for her to like someone, then it's too soon.

Speaking of her, she just returned with the pizza. I'M STARVING. I'll have a slice for you, the fictional person who's definitely not reading this. Goodnight!

CHAPTER 8

"Can you imagine living in a place like this?" Ada stops in front of a massive mid-nineteenth-century home. It's pristinely white, surrounded by an intricately-patterned wrought iron fence, and plants that have obviously never been left unattended for a single day. A strategically placed American flag flutters in the breeze, the blue perfectly complimenting the shade of the home's painted front door.

"Not even a little bit." My pupils have to expand to their full extent just to take in the level of curb appeal. "It's gorgeous, but also definitely haunted."

"Yeah, right." Ada begins walking again, turning over her shoulder to give me a look of narrow-eyed skepticism. "Ghosts aren't real."

"She says on the grounds of one of the most haunted cities in the world." I fight to contain a smile. "I'd choose my words a little more carefully if I were you."

We're walking along Jones Street, which is deemed the most charming street in Savannah. Homes similar to the one we just stood in front of line both sides, and each one is more likely to trigger your sense of jealousy than the last. Oak trees grow along the sidewalk. Their branches extend over the street, providing delicious shade and creating artful patterns on the concrete as the sun filters through them.

Ada grabs a piece of moss from the sidewalk and throws it at me. "Well if these supposed ghosts decide to come after us, they'll go for you first because you're the annoying one."

"Are you trying to give me red bugs?" I flick the moss from my shoulder, shivering as I imagine the tiny insects that inhabit it taking over my body. "You should be a little nicer to me if you want me to continue to play photographer for you today."

Last night she found an article on the most Instagram-worthy spots in Savannah, so that has become the first order of business on our agenda today. Luckily I wanted to visit most places on the list anyway, Jones Street being at the top. We've spent the last twenty minutes trying to get the perfect shot of Ada in the middle of said street, dodging cars and bicycles as they came along.

"Hey, I need good photos for my sewing account." She straightens the shirt she is currently wearing. It's one of her own creations—two black, thrifted band tees that have been cut in half then sewn together down the middle. A white Peter Pan collar lined in fake pearls finishes the top off.

"*Who is MetallDC?*" I had asked when she exited the bathroom this morning. Her response had been a middle finger.

"I know." We reach the end of Jones and take a right. "In all seriousness, I do think the shirt is cool. You know I'm only jealous of your ability to have a style."

"You shouldn't be." She eyes my navy tank top and

khaki shorts. "You have your own, you just don't realize it. You're very classic."

The compliment means a lot. I stand a little taller and re-adjust my backpack straps. At the same time Ada reaches underneath her hair to tighten the knot in her scarf. She's wearing a new cerulean one she purchased in a boutique yesterday.

This part of the city seems to be primarily residential. There are fewer and fewer tourists as we move further away from the restaurants and shops near the river. Locals are out taking walks with their families and dogs. Many smile and wave at us as we pass. I catch a whiff of something sweet and floral as we stroll by a fence covered in flowering vines. I breathe deeper, savoring it. A true sense of peace comes over me as I breathe out. The moment is rare and appreciated.

I've been thinking about Matt less and less each day. I mainly wonder what he's up to; if his life has changed significantly in the past few weeks. Maybe he *is* getting serious with the barista. Maybe he's decided to throw himself even deeper into software development. Even though I'm not sure it's possible for him to dive any deeper. All I can be certain of, is he hasn't attempted to contact me. For that I'm thankful.

Thoughts of Matt lead to thoughts of Orlando, which lead to thoughts of Sloan. We've texted a few times over the past week. What I mean by that is I've been bombarding her with various photos from the trip, and she'll occasionally respond to tell me how jealous she is. Then I'll reiterate to her for the millionth time that she really needs to look into taking a vacation.

She constantly travels for work, and when she's home her dedication to her job is equivalent to Matt's. How did I, one of the least-structured human beings on Earth, end up with a boyfriend (well, ex now) and good friend who take life so seriously?

"I see Forsyth Park!" Ada's voice brings my attention back to the present. I look to where she's pointing. Indeed, the Forsyth Park Fountain is in the distance, surrounded by throngs of tourists. We've made it to the next stop on our Instagram list.

"This is sooo pretty!" Ada skips through the park entrance, moving gracefully over the brick path. Lush, green grass hugs the walkways. People lounge on the expansive lawn, having picnics, sunbathing, and even playing instruments. The fountain is the focal point and one of Savannah's most iconic symbols. Nearing the edge, its mist offers a much needed refresh to my dewy face.

Ada opens the camera on her phone and passes it to me, then perches on the fence surrounding the fountain and poses flatteringly. I discreetly snap a couple of photos before she's ready, hoping she'll appreciate the candidness of them. Instead of her usual serious model face, she gives a genuine smile for each picture. Sneakily, I text one of them to myself before giving her phone back. I'll send it to Mom later—she'll love it.

We find a shaded area of grass and plop down amongst everyone else who is enjoying the summer day. Ada scrolls through her camera roll, seemingly pleased. For once, she's appreciating herself instead of going straight for the self-insults. "I actually look kind of good in these," she says confidently.

"Contrary to what you believe about yourself, you're gorgeous. Extremely." I'm not sure how much influence my statement will have, but I say it anyway.

"Not like a lot of girls." She toys with the edge of her scarf. "Not like that girl at the coffee place, or Gemma…"

"One day you'll understand that's not true." I remove

my sunglasses and lean back onto my elbows. "Or at least you'll try to."

I still struggle with this myself so I can't get too preachy. Everyone has insecurities. Ada has her trich. I have my weight. There are a multitude of traits and disorders that cause people unnecessary distress. Why do we create these demons for ourselves? Enough unavoidable issues do that already—such as losing loved ones too soon.

What would Dad say to Ada in these moments? Would he do a better job of getting through than Mom and I?

"Hey Ada?" I ask. She lies next to me on the grass and grunts in response. "Have you been getting Mom's texts the past couple of days?"

"Yeah, I have." She flings an arm over her face to block the sun. "Why?"

"I talked to her last night and she said you haven't been responding." She doesn't say anything. I glance over at her.

Several seconds later, she props herself up on her elbow, resting her face in her palm. "It's only been like two texts. I don't see what the big deal is. When did you even talk to her?"

"She called while I was getting the pizza from the lobby last night." I leave out the fact that I took the call down there on purpose. I knew Mom would be wanting Ada updates.

Ada sighs dramatically. She pulls a few blades of grass from the ground with her free hand. "Can I be honest with you about something, Amry?"

"Yes, always."

"I need a little break from her sometimes," she starts. "And this is the first time I've ever had the opportunity to be fully away from her."

I listen, saving my reply because I can tell she's not finished.

"Like I know she wants to hear about my day, but all of her questions are a gateway to asking about the only thing she *actually* cares about—and that's whether I've been pulling or not." Her cerulean scarf glints brightly in the sun, playing off of her equally shimmery eyeliner.

Her feelings make sense. In her mind, Mom doesn't care about anything other than her disorder. While it's not true, I hate that it seems that way. Ada has been overwhelmed by her trich for so long that she thinks it's the first thing on the mind of anyone who loves her. Having it at the forefront of her own mind is already taxing enough.

"I hear you, I do. And I promise I'm not going to force you to text her back if you feel like you need this week to breathe." She looks relieved. "However... I'm also going to encourage you to try and remember that Mom does care about *all of you*. The little parts just as much as the big parts."

She purses her lips but doesn't argue. "That's fair enough."

"So we're on the same page." Sitting up beside her, I reach for my backpack. "Should we move on to the next part of our day? Do you want any other pictures?"

"No." She smiles at me and gathers her own things. "We can go to your nerdy bookstore now."

———

A FAMILIAR CAT is on the roof of the bookstore. "So, we meet again." Looking up, Ada places her hands on her hips and gives it what is supposed to be a menacing stare. It gives us its signature hiss and darts further up onto the roof, disappearing from sight.

"I think it dislikes you because you smell." My butt

barely escapes Ada's kick as I dart around the corner of the brick shop.

The front door is yellow and cheery. A bell tinkles when I push it open. I'm immediately swathed in the combined scents of paper and old house. I draw a deeper breath through my nose, wishing the smell existed as a candle. Ada comes through the door behind me and pinches me on my left butt cheek. I stifle a yelp.

"Hello there!" An elderly man peeks over a stack of books on the front counter. "All of our canvas totes are 50% off today. Let me know if I can help y'all find anything specific. All rooms are organized by genre."

We thank him and veer into the room on our left. It's obvious that the shop used to be a residence. I would guess it was built sometime in the mid-1800's. A table of bestsellers and a wall full of bookmarks and small art pieces fill the space we've entered. It takes every ounce of my self-control to not immediately fill my arms with things that catch my eye.

Ada takes a short set of stairs into the next section. She trips on the second step, barely catching herself on the banister. Looking down, she identifies the obstacle. It's a cat—the exact cat from the roof.

The Matt cat.

"You!" She squats to make eye contact with our nemesis. The cat stares at her cooly, its pale, green eyes bright against its body full of thick, orange hair. Ada hopefully extends her hand. The cat forcefully smashes its face into it, purring loudly on contact.

"So he's not a total asshole." I descend the steps and bend to scratch behind the cat's ears. "How did he get in here?"

"She, actually." The shop owner's Rhett Butler-esque

accent pipes up behind us. "Let me guess, you saw her on the roof outside?"

"She hissed at us—twice." Ada sounds offended, but her face melts into contentment as the cat begins to wrap around her ankles.

The shop owner laughs. It's a big, booming sound that rattles the walls. I like it. He probably won the superlative for "best laugh" in high school. I peer at his name tag—"Martin."

"Her name is Prima Donna for a reason," Martin says. "Donna for short. She can be grumpy sometimes, but is really very friendly. As you can see."

Donna is now aggressively rubbing her face on my foot.

"I get it Donna." I give her another head scratch. "We can all be grumpy sometimes."

"Here, follow me." Martin joins us at the bottom of the stairs and walks to the far wall. Half of it is taken up by an ancient-looking brick fireplace; the other half, wooden shelves full of children's books. "We never used the old fireplace, so I created a secret entrance for the gal."

Martin's booted foot nudges the wood panel covering the fireplace, revealing a hidden, swinging pet door. Donna runs through it twice, as if to demonstrate.

"How cute!" Ada drops to her knees and gives the little door a push before returning her attention to Donna, smiling as she crawls onto her lap. It's the beginning of a beautiful friendship.

"Enjoy looking around!" Martin backtracks to his post at the register. "Let me know if you need anything."

"I'm going to explore." I mosey towards the entrance to the next room, trailing my hand across the bookshelves as I walk. "You ok to stay here?"

With Donna still mid-snuggle session, Ada settles against the brick wall of the fireplace. "Obviously."

They stare at me with matching expressions—two sets of eyes, one brown and one green. I feel as though I'm being scrutinized by two teenagers instead of one, and give them a lame wave as I depart.

The next room is the young adult room. Shelves of moody-colored book spines surround me; blacks and browns and jewel tones. Assassins, vampires, fey, and other popular fantasy characters stare up at me from stacks on a giant table in the middle of the room.

In the corner, a collection of pastel rainbow covers represent the contemporary section. I do a quick search for titles I may have helped edit. Working with mostly indie authors, I don't find many of my books in stores, but there can be nice little surprises every now and then.

In the next room, a quote on the wall catches my eye.

"I love you, and that's the beginning and end of everything." - F. Scott Fitzgerald

Paper hearts hang from the ceiling at varying heights. Dim, pink fairy lights line the shelves. I've entered romance territory.

I should walk straight through without stopping. Too bad I get distracted by a cover containing a woman in an emerald green ball gown. She's being embraced from behind by a buff, tan, man with copious amounts of dark hair on his head. I'm not sure if it's the dress or the man that reels me in, but I find myself flipping through the pages and reading different passages. Landing on a partic-ularly intimate paragraph, I blush when my lower abdomen tightens unexpectedly.

What in the world, Amry? It hasn't been THAT long.

I slam the paperback shut and drop it back on top of its stack. Closing my eyes, I take a deep breath through my nose and focus on the bookstore smell I love so much. Another customer enters the room and I snap out of my makeshift meditation, opening my eyes to give them an awkward smile. They ignore me and exit to the young adult room.

I revisit the book with the green dress and tuck it beneath my arm. Maybe a steamy, cheesy love story is exactly what I need while on vacation this week? Maybe it will fill the lonely—ok fine, somewhat amorous—hole in my heart? For good measure, I add two more historical romances to my collection.

But how can I be expected to leave without a more contemporary romance? Or three? I love the covers with their pun-filled titles and charming, hand-drawn illustrations. One in particular catches my eye. The little illustrated man has an arm full of tattoos. Closer inspection reveals a big, friendly smile and curls that beg to have fingers buried in them.

Jace?

This guy has entered my thoughts more in the past two days than the rest of my life combined.

The book joins the others underneath my arm—for the plot, of course. I didn't read the synopsis. But it must be good.

See you tmrw, maybe?

His text from last night sits unanswered in my phone, which my free hand suddenly begs to reach for. Do I want to see him today? It couldn't hurt to catch up with him this week, right?

Stop it, Amry.

The only things I need to catch up on this week are relaxing and forgetting. And spending time with Ada. If I run into Jace again before the wedding, that's one thing. But I don't need the extra commitment. Or, if I'm going solely off the signals my body and brain are putting off, I don't need the extra *temptation*.

Unless I do?

"Are you almost ready?" I jump at the sound of Ada's voice, fumbling the four books. They fall to the floor; *thump, thump, thump, thump* on the worn wood. Bending to help me pick them up, she eyes the green dress cover skeptically as she passes it to me. "What…is this?"

"They're good vacation reads." I snatch the book and hug it to my chest with the others, turning on my heel to make a beeline through the sci-fi and horror room that separates me from the cash register. Martin takes my stack and scans the barcodes. Ada saunters up behind me, wearing her full-on judgment face.

"Don't let anyone shame you about reading romance." Martin places the books in a canvas bag and passes it to me. "For many, it's where the love of story crafting begins."

"Thanks, Martin," I say. "Your place is the best."

Outside, Donna has assumed her station on the roof. When Ada tells her goodbye, she doesn't hiss or run away.

June 10, 20193:15 PM
From: matthewgeralds@casanasoft.net
To: amry_edits@tmail.com
Subject: How are you?

Amry,
Hey, I hope you're having fun in Savannah. Not gonna lie…I'm kinda jealous. I need a vacation so bad! Anyway, wanted to say a quick hello. Give Casey and Ed best wishes from me at the wedding. Can we meet up when you're back in town next week?
See ya,
Matt

CHAPTER 9

A driblet of peach-flavored slushie snakes down the side of my plastic cup, narrowly missing my khaki shorts on its fall to the sidewalk. Hoping to avoid another overflow, I shove the straw in my mouth and take a large sip, spluttering when I ingest a mouthful of rum.

Ada stifles a giggle and sips her own virgin version with a bit more grace. "I remember my first drink."

My eyebrows nearly fly off my forehead. I gape at her. My throat burns from the rum and another coughing fit fights its way up. She doubles over on the bench, laughing so hard she almost drops her cup. "I'm joking, Am. I've never seen you look so much like Mom."

Savannah City Market foot traffic filters around us as tourists veer off into the surrounding bars and bistros. The sun is setting, but the Georgia heat still lingers. People look exhausted–sweaty and sunburnt from their long days. Smells of grilled meats and other Southern delicacies drift from open restaurant doors.

"Can you believe how many flavors they had?" Ada swirls the contents of her cup and nods at the bar next to us. From our bench, I can see the wall of colorful, frozen drinks swirling in their prospective machines. It had taken both of us ten minutes and several samples to decide on the peach.

"We'll just have to try more tomorrow!" I cross my legs and focus on stirring the drink so it doesn't separate. "And the next day, and the next day."

We sip in silence, people watching and scrolling through our phones. A couple of Ada's photos from the day pop up on my Instagram feed. I comment a few fire emojis on one and "Vibes" on the other. Her elbow finds my ribs when she sees the notification.

"Who knew vacations were so exhausting?" Ada yawns, placing a hand over her mouth. "How have we been here for two full days already?"

"Are you having fun so far?" I ask.

"Yeah, Savannah is awesome. Well, other than the fact that it's a thousand degrees every day." She smiles sheepishly.

"You should be used to that." I point out.

"Are we calling it a night after this?" Ada stifles another yawn.

My phone buzzes with a text, distracting me from responding. Jace's name flashes across the screen.

JACE ADAMS

> Would you and Ada be up for a ghost tour tonight?

My thumbs freeze in their position over the keyboard. The serotonin rollercoaster in my brain reaches its peak and teeters on the edge. My ability to think pauses with it. I'm happy, but why? I'm excited, but WHY?

"Who is it?" Ada leans over, trying to peek at the screen. "Why are you smiling?"

"Don't be nosey!" I swat her away. I need to think. Do I want to go? Rather, do *we* want to go? I remember Ada's remark about being tired. And a cool, cushy bed does sound great. Not to mention I have a bag full of books that are too heavy to haul around the city a second time. But ghosts could also be fun? *Jace* could also be fun. Another text comes in as I struggle.

JACE ADAMS

It was Gemma's idea for the four of us to go. Totally get it if you're scared though.

Oh. No. He. Didn't. The rollercoaster finally drops. I want to throw my hands into the air and enjoy the ride. Instead, I use the energy to type a contained response.

AMRY

Sounds fun! But I have a bag of books I need to take back to the hotel first.

"Hey Ada, you know those ghosts you said you don't believe in?" I return my attention to her.

"Mmmmhmmmmmm." She stares at me out of the corner of her eye.

"Want to meet some of them tonight?" I give her the details and wait for another text from Jace.

JACE ADAMS

Meet y'all in the lobby in 30?

———

I'VE NEVER SEEN anyone look so good in green.

We follow Jace through the evening crowds towards Madison Square, the meeting spot for the ghost tour. I should be thinking about the potential impending doom of being followed home by a spirit, or appreciating how comfortable Ada seems to be around Gemma. But, here I am, obsessing over the way Jace's t-shirt coordinates with tonight's plaid shorts and brings flecks of colors to the surface of his tattoos.

Would anyone notice if I reached up to give myself a swift slap on the face? Being single has altered my brain in some strange way.

Every few minutes, he turns to make sure we're all still behind him. The cute gap between his front teeth is on display each time he smiles. It's the same grin from the days he would play pranks on Casey and I at her grandparent's house. Said pranks were only successful 90% of the time. The remaining 10% consisted of an indoor water hose attack that left us (and his Grandpa's brand new leather recliner) soaked, and him grounded for a month. He had continued to gloat about it year after year, insisting the punishment was completely worth it.

The square is eerily dark and quiet amidst Savannah's nightlife. An easy breeze and yellow-hued streetlights collaborate with the square's shrubs and tree branches to create constantly shifting shadows. They seem to follow us as we make our way to the meeting point. A shiver creeps down my spine, and I wonder for the first time if I'm mentally stable enough for a ghost tour. I can't even read horror books. I once edited a paranormal romance novel that wasn't scary at all by most standards, and still didn't sleep well for weeks.

Jace comes to a halt in the center of the square. I stop mid stride to avoid colliding with his backside. Ada and Gemma are so caught up in their chatter behind me that they don't catch the memo and face plant into my shoulders. They immediately start giggling. Apologizing, Gemma tries to rub her foundation off my shoulder. If the two of them are nervous about the tour, I can't tell. Hopefully, I can play it cool too.

"We're a few minutes early." Jace turns to us, checking his watch. "Last chance for anyone who wants to back out." He waggles his eyebrows.

Why was that so cute?

The aforementioned park shadows seem to be encroaching on us now that we're standing still. The tour hasn't started, but I'm already struggling to keep my face in a neutral expression. Savannah is a completely different city in the dark.

"I don't believe in ghosts." Ada shrugs. How is this the one time in her life that she's not secretly worrying herself to death? And she legitimately isn't worried—I know all of her anxiety signs, and she's displaying none of them. Maybe she's utilizing the same sorcery she uses to keep her makeup consistently flawless to pass her paranoia over to me for a couple of hours.

"I'm just excited!" Gemma bounces up and down, optimistic energy radiating from her.

More people wander into the center of the park. We all do that thing where we glance at each other to try and determine if we're waiting for the same activity. There are even a couple of children in the group. They couldn't look less worried about the fact that they're about to go hunting for lost souls. Am I the only sane person here?

"You're awfully quiet." Jace's voice pulls me out of my people watching stupor. He's bent to my level. His face is shockingly close when I turn to look at him. Instinctively, I take a step back.

"Oh, I'm just...thinking about how stoked I am for this!" Pinnochio is a better liar than I am. Jace's smirk shows that he's thinking something along the same lines.

"I did a similar tour in New Orleans once," he

remarks. "I promise, it's all good fun. Nothing too outlandish."

"What if we have different definitions of fun?" I argue.

He laughs out loud. "I guess we'll just have to do this tour and find o—."

His sentence hangs unfinished in the air as Gemma pokes him in the ribs. She's pointing across the park. He closes his mouth and squints in the direction that everyone else is now staring. A light is drawing nearer—a floating light. It sways back and forth in the darkness beyond the street lamps. Realizing I've stopped breathing, I force myself to take a deep breath.

The glow arrives in front of us. Someone is attached to it. A man dressed in a 1900's style black cloak and matching bowler hat steps into the crowd. An old-fashioned lantern with a real flame creaks and swings in front of him. He sets it on the ground, casting all of our faces in darkness.

"Good evening, brave friends," he says in the type of posh, Southern drawl that you only hear in the movies. "Are y'all here for the eight o'clock tour?" He pushes a pair of round eyeglasses further up his nose and flashes a grin that is barely visible behind his thick mustache.

Everyone moves closer to him and his lantern, drawn by light and curiosity. Ada's arm brushes my right side, and Jace's my left as the group presses into the smaller space. He apologizes, his cheeks pinkening. Is it a blush, or a result of the ambient lighting?

"It's lovely to have y'all joining me tonight," the Cloaked Man continues. "My name is Jefferson and I'll be your guide on this two-hour walking tour. We'll be visiting and learning about three famously haunted buildings here in Savannah. You'll even have the opportunity to step through the front door and walk the halls of one of these homes. You can see it on the corner, just over there."

We all turn to look at the building he's referring to. From this distance, it's difficult to see the details. It glows orange in the dark; the yellow-lit windows stare at us through the square's trees. Gemma whispers something indecipherable to Ada and they both giggle. What could possibly be humorous at a time like this?

When did I turn into such a boring scaredy cat? (No offense, Donna.)

"But that will be our grand finale!" Jefferson bends to collect his lantern. He walks forward and the group parts around him. "Let's proceed. Please keep up and feel free to chat as we go. I only ask that you are quiet and courteous to those around you at each stopping point."

We fall into step behind him, looking somewhat like a kindergarten class walking to the lunchroom with their teacher. Ada and Gemma traipse along in front of Jace and I, shoulders bumping as they navigate the uneven brick path in the dark. Gemma links her arm through Ada's and I want to do a celebratory dance. I can't recall the last time Ada made a new friend.

"Do you remember being a teenager and bonding with people over nothing other than the fact that they were also a teenager?" Jace seems to read my mind.

"Things were so much easier back then." I sigh dramatically. "But also, at the same time, way...suckier?"

"Oh, the suckiest!" He screws his face into a look of dramatic disgust. "We had to do homework and live rent free and eat food other people cooked for us. The worst."

"Vulgar." I stick my tongue out at Ada when she turns over her shoulder to roll her eyes at our conversation.

The warmth of the evening adds to the stickiness already on my skin from a day full of exploring and perspiring. I had attempted to freshen up while dropping my books off at the hotel, but only had time for fresh deodorant and a splash of cold water to my face.

Sounds of shuffling feet and scattered conversation float along with our troupe. Jace and I have moments of silence between our own varied discussions, but the silence is comfortable. I've almost completely forgotten that I'm on a ghost tour—until we slowly come to a stop in front of an ornate mansion surrounded by a pointy, wrought iron fence. Magnolia trees bloom all around the grounds, the sweet fragrance more ominous than inviting.

Jefferson waits for us to settle in front of him. "Who here has read *Midnight in the Garden of Good and Evil?*" A couple of tourists, including Jace, raise their hands. Ada is staring at me expectantly but I shake my head at her. It's one of the many books on my to-be-read list, but hasn't happened yet. And may not ever happen if there are ghosts in it.

"It all seems less scary if you expose yourself to it intentionally every now and then." Dad had always tried to recommend his coveted horror and thriller novels to me. The bookshelf that still sits dusty and untouched in his home office is made up of ninety-percent Stephen King. The disturbing covers always frightened me as a little girl, but I could never resist wandering into his office to look at his vintage ink and quill sets that also still live there. Mom is constantly telling me to take them because he would want me to have them. I would, but I feel like they belong amongst Dad's shelf of spooky books. When the time is right, I'll make them mine—and maybe the books too.

"Those of you that have," Jefferson continues in his feigned accent. "You'll recognize this home as the site of those raging parties that Joe Odom threw so frequently." I hear Jace *ah* in recognition beside me. "Now, let's dive into the creepy stuff."

My eyes roam over the inn and surrounding property as Jefferson tells us about the history of owners and tenants. I'm ready to peace out as soon as he mentions a doctor that performed autopsies in the home, but then find it impossible to stop listening when he jumps directly into details on the death of a young girl who tumbled down the stairs. Jace is hanging on every word. Gemma shifts closer and closer to Ada with each story. Like me, she's unwilling to look at any particular window or shadowy corner for more than a second or two. We look at each other, our eyes the shape of saucers.

"As you can probably tell, the inn is now a modern, luxury bed and breakfast. Multiple guests over the years have reported sightings of a cigar-smoking ghost, and unexplained sounds of laughing children." Jefferson finishes his speech and pauses for questions from the crowd.

"I should have stayed here this week." Jace leans down to whisper to me, his breath warm on my cheek.

"You couldn't pay me enough," I respond, subconsciously reaching up to touch my tingling face. His eyes linger on mine for a second too long. The feeling in my pelvis, although frustrating, is a welcome change to the worry that a spirit has attached to me and is planning to follow me home and haunt me for the rest of eternity.

Our group has continued without us and we have to jog a few steps to fall in line behind Gemma. She's clutching Ada's arm tighter than she was earlier.

"This is fun!" Ada turns to grin at me and I wish I could agree.

I have no idea where we're going next until we're there, halted in front of another historic mansion. This one is red brick, with concrete balconies protruding from different areas of the foundation. The window in the front door frames an expensive chandelier that emits a very small amount of light inside the home. Curtains in all of the upstairs windows are closed tightly, and I'm thankful for a lesser feeling of being watched by someone hiding in the dark interior.

"Welcome to our second stop." Jefferson's voice fills the stretch of sidewalk. "Built in 1892 by Mr. and Mrs.…."

The chronicles of the Irish immigrant who built the home are less spine-chilling than those of the previous residence. I'm actually able to listen in appreciation. Or maybe, the heat coming from Jace's close proximity is lulling me into a trance. I move slightly further away from him, watching out of the corner of my eye to see if he notices. He only crosses his arms, fully entranced by the story.

"Oh my God, what was that?!" Ada whispers, clutching onto my elbow. I jump what feels like a mile into the air.

"What? Where?" Frantically, I scan the windows of the house and check behind me for good measure. My heart thunders in my ears as I prepare for a sight that I already know will stick in my mind for years to come. I've never appreciated my solid sleep schedule enough. Now it may be gone before I've even had the chance.

Jace, Gemma, and Ada are holding their hands to their mouths, attempting to cover the sounds of their snickering. "I'm sorry, I couldn't resist!" Ada says into my ear. I snatch my elbow from her and step away from the three of them.

"The bodies of the two children were found in the chimney…" Jefferson's voice comes back into the foreground at just the wrong time, doing nothing to slow my heart rate. Rude sisters and all of these stories about creepy kids—I'm questioning my ability to make it through the final part of the tour, not to mention, my sanity.

Jace falls into his place beside me as we trek to the final (thank God) destination. "You have to admit, she got you pretty good."

"Yeah, yeah, yeah…" I refuse to look at him.

"Okay, okay, let's change the subject. We'll talk about anything other than what we are doing right now." He pretends to cross his heart over his t-shirt. His perfect green t-shirt that is the same shade as the dress on the cover of the historical romance I purchased earlier.

"Uh…um, how are your grandparents? Your mom's parents?" My tongue is tied in knots. I focus on the ground in front of me.

"They're great! They'll be at the wedding on Friday. You can say hi."

"Do you think they'll remember me?"

"Amry." Jace turns to me, eyes twinkling. He swings his arms back and forth, his energy suddenly nervous. "Since you were just embarrassed, I'm going to tell you something to embarrass myself. But you have to promise not to laugh or give me shit about it."

"Okay?" I look ahead, wondering what he could possibly say. We're mere feet away from the creepy, orange house. I wish he would hurry up and spit it out.

"I kinda…" He runs his hands through his hair and releases a long breath. "Sorta, maybe, had a small crush on you at one time."

The confession hits me like a brick from left field. I never saw it coming.

I always assumed he thought of me as his cousin's chubby friend. Because in my mind, he was always my best friend's geeky cousin. There never seemed to be room in the equation for secret crushes. But apparently that doesn't mean they weren't there. A grin spreads over my face. I decide to blame it on the element of surprise, since there's no other reason it could possibly make me this happy.

"Oh." It's the only response I can formulate. "Wait, what does that have to do with your grandparents though?"

He runs his tongue over the gap in his teeth. The action draws my gaze to his mouth. "Let's just say they used to hear your name all the—"

"Here we are, at our final destination!" Jefferson's voice interrupts Jace's confession. I want to kick him in the shins. Or smash his lantern. "It's time to put your true bravery to the test as we learn one more round of history. But this time, let's go inside, shall we?"

Please no.

Jace gives me a look that conveys we'll finish our conversation later. We enter through the gate one by one to climb the concrete stairs and clump back into the group on the front porch. Ada grabs my hand and squeezes it. "I swear I won't try to scare you again."

I believe her.

The front door swings open to reveal a middle-aged man in khakis and a button-up shirt. (Wait, do ghosts wear khakis?) Jefferson speaks to him before ushering us into the foyer. The interior is clean and obviously well-kept, but the air holds a stale smell that is most likely impossible to get rid of. In my mind, it is officially the smell of ghosts. The foyer light is the only one shining, turning the surrounding rooms into pitch black caves.

"This is Richard." Jefferson snuffs the flame in his lantern and raises it in the direction of the man in the khakis. Our group says hello. "He'll be guiding us through this portion of the tour."

"Welcome, everyone," Richard begins, his Southern

accent much more modern than Jefferson's. "This home is primarily used as a museum now. In addition to our ghost tours we're known for our architecture, due to the combination of Greek Revival and Regency styles the house was constructed in. Here, let's walk as we talk."

He leads us to a grand staircase. My legs may as well be filled with concrete. Escaping from the first floor would be one thing, but the second floor brings entirely new obstacles. Ada nudges me encouragingly. Jace ascends the steps with me at my pace. To my relief, a second light automatically clicks on as we come into the upstairs hallway.

Most doors in the hall are closed. We follow Richard, listening to his account of the home's history. Children in the tour group are now holding their mom's hands. It makes me feel better to know they're also under a little more stress, even if they are less than half my age. At the end of the hallway, Richard opens the final door on the right, sweeping an arm in front of him to invite us all through.

The room is bare except for a fireplace and two armchairs. It's also particularly small, which forces us to squish together in a semi-circle around the fireplace. I'm smashed between Jace and Gemma, focusing on the floor and distracting myself with a game of "Is this threadbare carpet the original?"

"There are a few different spirits residing within the home," Richard explains. "But perhaps our most famous ghost is the late wife of the original owner. This was her sitting room. She ended her life in 1859, after discovering that her husband was having an affair."

The lights go out.

I shit you not, we're submerged into complete darkness the moment Richard finishes his sentence. Gasps fill the air. Someone screams. Was it me? No, it wasn't me, thank God.

Everyone is silent, too terrified to say anything, and I...I'm in Jace's arms. My own arms are snaked around his waist, holding on for dear life. I release my grip, but can't move away because he is squeezing me just as tight.

We're breathing so heavily I can't tell whose breath is whose. His shirt is a soft layer between my face and his chest. I'm about to snuggle closer when I remember that we've just been plunged into night inside a haunted house —on the *second floor*. A shudder makes its way through my body.

"They must have forgotten to pay the electric bill," Jace jokes. I pull my head away from his chest and my eyes slowly adjust to the darkness. I can barely see the outline of his mouth and nose. Our bodies relax, and I prepare for him to release me.

Instead, he closes the distance once more. Then his lips are on mine. It's the softest touch; the slightest sensation of skin to skin. When he does pull away, leaving behind the faintest smell of Ivory soap, I can't help but wonder if it even happened at all.

MOM

Hey! What did y'all do today? Did you get a chance to talk to Ada for me? I still haven't heard from her. Love you both so much.

AMRY

Hi! Just getting in from a ghost tour. Probably won't sleep at all tonight. I did talk to her today, she's working through some stuff but she's ok. We love you too!

ADA'S PRIVATE ANXIETY THOUGHTS

(SERIOUSLY...NO ONE WILL EVER SEE THESE.)

June 10, 2019

Well, the secret blog is no longer secret.

It's 11:00 PM and Amry would normally be snoring by now, but she's still wide awake. The ghost tour we took this evening is 100% the reason for this. She hasn't turned her bedside lamp off and she's been going back and forth between staring at her phone and the ceiling. All this is to say, she just asked me what I'm doing on my laptop.

I had no choice but to tell her. Her response was an "I told you so" smile, but she didn't ask to read it. Thank God, because I'm not ready for that yet. Maybe one day.

Tonight was amazing. I can see ghost tours becoming a possible hobby of mine. I truly don't believe in ghosts, but the idea is fun. You may be wondering, how can someone with such high levels of anxiety have zero worries about ghosts? It's a pretty easy answer—I feel like it's a fear I can control. Kind of like how I wasn't afraid to climb those "death stairs" yesterday. Maybe it's because my brain just doesn't have any space left for those types of fears?

Failure, judgment, loneliness...those are the things that really scare me.

Look at me, trying to be deep! Before I move on to a different subject, I would also like to briefly mention that I haven't pulled in two days. Whether it's because we've been busy, or I'm just happier this week—I don't care. It's been a while since I went even a single day without messing with my hair.

Now, blog, it's time for us to have a discussion. May I present tonight's main topic: love.

Sorry, one more side thought that does relate to the love discussion—and that is that I totally think Amry and Jace have a crush on each other. Thanks for coming to my Ted Talk.

This isn't about them though, at least not right now. This is about a realization I recently had, and that is that Mom, and even Amry, rarely make comments to me about relationships. Shouldn't Mom be worried about me sneaking out of my room at night to hook up with boys? Shouldn't Amry make more remarks to me like the one she made in the car about me meeting a cute Georgia guy? That's not the case though, and I've figured out why.

It's because I never talk about these things myself. I was fifteen when Dad died. While most kids my age are consumed by hormones and first loves, I've been consumed by grief, anxiety, and trich. I've only recently begun to ask myself what I might like in terms of dating...WHO I might like in terms of dating.

And I, without a doubt, like people who identify as girls.

You have no idea how much more free I feel after just typing that. It's something I've known in the back of my mind for quite a while, and something I've now fully accepted and am excited about. Yet, I'm also extra self-conscious around anyone I find attractive, like the girl at the coffee shop, or Gemma...so how is that fair? I guess it's something I'll just have to take one step at a time. Plus, it's not like I've met anyone who would return the feelings anyway.

Which may ultimately be a good thing, considering I don't want to develop feelings for someone anytime soon...not while I'm still fighting this never ending battle of re-growing and pulling my own hair out of my head. Not while I so often feel overwhelmed by my own thoughts that I could explode if it were physically possible. I want so badly to be able to control this.

And I don't want to "pull" someone else into my mess until I have a handle on it.

CHAPTER 10

The mission is simple.

Get to the lobby. Get the coffee. Get back to the room.

Get to the lobby. Get the coffee. Get back to the room.

I repeat the mantra in my head as I scurry out of the elevator, flip flops smacking on the shiny, tile floor. My polka dot pajama shorts are making a public appearance, but I did manage to put on a bra, so I'm proud of *that* last minute thinking. Besides, it's 6:00 AM. How many people can possibly be wandering around at this hour?

I didn't sleep at all last night. Between being wound up from the ghost tour, and even more wound up from what I've convinced myself was a ghost kiss, it had been impossible to calm down. I finally managed to doze off around 2:30, but when I woke up at 3:00 to pee, Ada had turned my lamp off and I went into a panic trying to locate the switch in the dark. Thus, the cycle of "Holy shit, there's a demon in the corner," and "What did the kiss mean?" restarted.

The lights in the last house had flicked back on mere

seconds after Jace kissed me. I still don't know if the whole thing was an accident, or what Ada called a "tactical jump scare attempt." I don't really care—my brain was done for at that point regardless. I floated through the rest of the night in a daze. Jace and I barely spoke on the walk back to the hotel. I have no idea if he even tried to make eye contact with me because I was too terrified to look at him.

The coffee station provides a temporary distraction while I try to decide between original or hazelnut roast. Opting for the latter, I pull a styrofoam cup from the stack and press down on the lever. Steam fills the air and the hot liquid quickly heats through the reusable cup, warming my hand. A bit of creamer and one lid later, I'm backtracking to the elevators.

Ok, Amry. Two down, one to go. Let's get back to the room.

I pass a couple of other guests in their pajamas. They stare longingly at my coffee. The normally crowded seating areas are quiet and empty as I speed walk through them, eager to get to the room and make plans for the day. Maybe I can wake Ada up for an early start.

The elevator is mere feet away. I'm almost there!

But then I see a familiar face sitting on the last sofa between me and freedom.

Jace is also in his pajamas (not plaid!), staring down at a book in his lap, coffee perched on the arm rest beside him. His left ankle is crossed over his right knee and his foot jiggles as he flips to the next page. The site is attractive enough to halt my pursuit of escape.

Dammit.

I'm somewhere between "pretend you didn't see him" and "say good morning" when he looks up and the decision is made for me. He waves, then uncrosses his legs and shuts the book. Swapping my cup to the opposite hand, I wave back. He pats the empty seat beside him and I'm drawn over by what I can only describe as a magnetic force.

"Hey." His eyes are still puffy from sleep, his morning voice an octave deeper than usual. Both characteristics make me want to jump on top of him. I find it super unfair that my own morning breath and sleep-deprived state aren't equally as cute.

"You're an early riser." I sit my coffee on the table in front of him, instinctively pulling my shorts down to cover more of my thighs before I drop onto the sofa. His eyes linger on my lower half before roaming up to my face.

"I could say the same about you," he simpers. "Nice polka dots."

In true Ada fashion, I give him the middle finger. He laughs loudly, like I'm much funnier than I actually am. It boosts my confidence slightly, and I let my shoulders relax. We sit in silence for a few moments, sipping our coffees and watching as the lobby slowly comes to life.

The cover of his book catches my attention: *Midnight in the Garden of Good and Evil.*

"Wait, wait, wait..." I grab the book from the table, thinking back to last night. "You can't say you've read a book if you haven't actually finished it!"

"I practically HAVE finished it!" He seizes it and flips to a dog-eared page that makes me cringe. "Look, only like three chapters to go."

"It still doesn't count." I cross my arms and lean back into the firm cushion. "You're a book poser, Jace Adams."

He waves me off and returns the book to the table. His shoulder brushes mine as he leans back next to me. "Yeah, yeah, yeah. We can't all hold ourselves to such high reading standards."

The conversation has further lightened the mood (book chats have a way of making any situation more comfortable), but the aura of an unfinished discussion still lingers. I open and close my mouth a few times, trying to decide whether to bring up the teenage crush conversation, or the even heavier-pressing kiss debacle. Neither seems appealing.

Do I address the kiss and shut him down, using my very fresh breakup as an excuse?

Do I admit my attraction and get to know more about the person he is now?

Or maybe there's a third option where we just succumb to physical attraction and old familiarity and enjoy the rest of this vacation for what it is?

"So, you used to have a crush on me, huh?" I ask at exactly the same time he says "Are we going to talk about last night?" Red tinges both of our cheeks. We look everywhere but each other, our shared moment of courage gone. He nervously jiggles his leg and his thigh falls against mine and stays there. The warmth is nice in the chilly lobby.

"Let's start with your question," Jace speaks first. "I did. It started around the time I was thirteen and you were fourteen. I nursed my wounds for ages when you and Matt made things official." He gets a far off look in his eyes and shakes his head, developing the memory like a Polaroid.

"I had no idea." Would anything have been different if I *had* known?

"It's a miracle you didn't figure it out," he continues. "Casey knew. She would even make sneaky jokes about it when we were all together."

"*Casey* knew?" I tuck my legs beneath me and turn to face him. "Damn, I must have been really unobservant. She never told me, though!"

Jace takes a swig of his coffee and grimaces. "Too

cold." He gives the cup a frustrated stare and sits it on the table.

I think back, trying to remember times where signs of Jace's puppy love could have been evident. But it's been too long.

Until two days ago, Jace lived in my mind as an old friend; one who I always considered to be such a baby even though he was only a year younger than me. Just like any other teenager (well, most—Ada, for example, never worries about dating), I had a one track mind, and that track belonged to Matt. His face is at the forefront of my high school memories. Casey is slightly off to the side. Everyone and everything else is in the background, a little bit hazy and therefore, indecipherable.

"Sorry you were so freaked during the ghost tour." Jace maneuvers so we're face-to-face.

"It's no big deal." I sigh dramatically and grab my coffee for moral support. "I can be a big baby when it comes to stuff like that."

"More importantly," he goes on. "I'm sorry I kissed you so unexpectedly. You were scared and I took advantage of the situation, which kind of sucks on my part."

Unexpected? Maybe. Unwarranted? Hardly.

The apology is sweet, though. He obviously has no idea how much I've been thinking about him and his stupid lips and tattoos and strangely endearing plaid shorts over the past 48 hours. I essentially manifested it.

I shouldn't be wanting this to happen, but I can't stop it now.

"I was a little surprised, but also not as uninterested as you might think." I bite my tongue as if that will retract the confession. Jace doesn't seem to notice.

"The past couple of days have had me feeling super strange, you know? Like I've had this blast from the past and even though it's been years you still feel so familiar and —" He stops mid-sentence and crinkles his nose. "Wait, did you just say you weren't uninterested?"

The nose crinkle is distractingly adorable. A claw clip holds his untamed hair, making his face open and vulnerable. There's a pocket on his white tee and for some reason I want to stick my hand in it. His casual appearance is a stark contrast to Matt's perfectly gelled hair and wrinkle-free shirts. Matt also wouldn't be caught dead wearing pajamas in a hotel lobby.

Even more reason to think Jace Adams is darling.

I escape his gravitational pull and land safely back on Earth. "I actually totally relate to feeling strange. Running into you has been jarring...but in a good way!"

His face transitions to a look of exaggerated smugness. It's the same expression he used to wear when his grandparents would take his side over Casey's in a disagreement. Only now, I find it hot instead of annoying.

"I always knew I'd have my chance," he jokes.

Something unfamiliar wells in my chest—a feeling I haven't had since I found out Matt had a crush on me back in sophomore year. For the first time in over a decade, I'm experiencing the pure elation of new attraction, the excitement of connecting with someone on a deeper level than friendship.

The problem is, as good as it feels, my life isn't in the right place to hold on to it. The physical element, perhaps, but the emotional aspect—that seems like a lot. My shoulders slump with the realization.

"What's wrong?" Jace picks up on my change in demeanor.

"Um..." I squeeze my coffee cup so hard the lid pops off. "I feel guilty for having feelings like this right now. Seeing as I just got out of a ten-year relationship and all."

He scoots forward to perch on the edge of the sofa, his face serious again. "I understand."

"You do?" I wait for him to continue.

"Amry." His voice waivers. "I was engaged. Things ended three months ago, and it was for the best. But I feel wrong in the same way you do."

My mouth falls open slightly. "I had no idea. Casey never mentioned anything."

"Why would she?" His question is direct. "Sadly, my family saw the end result of the relationship before I was capable of it. We never even took a single step towards planning the wedding."

He stares down at our flip-flopped feet. Maybe our expectations are more on the same level than I thought. Matt and I may have been together for ten years, but at least an engagement didn't add to the messiness at the end.

"I'm sorry, Jace." Following my instinct, I reach for his hand. He allows me to take it, then threads our fingers together. His palm is cool and dry against mine. We sit contemplatively in the awakening lobby. I can see the fully risen sun through the glass doors.

Ada is probably wondering where I am.

"Good talk, Phillips." He squeezes my hand before releasing it. "But...what do we do now?"

His hazel eyes are deep green in the morning light. His lips are still red from the warmth of the coffee. Are they warm to the touch, too?

"How about this?" I stand and fight the urge to stretch. "I need to go upstairs and check on Ada. Let's take the morning to think about how we want to act around each other the rest of this week?"

He laughs and gathers his book and cold coffee. "Deal."

We mosey into the waiting elevator and reach for the ninth floor button at the same time.

We're on the same floor.

I feel faint. Have I fallen into one of the romantic comedies I edit? It sure feels like it. I can see the hook now: *Newly single woman bumps into a childhood friend on vacation, then summer romance ensues.* The doors open onto our floor. Jace exits right and I turn left.

"I'll text you," he promises, swiping his key to enter 912.

I find Ada still in bed, reading one of my new romance novels. She chucks it across the room. It lands face down on top of my suitcase.

"Doing some reading, I see?"

"I was bored!" Ada flings the covers off of her lap. Her nightcap is still on her head. "Where the heck have you been?"

"The lobby, for coffee. Then I ran into Jace." I walk to the window to pull the shades open and shade my eyes against the morning light. River Street looks relatively quiet. The first water taxi of the day is backing away from the hotel's dock.

"Ooooh, Jaceeeee," Ada says in a sing-song voice. "What are we doing today?"

I remove my phone from its charger and plop down into one of the chairs by the window. "Whatever you want to do! Any ideas?"

She climbs onto the other chair and stares down at the water, thinking. "Maybe we could drive to Tybee Island? Get some lunch? Go to the beach?"

It's the second time this week that she's suggested a water-related activity. Why does she all of a sudden want to do things she usually hates? I'm about to press her on the subject when my phone dings with a text. My vision blurs at the sigh of Jace's name on the screen.

JACE ADAMS

I know it's been all of 10 minutes since we saw each other, but I've come to a conclusion.

A pit of anticipation forms in my stomach. Three dots appear, showing that he's typing another message. Ten minutes isn't a lot of time to think. What is he going to say? Will I like it? Will I hate it? *What is happening?*

JACE ADAMS

I'm glad I ran into you this week. I'd like to continue hanging out and having a good time...wherever that may take us?

My first instinct is to fist pump like I'm at a Metallica concert. (There's fist pumping at those, right?) I settle for a couple of excited feet taps instead. A hand on my shoulder startles me. Ada is sitting on the arm of my chair. "Hello, are you listening?"

"Yeah...sorry! Tybee Island is perfect." What was I going to ask her? Unable to remember, I return to Jace's texts. My fingers tremble from the heightened level of adrenaline in my body.

AMRY

A bit of summer flirting never hurt anyone, right?

I hit send and my heart skips a beat. *Who am I?*

Ada is rummaging through her clothes for a swimsuit. The already sunny day is now even brighter. I can't hear them, but I'm positive birds are chirping outside. Relaxing into the chair, I let my eyes fall closed. Possibilities swirl around my head and I seize one of them.

"Should we invite Gemma and Jace?" I ask.

Ada is diving onto the bed to grab her phone before the question has fully escaped my lips. "I'll text Gemma!"

One hour later, we're in the parking lot with Jace. He's already whipped out his keys and insisted upon driving, even though I was fully prepared to. He leads us to a bright blue Camaro and pops the trunk. The urge to take one more shot at offering my Toyota is quelled.

"Whoa, *this* is your car?" Ada drops her stuff into the trunk and runs around to peek through the passenger window. "It's so cool! And much cleaner than Amry's." I narrow my eyes at her and she shrugs.

"Don't be fooled, I cleaned it right before I left Nashville." Jace winks at me. "It doesn't always look like this."

The sound of shoes clapping on the pavement fills the air. I look over my shoulder to see Gemma running toward us. She's carrying a volleyball under her arm, looking like the epitome of summer in her yellow sundress with her perfect tan. She tosses her things into the trunk and Jace closes it.

"Sorry I'm late!" She gives me a quick side hug and moves to do the same to Ada. "Mom was giving me a lecture on sunscreen. And don't forget, gotta stay hydrated! I was like, come on Mom, I'm basically a legal adult." She rolls her eyes.

"Relatable." Ada gives her a knowing smile. They scramble into the backseat and buckle their seatbelts.

It's barely mid-morning and the leather seat is already warm against my exposed thighs. Starting the car, Jace immediately turns the AC on and readjusts the vents so everyone can feel the cool air. Indie music blares from the speakers as his phone connects to the bluetooth, startling all of us.

"My bad." He turns the volume to a more suitable level. "Alright, everyone good?" He looks at Ada and Gemma in the rearview mirror then turns to me. We all nod. "Let's hit the road then." His eyes crinkle in the corners when he grins at me. His hand momentarily rests on my thigh before he clutches the gear shift.

Goosebumps spread over my legs, and they're not a result of the air-conditioning.

SLOAN PINNER

> Hey, Am! I know you're on vacation, but would you have time for a quick phone call later? I miss you and could use a friend chat.

CHAPTER 11

We circle the public parking lot three times before finding an available space. The second he sees brake lights, Jace reverses to let a Jeep back out, then swoops in for the claim. Gemma sarcastically cheers in the backseat.

"You think you could have done a better job?" Turning to face her, he removes his sunglasses and gives her a challenging stare.

"No doubt." She grabs hold of his seat and shakes it. "Does that mean I get to drive home?"

"Not in a million years. Your mom would kill me."

I climb out of the car and flip the passenger seat up for Ada and Gemma to clamber from the backseat. I fill my lungs with the salty air, basking in the calming sound of waves in the near distance. The ocean breeze whips a strand of hair into my face and I tuck it behind my ear. Ada's scarf flaps aggressively in the wind. She shoots me a worried look and reaches underneath her hair to tighten the knot.

"It'll be fine," I whisper, reaching out to squeeze her

arm gently. Her face relaxes and we join Jace and Gemma at the trunk. Jace loads a plastic cooler with the drinks and snacks that we stopped to buy just outside of Savannah. Gemma hangs her beach towel around her neck and bounces her volleyball on the pavement impatiently.

"Ada and I will go claim a spot!" She snatches the ball from the air mid-bounce and slings an arm around Ada's shoulders. They skip off towards the water, Gemma's blonde head bobbing half a foot above Ada's orange-scarfed one.

"I can't believe Ada is so comfortable around her." I accidentally verbalize my thoughts.

"Is she shy or something?" Jace wipes a bead of sweat from his forehead and glances at their disappearing figures.

"Or something."

"Gemma has always been a social butterfly." Jace dumps ice over the canned drinks. "She's like Casey, in that regard. She's a good kid."

"Do you need any help?"

Shaking his head, he closes the cooler's lid. More sweat trickles from his brow, making it to his chin before he swipes it away. I focus on gathering my things from the trunk, hoping he didn't catch me staring. Oh, to be one of those sweat beads.

Gross, Amry.

"I think that's everything!"

We reach to close the trunk at the same time. Jace's hand brushes mine and we both freeze. With our arms in the air, I can smell the slightest hint of his Old Spice deodorant. We lock eyes through our sunglasses. Standing behind the car, it feels as if we are blocked off from the rest of the world. My heart rate increases, drowning out the surrounding waves and beachgoers with its quickened rhythm.

"Do you want to kiss me as badly as I want to kiss you?" he asks hopefully.

Taking a step forward, I close the tiny distance between us. The heat from his body immediately increases my sweat production, but I couldn't care less. Removing his hand from the trunk, he gently wraps his fingers around the back of my neck and pulls my face to his.

His lips are smooth and full. They easily part mine to deepen the kiss and the rhythms of our mouths sync naturally. Our sunglasses clink together. His tongue is warm and curious. Rising to my toes, I lean into his chest. *This* is no ghost kiss. Later, I won't find myself wondering if it actually happened.

His other hand threads into my hair then slides to one of my cheeks to cradle my face as we separate. I open my eyes and laugh, despite my attempt not to.

"I'm sorry!" My voice cracks. "That was...awesome. I just can't believe this is happening!"

Are cheek cramps a thing? Because that's how hard I'm grinning. I could float down to the water instead of walking.

"I get it! I'm the one living my teenage dreams here."

He slams the trunk and bends to retrieve the cooler. We head to the beach, stopping to kick our flip-flops off just before we reach the sand. He gives me another peck on the lips and my knees go weak.

So far, I'm very pleased with the direction we've decided to take this.

I spot Ada's orange scarf. She and Gemma are setting up their towels, placing random objects on the corners to keep them from blowing away. It isn't working very well. Ada manages to tame hers as we approach, but Gemma gives up with a dramatic huff. She yanks her sundress over her head and spikes it to the ground.

"Last one in is a loser!" She takes off running, toned legs and arms pumping. She crashes into the water, disappearing into a wave once she's waist-deep.

Oh, to be that carefree. My boobs would have bounced out of my top twelve times.

Ada watches Gemma with a fond expression and removes her own sundress to reveal another black bathing suit-—this time a one piece with scalloped edges. She gathers her free hair into a ponytail at the base of her neck and begins a much slower approach to the water's edge. After a beat of hesitation, she wades in up to her knees.

I'm proud of her. I don't know why she's suddenly so eager to step out of her comfort zone, but I would never discourage her from doing so. This week has been full of surprises so far.

Jace lays our towels out side by side. There's barely an inch between them. He grabs two mango White Claws from the cooler and hands one to me as I settle down beside him. I dig around in my bag, searching for the sunblock.

"Those two probably didn't put any of this on." I give the bottle a shake and squeeze a glob onto my legs.

"We'll chase them down in a few." Jace peels his tank top off and holds his hand out. "Can I have some of that?"

I'm hypnotized by the sight of him shirtless. He's long and lean; his skin a shade of bronze in the unrelenting sunlight. The tattoos on his right arm go all the way up and curve onto his upper back. I discover something new every time I look at his sleeve—it's like playing a game of "I Spy" without the clues. Random words and dates are speckled throughout the mountains, sunrises, and plants, serving as barriers amongst the sea of nature.

"Amry?" His open palm is still suspended in the air between us.

"Oh." I shake the bottle with more aggression than necessary and dispense some into his hand. "Of course."

I take off my dress and finish lathering up, being sure to cover the awkward spots between the strappy details of my suit. The combination of sweat and sunscreen always makes me feel itchy. I focus on my breathing until I forget about it.

Out of habit, I scan the horizon for Ada. She's sitting in the shallow water, judging Gemma's attempted hand-stands, which are short-lived thanks to the waves. Satisfied the girls are safe, I lean back onto my elbows.

"When did you start getting tattoos?" I ask between sips of White Claw.

Jace furrows his brow in thought. "About five years ago now. Do you have any?" He scans my exposed skin.

"Nah," His gaze makes me feel the need to pull my bottoms up over my stomach. "They're cool. I just have no idea what I would want to permanently commit to."

"Everyone without tattoos says that." He runs a hand from my shoulder to my wrist. "It's as easy as getting something you love, or something you want to remember. Then you can look at it every day and think about the memories and good times attached to it."

"That's beautiful," I say. "But the bigger issue is I'm a weakling and the whole jabbing needles into my skin thing sounds torturous."

"Oh, you could handle it!" He lies back and drapes an arm over his face to block the sun.

I do the same, letting my eyes close. Seagulls fly some-where overhead, filling the air with screeches and chaos as they scour the ground below for any sign of food. Chil-dren's feet patter back and forth on the sand around us. Country music plays from a speaker further down the shore.

The beach always reminds me of Dad. Images of him holding me steady on my old purple and blue boogie board slide across my eyelids. He used to take me deep into the waves, never letting his attention leave me for one second. When I went under, he went under. If I took an accidental gulp of salt water, he would do the same to make me feel better. Mom would watch nervously from her beach chair. I was never scared. When Dad had my back, there was no reason to be. That's how he made me feel in every area of my life. Even when he was feeling scared and overwhelmed himself.

A single tear slides down my face. It drips off my ear and hits the towel underneath me. The saddest memories always seem to come in the quietest, most relaxed times.

Jace naps beside me, his breathing slow and even. Rolling over, I find my cell phone. Mom has sent me a picture of her enjoying coffee on the front porch. I reply with a sneaky picture of Ada sitting in the distance. Her orange scarf is blinding against the cloudless sky. I start to respond to the text I received from Sloan on the drive over, but decide to do it later.

I still need to respond to Matt's email as well. Unlike Sloan though, he doesn't deserve a response. I'm sure he just wants to make sure I haven't flung myself off a bridge. Or...what if he wants to apologize? What if he regrets everything and wants to get back together? Is there a version of the present where I would still want that?

Maybe. Matt's blue eyes make a brief appearance in my mental collection of things I miss.

But, maybe not, I dispute, looking over at a peacefully sleeping Jace.

Ada and Gemma approach silently, dripping and covered in sand from the knees down. Gemma holds a finger to her lips and nods at Jace. She tiptoes to his side and pulls her drenched hair over her shoulder, then wrings it out on his bare chest. He shoots up and looks around frantically.

"What the—?!" His shock fades to nonchalance when he sees Gemma. "I swear, for an only child, I sure do feel like I have a lot of obnoxious siblings."

"It comes with being a part of the Adams family." Gemma circles around us and flops onto the sand beside her crumpled towel. She opens the cooler for a bottle of water and offers one to Ada. Their hands touch, and maybe it's only the sun doing its thing, but I swear Ada blushes. They tear open a bag of Cheetos and pass it around our circle.

We munch in silence, staring out at the horizon and devouring the entire bag. Jace finishes a second White Claw and stands. He walks backward toward the water. "I'm going to take a quick dip, but after that would anyone be up for a little volleyball competition?"

"Yes!" Gemma whoops and downs the rest of her water. "Me and Ada versus you and Amry!"

Ada and I raise our eyebrows at each other. Our family has never been known for athleticism. But if we're going to be split into teams with two people who do have some form of stamina, maybe one of us will have a chance.

———

"ALRIGHT, HERE ARE THE RULES." Gemma drags a heel through the sand to complete the final makeshift boundary line, then jogs back to join us. "No more than three hits to get it back over the line. You have to be behind your back boundary to serve. And no hitting it back after a bounce. We'll play to eight points. Sound good?"

We all nod. She tosses the ball to Jace. "Cool. Old people serve first!"

Ada doubles over in a fit of laughter. Gemma looks proud of herself. Scoffing, Jace and I walk to our side of the "court," being careful not to drag our feet through any of the lines drawn in the sand.

"We're gonna show them," Jace huffs beside me.

"I wouldn't count on that." My foot slips in the sand and I stumble. "Hand-eye coordination isn't my strong suit. Or any physical coordination for that matter. It's not even an honorable mention."

"Don't worry, just follow my lead." He steps into the back right corner and tosses the ball in the air, testing the weight. I try to determine the last time I served a volleyball and decide it had to have been high school Phys. Ed.

We're in trouble.

"Wait!" Ada yells from the other side of the court. "What are the stakes?"

"Why do we need stakes?" I yell back. "Let's just have fun!"

"No way!" Ada interrupts Jace's serve a second time. "I want to make a bet. Meet me in the middle!"

First she wants to come to the beach, and now we're making bets? What has gotten into my sister?

We trudge back to the center and find ourselves in a face-off. Ada and Gemma place their sunglasses on top of their heads and squint at us. Jace and I mirror their actions, forcing ourselves to look intimidating.

"Since when are you so competitive?" I cock my head at Ada.

"Since today," she snarks. "We can keep it between us. For motivation."

Motivation? I supposed I could use any help I can get.

"Fair enough. Name your price."

Contemplating, Ada bites her lip and searches for inspiration. Her eyes land on Jace's tattooed arm. A Grinch-like grin curls across her mouth.

She better not, I swear to—

"If Gemma and I win..." She does a little excited hop. "You have to get a tatt—"

"Ada—"

"Hold on, let me finish, please." She mocks politeness. "You have to get a tattoo of my choice—tomorrow."

"Oooooh!" Jace and Gemma explode into heckling sounds. I stare at Ada unblinkingly, waiting for her to tell me she's just joking and give me her actual proposition.

She doesn't crack.

I continue to stare at my sister in her orange scarf. Her skin is pink from a few days in the sun. She stands tall and confident, perfectly comfortable in our company. She's been up for anything this week, full of some sort of newfound zest for life that is still a mystery to me. Waves crash behind her, adding to the power of it all. *Her* power, which at one point, Mom and I thought may be gone forever.

If she can do it, why can't I? I've said yes to Jace this week. Why can't I say yes to the rest of life?

"I...accept."

Fully taken aback, she shakes her head in disbelief and pretends to check her ears. "Wow. Okay. Now name *your* price."

I did have one idea the moment she mentioned wagers. It extravagantly pales in comparison to hers, but I'm feeling put on the spot. And perhaps a little in shock. It's also not like I can take her home to Mom with her own tattoo, or a facial piercing. (Even though Ada would love that.)

Where is my first-grade thinking cap when I need it?

"You have to wear a color other than black, navy, or gray to Casey's wedding on Friday."

Her expression remains flat. She simply sticks her hand across the line. I shake it and we go back to our prospective sides.

"We have to win this game," I grumble to Jace, nerves setting in.

What did you just agree to, Amry?

Jace claims his serving position. I adjust my bathing suit top and squat into what I think is a "ready" stance. The sand is burning straight through the soles of my feet.

"Here it comes!" Jace tosses the volleyball into the air. Sand flies in every direction. His hand makes successful contact with the ball, producing a *smack* sound. It flies across the middle line, straight to Gemma. She professionally bumps it back to us and I manage to tap it into the air. Jace runs up and spikes it perfectly into the empty space between Ada and Gemma.

The loud squeal I emit is borderline mortifying. Jace runs over to hug me from behind, lifting my feet slightly off the ground. The feeling of his bare chest against my back is almost enough to make me forget the dire predicament I'm in.

"That's one for us!"

Ada kicks sand and Gemma rolls the ball back to us a little too forcefully. Jace tosses it to me with a wink that makes me want to melt more than I already am in the midday sun. "You're up, Phillips."

Mentally reviewing volleyball serving mechanics, I walk slowly to the corner of the court. The ball is sticky in my palms. And have volleyballs always been so heavy? I hold it out with my left hand and crush my right into a fist, then pull my arm back to add momentum to my swing. My fist connects with the ball and it flies over the center barrier, landing just out of bounds on the left side.

"No good!" Gemma runs to retrieve it. "That's our serve!" She takes her place while Jace and I regroup. He gives me a motivating thumbs up. I would prefer another hug.

Ada and Gemma score on the next volley. Jace and I come back with another point, then they land two in a row, which puts them in the lead by one. We're all sweating buckets; the sand is turning to mud on our bodies. The need to win becomes less and less critical as we trip, laugh, fall, and collide. Jace helps me to my feet after an unsuccessful dive save and rests his hands on my hips. As the game continues, he finds more and more reasons for us to touch.

The girls have to be on to our secret by now.

It's Ada's turn to serve. Her scarf flutters dangerously in the breeze as she walks to her corner. It sits further back on her head than usual. The knot needs to be tightened. I watch nervously, preparing to call a timeout and pull her aside. Before I have the opportunity, a rough gust of wind comes through. The scarf blows off of her head and floats through the air in slow motion before finding a landing spot behind Gemma.

"Hope you're still ready to lose!" Ada yells, aloof to what just happened. Her grin fades when no one responds. She looks up from the ball to find us staring. Patches of her scalp flash white in the sun. Strands of new growth, only a fraction of the length of her healthy hair, stand straight up in the wind. She sees the panic in my eyes. I hold eye contact with her, hoping I can somehow keep her calm without speaking.

The volleyball falls from her fingertips and rolls away. Her hands fly to her head. She takes off running in the direction of the parking lot, auburn ponytail flying behind her. The scarf lies abandoned in the sand.

"Um, time out," I say to Jace, coming to my senses. I sprint to the scarf. Seeing me coming, Gemma retrieves it and shakes it off before handing it to me. Her usual happy demeanor is gone, replaced by something more serious. Not judgment, or discomfort–but concern.

"Can I come with you?" she asks, grabbing my elbow. "I know about her condition. Most kids at school do. I just...don't know if she knows I know. Maybe I can help somehow?"

I want to hug her. But it'll have to wait until later.

"Give me a few minutes alone first. I'll feel the situation out." She nods, understanding. I thank her and keep moving, fighting to pick up momentum in the sand.

Ada isn't in the parking lot. Panic shoots from my head to my scorched feet. I hop from one sole to the other, searching for any possible hiding spot. My eyes land on a small, public restroom and I speed walk to the entrance, where I have a hurried inner debate about whether or not it's ok to enter without shoes.

"Ada?" The bathroom is seemingly empty, quiet. I push open the first few stalls and find nothing but toilets and a couple of...other things. Stifling a gag, I stop and listen for sounds of life. Quiet sniffles become audible over the erratic drip, drip, dripping of a broken sink. I continue down the row of toilets, pushing open more doors and finding more empty compartments. My palm connects with the final door and it doesn't budge.

Someone draws a deep breath on the other side. Then, silence.

"Are you holding your breath right now? I can see your feet." Tapping on the door with my knuckle, I glance nervously at the bathroom entrance. If anyone else comes in, she definitely won't come out. Her breathing resumes in a big whoosh, but she says nothing.

"I have your scarf. Open up and we'll get you fixed." More sniffles. I lean against the bathroom wall, wracking my brain for the correct way to handle this. Mom would be beating the door down, but I know that's not the way. Instead, I stay put and hope she at least feels the support of my physical presence.

"Do they hate me now?" she speaks, her voice wavering.

"Huh? Who?"

"Gemma and Jace. Do they think I'm a freak now?" She starts to sob and my knees go weak.

Hearing my baby sister say things like that about herself crushes my soul. And on the opposite spectrum, makes me furious. Every time I have ever felt left out or rejected could be combined together and still not outweigh the pressure that Ada carries on her shoulders daily. It's something I simply can't understand.

I tried it once. Pulling, I mean. I was curious. Why does Ada do it? Why did she start? Why does she continue? I wanted to know what it felt like—what it could possibly reward her with. I only pulled two strands before I was sick of it. It hurts, and not in the way that makes you believe the pain feels good. At least not to me.

But obviously, Ada finds comfort in it.

"Ada, that's so far from the truth." I lean my forehead against the cool, metal door. "Can you please let me in?"

Eventually, I hear the click of the lock releasing. The door creaks open and I step into the small space with Ada. Her eyes and nose are red and swollen. The scrunchie has nearly fallen out of her ponytail. Her shorter hair is wind-blown and sweaty. I fold the scarf into a triangle and pass it to her. She unsuccessfully attempts to tie it around her head with trembling fingers.

"Here, let me help." I hold my hand out. She shakes her head no but I take it from her anyway. "Turn around."

She faces the wall. I remove the scrunchie and use my fingers to smooth her hair into a new ponytail. She stiffens each time I brush over the crown of her head, but doesn't fight me. I secure the scrunchie, then reposition the scarf at her hairline and tie a snug knot at the base of her neck.

"You're not a freak, Ada. Jace and Gemma would never think that," I say softly. "Gemma is actually really worried. She knows more than you think, and it's not because of me."

She turns to face me, eyebrows pinched in the center of her forehead. "Really?"

"Really, really." I tuck a stray section of hair into her scrunchie. "Look, you can't control what assholes at school say about you, but you can control what you say about yourself. And those things should always be nice. Well, sometimes strict to keep yourself on track, but mostly kind and empowering and—"

"I get it!" she interrupts my monologue, rolling her eyes. "I need to stop figuratively beating the shit out of myself."

"No? Well, yes?" I sort through the statement in my head.

Her eyes well up. More tears spill down her cheeks and splatter onto her bathing suit. "I've ruined our good day."

"You have not!" I gather a wad of toilet paper and dab at her face. "This is still a wonderful, fantastic day. I've been thinking about how proud I am of you all morning."

She stops crying again and continues to breathe deeply. I wait while she calms herself, ready with more encouragement on the tip of my tongue and more toilet paper to dry her tears. Abruptly, something switches within her. She stands up straighter and smooths her hands over her scarf.

"I think I'm good." She opens the door and waits for me to leave. "But I do actually need to pee. Meet you outside?"

I study her face to determine whether or not she's lying. Her eyes are clearer–calmer. Deciding to trust her, I give her a hug and leave the stall.

Gemma is waiting in the parking lot with two cans of Coke. Tears jump into my eyes now, because I can see she cares. Ada needs more people who genuinely care. Her friends usually ignore her disorder for the sake of their own comfort. They are teenagers, to be fair. But Ada could use a Gemma in her life.

"Hey!" She runs over to me, eager. "Is she ok?"

"She is." Nodding, I wrap an arm around her shoulders. "Thank you for checking on her."

"Of course! Do you think she'd be ok if I went in?" She looks at me expectantly.

"Yes," I say truthfully. "But Gemma, do me one favor? If she trusts you enough to talk about it, please don't let what kids at school say affect your opinion."

I don't want to question her kindness, but I need to know I can trust her.

"I already don't. Those kids at school–they're ignorant." She rushes into the bathroom.

"You two meet us back at the cooler!" I call after her.

Closing my eyes, I let my shoulders relax and release a pent-up sigh.

MOM

These pictures are the best. You two truly are my whole world.

CHAPTER 12

"So it started after your dad passed?" Jace stares down at the encroaching tide.

We walk slowly, ankles dead weight as we drag them through the water. The evening sky paints a pink horizon that casts the slightest aura around Jace's curls. Beachgoers are slowly packing their things and trickling back to their cars and beach houses. Once crowded and chaotic, the stretch of sand is now peaceful in deepening dusk.

"Yeah, just a few weeks after." The tang of the tartar sauce and fried shrimp I inhaled for dinner sits heavy on my tongue. "It was a confusing time, to say the least."

"I can imagine." Jace purses his lips. "I know anxiety and depression manifest in a lot of different ways. But this is the first I've ever heard of trich."

I hop over a clump of seashell fragments. "Ada was our introduction. Most people don't realize a disorder like that is even possible. That's because those who have it do everything in their power to hide it."

"I'm so sorry." Jace turns to look back at our spot by

the cooler. Ada and Gemma are hunkered over their takeout containers, eating and intermittently stopping to hold their phones up and take what I can only assume are Snapchats or Instagram stories. "Ada's a cool kid. I know it can't be easy."

"She's the coolest kid." I smile sadly.

He reaches over to tuck a lock of hair behind my ear. The gesture is thoughtful, exactly what I need in my current state of dejection.

"I hate that *she* doesn't know how cool she is. She's too consumed by what other people will think of her when they do find out; too worried about how she'll be treated differently before it even happens."

Jace takes my hand. My mood becomes a little less somber, like he's extracting the emotion through my palm. We wander in silence for a few minutes, watching the sun get lower and lower in the sky.

"Did you ever feel like that as a teenager? Like you were living in constant fear of being rejected?" I ask. "I always did somewhat, with my weight, but don't have a way to relate to her on the same level."

"Definitely." He releases my hand long enough to push his hair out of his eyes. "Being multiracial wasn't the easiest experience. Then after Mom and Dad's accident, I was the multiracial kid with dead parents. My classmates were either walking on eggshells around me, or going out of their way to be mean and ignorant."

His answer is heavy. It deserves more than the "I'm sorry" that I give him. We were friends back then, and I'd been too blind to see how badly he was actually struggling. His experience is something I can never relate to, because of the place I was given in life. It's different, even, from Ada's situation.

"It's ok." He squeezes my hand and flashes a smile. "It is a big reason I moved away from Jacksonville the second I got the chance, though. I miss being close to my family, but what I really needed was to learn and grow through my own adventures. I had to figure out who I was outside of the box I grew up in, ya know?"

I don't know. Because I've never done the same for myself.

The current me is a product of molding myself to Matt, and my responsibilities as a sister and daughter. Those aren't bad things within themselves, but I've never thought, "Hey Amry, where would you like to live?" or "Hey Amry, besides books, what do you want to do? Where do you want to go? Who do you want to be?"

But these are epiphanies to work through at a later time.

"For sure," I lie.

We stop walking and stare out at the quelling waves. My sundress can't block the evening chill and I shiver involuntarily. My face is warm, but I'm not sure if it's a developing sunburn or the result of holding Jace's hand.

"Anyway." Jace pulls on my arm to lead me back to Ada and Gemma. "Ada will have the opportunity to do the same for herself. Maybe that will be tomorrow, or maybe it will be a year or two from now. The important thing is it will happen."

Cute, funny, and thoughtful—he's the trifecta. It's making the "let's have fun and see where the week takes us" plan increasingly more difficult. I release his hand as we near the girls.

"I need your help with something," I whisper before we're in earshot. "Ada and Gemma technically won the volleyball bet, but if I'm the one to bring it up Ada won't get the same level of satisfaction from the victory…"

"Are you saying you want to sacrifice yourself and let your sister choose your first tattoo?"

"Yes?"

"Then say no more. I hope you're decent at improv."

He jogs the rest of the way through the sand. I trail behind and question my decision-making skills.

———

THE INSIDE of Jace's car smells like a wet dog. Specifically one that has been at the beach all day.

All I can focus on is a shower. Lucky for me, it looks like I'm going to get one the second we step out of the car. Rain pelts the windshield; sheets of it blow sideways in the headlights as we arrive at the hotel. Jace shifts the Camaro into park and looks at me out of the corner of his eye.

It's about to happen.

"Oh no, Amry!" he yells, waking Ada and Gemma from their half-induced slumber in the backseat. "You know what I just realized? We lost the volleyball game earlier. Rats." He snaps his fingers and gives the girls an "oh shucks" look in the rearview mirror.

This is already the worst acting performance I've ever witnessed.

But I'll go along with it. "Ugh, why did you have to bring that up? You know Ada and I had a bet!"

Ada's face appears between Jace and I, eyes wide with anticipation. "Oh my gosh, yes! I had forgotten!"

She grins crazily. Lightning flashes, illuminating her face. Rain falls harder on the roof. I can't help but feel like I just made a deal with the devil himself.

"This is amazing," Gemma says between yawns. "My brother would never agree to something like that."

"Well, that's probably because he's twelve," Jace says sarcastically.

Great. A twelve-year-old is smarter than I am.

"Let me out of this car!" Ada tugs on my hair. "I have research to do!"

My dress is soaked through before I've even flipped the seat for Ada and Gemma to climb out. We scramble madly to get our things out of the trunk, almost locking Jace's keys inside in the process. Giggling, we slip and slide on wet flip flops to the hotel entrance. Nothing makes you feel more alive than rain on a hot summer night.

The air conditioning freezes the smile on my face when we step into the lobby. Our teeth chatter as the elevator rises at a glacial pace. Gemma exits on the seventh floor with a wave, and then we're finally on the ninth.

"Bye, Jace!" Ada runs down the hallway and swipes into the room, leaving him and I dripping on the green, carpeted floor. He pulls mine and Ada's towels from around his neck and passes them to me. They're heavy, sodden with rain. I cradle them against my chest and more water seeps down the front of my dress.

"Today was a lot of fun." I fall victim to the fact that I'm not sure how I should say goodnight to him. "Thanks for driving. You're a terrible actor, by the way."

He pretends to look offended. "That was an award-winning performance. You obviously have no taste."

"Whatever you say. I'm going to take a steaming shower and begin mental preparation for tomorrow's torture…I mean, tattoo session."

"Good luck with that. Sweet dreams, Am." He hugs me and hesitantly inches toward his room, disappearing through the door with a smile that seems to be hiding disappointment.

Ada is already in the shower. The mirror TV blares

over the sound of falling water. I dump the towels on the floor and fling my bag onto the bed. Sorting wet items from dry, I unpack everything. The edges of my paperback are wet and wrinkled so I sit it on top of the air conditioning unit to dry. I pull my phone out last, pausing.

Didn't I already put my phone on the charger?

I tap the screen. A wallpaper of the Grand Canyon greets me, confirming this phone definitely isn't mine. The wallpaper points to one person, and one person only.

"Ada!" I knock on the bathroom door. "I have to take something to Jace. I'll be right back!"

"Whatever!" she yells over the TV.

I grab my key and step back into the hall. It only takes twelve steps to make it from our room to Jace's. Lifting my fist, I tap lightly on the door. There's no response. I knock again, a bit louder this time.

"Just a second!" he yells. The deadbolt unlatches and then he's in front of me, naked from the waist up. His swimming trunks still hang around his hips.

I can't remember what I'm doing here.

"Miss me already?" He looks both amused and curious, raising his eyebrows and cocking his head to the side. I can hear his shower running in the background.

"I believe this belongs to you." I hold the phone up with two fingers and dangle it in front of his face. "Also, you're wasting so many gallons of water right now."

"Well, I would be *not* wasting water but someone knocked on my door and interrupted me." He takes his phone from me. "Thanks. But this could have waited until you weren't soaked and freezing to death."

He's right. I'm currently composed of 90% goosebumps. "Ada beat me to the shower, so I have to stay strong for a few more minutes."

"Can I interest you in a cup of shitty hotel room coffee

while you wait?" He opens the door a little wider. "It won't be very good. But it will be hot."

Yes, it will be.

I peer down the hallway. Ada should be close to finishing. And I did tell her I would only be gone for a second. She had a tough spell today. Being alone may not be the best idea for her this evening.

On the other hand, spending a few minutes alone with Jace doesn't sound like the worst thing in the world. And what would Ada appreciate more? A little independence? Or a sister breathing down her neck like a second mom?

"Ok, you've sold me." I slip into his room. It's the same layout as mine and Ada's, with a small loveseat by the window instead of two chairs. A few clothing items are strewn about and the bed is unmade, but other than that it's tidy. Much tidier than my room would be if I were staying by myself. Ada has been passive-aggressively tossing things back into my suitcase since we arrived.

"Let me turn this off." Jace ducks into the steam-filled bathroom. I hear the squeak of a faucet being rotated. He re-emerges and I follow him to the small coffee maker on the dresser. Fiddling with the settings, he struggles to open a packet of French roast. His hands are shaking.

For the first time, we're truly alone.

"This better be the best coffee of my life." Leaning against the dresser beside him, I try to hide the fact I'm just as nervous as he is. His lean biceps twitch as he fusses with the machine. I take the coffee packet from him and open it.

"I can't believe I'll have one of these this time tomorrow." I trail my fingers over his tattoos, from his shoulder down to his hand, like he'd done to me on the beach earlier. His skin is warm and his muscles tighten in the wake of my graze. He grabs my wrist. His usual lighthearted expression is replaced by something more eager. His hazel eyes darken to brown. Yearning washes over me and I wonder if I look equally as wild-eyed.

Our mouths connect as the first drip of coffee splats into the pot. The kiss begins as gentle as the one from the ghost tour, deepens into a rhythm similar to the one at the beach, then tumbles into intense, full-fledged need. He pulls me closer, body firm and tight against mine. His hands drop from my hair, to my waist, and then settle on my butt. He squeezes and presses his chest even tighter to mine before he takes his mouth from mine.

"Wait, is this okay?" he asks, nose touching mine. Licking my lips, I lower my mouth to kiss his neck. I'm wet, salty, and covered in twelve pounds of Tybee Island sand. But I don't care because Jace is too. Matt would have never wanted to proceed in this situation.

But Jace isn't Matt.

He finds the hem of my dress and slowly pulls it up. It bunches at my chest. I put my arms over my head so he can remove it. Like him, I'm now standing in my bathing suit, freezing in the draft of the AC. My eyes are drawn to the protrusion jutting from his trunks. He reaches for my chest, retracting his hand twice before he allows himself to make contact.

"I have to tell you, Amry," he mumbles against the top of my head as he unclasps my top. "This is the last thing I expected to happen this week."

The top falls to the floor, bringing the new sensation of skin against skin.

"You're telling me," I murmur.

"But I'd be lying if I said I haven't been thinking about this since I saw you at the coffee shop the other day. Your lips were covered in sugar. It's the first time I've ever been jealous of a muffin."

"Maybe it won't be the last," I banter.

He palms my right breast and presses my back into the dresser. I run my fingers down his sides and hook them in the waistband of his trunks. When I hesitate, he puts his hands on mine and we guide them over his boxers together. They pool around our feet on the floor and he kicks them away.

Backing up, he holds me at arms length. His gaze trails slowly from my face to my feet. I fight the urge that I always get to cover myself when someone looks for too long. He takes his time, appreciating every curve, dimple, and inch of skin.

"You are stunning, Am."

He kisses my shoulder and the need to hide myself passes. *Stunning.* The word loops in my head. It could also be used to describe how he looks in his teal boxers. Who knew hiking could give you the body of a deity?

People who understand how exercise works, but I digress.

Grabbing my hand, Jace leads me to the foot of the bed and sits me down. Sand falls onto the comforter and I spring up. "We can't get in your bed like this!"

"I don't mind. Housekeeping will change it tomorrow." He presses his mouth to my chest.

"Ok…" His touch almost changes my mind. "No, wait. I'm serious, you can't sleep in a sandy bed tonight."

"You're right. Maybe I have a better idea anyway?" He arches an eyebrow.

"Do tell." I play it cool, like I have topless conversations on a daily basis.

"One second." He walks into the bathroom and the echo of the shower stream fills the room once again. His intention becomes clear.

I would very much like to take a shower with Jace Adams.

I stand and tiptoe to the bathroom. Outside the door, I pause to take a deep breath. I lost my virginity a decade ago, but the feeling in my chest is just like the one I had before my actual first time.

It's a mixture of excitement, nervousness, and pure, human want. Perhaps the want is even stronger than it was my actual first time. Because now, I know what to expect. I know how the desired outcome feels.

Ok Amry, you can do this.

No boxers in sight, Jace's bare ass is the first thing I see upon entering the bathroom. He leans into the shower to check the temperature of the water. Looking over his shoulder, he grins at me through the steam.

"Is this too hot for you?" he asks.

"I doubt it." I join him and stick a hand under the shower head, thankful I was able to comprehend that he was asking about the water and not himself. The answer to that question would have been a resounding "yes."

"Good." He steps into the stream and fixes his focus on my bikini bottoms. "I think you'll need to lose those."

My heart rate doubles. Partly from the idea of losing my final scrap of cloth to hide behind. Partly from the sight of water cascading down his body. He blinks at me patiently, droplets dripping from his dark lashes. I shimmy out of the bottoms, leaving them to their fate on the floor.

The water soothes my clammy skin and washes some of the nervousness away. Jace's wet lips glide effortlessly over mine, then move down my throat as he pushes me against the shower wall. His mouth continues to descend, brushing lightly over each of my nipples and then my rib cage. He becomes harder and harder against my thigh.

He grabs a bar of hotel soap and lathers it in his hands. We rub the suds over our arms and take turns washing each other's backs. Bending to swipe the soap over my legs, his face levels with the space between them. I suck in a breath. My pelvis aches, and though I can tell Jace is on the same page, we practice patience and enjoy the thrill of the moment.

Once the soap is rinsed away, Jace holds my hand to help me out of the shower. He grabs a clean towel, and wraps it around me. Back in the bedroom, I'm immediately cold again. We trail wet footprints along the carpet, ignoring them because there's only one goal in mind. He tackles me onto the bed, his weight solid and comforting on top of me.

"I guess a wet bed is still preferable to a sandy wet bed," I say between kisses.

"Any bed you're in is my number one choice."

"What if it was a bed full of spiders?" I joke.

"It's your lucky day. I'm not scared of spiders."

He stands and rushes to his suitcase. The muscles in his thighs flex as he bends over to dig through it. The foil wrapper of a condom flashes in the light. He rips it open, and I allow myself to stare as he rolls it on.

"You're still okay?" he asks, placing a knee on the bed between my thighs. I nod.

He wraps an arm around my waist and scoots me further onto the bed with surprising ease. My thighs open wider as he nestles between them. I wrap my arms around his lower back, and his eyes remain on mine as I guide him in.

Then I'm lost in another new moment with Jace Adams.

JACE ADAMS

This is the best week I've had in a long, long time.

Let's go out tomorrow night and have some fun. Just me and you?

AMRY

Ok, let's do it. But I'm paying for myself. ;)

Goodnight, Jace.

ADA'S PRIVATE ANXIETY THOUGHTS

(SERIOUSLY...NO ONE WILL EVER SEE THESE.)

June 11, 2019

Today was the best bad day I've ever had.

I know, that makes no sense, so let me explain. What happened on the beach today was my worst nightmare–a nightmare that I've already lived a few different times, unfortunately. My trich is my secret. If someone has to know about it, I would prefer to tell them, rather than have them find out by accident. Especially if it's someone I feel drawn to; someone I want to be a bigger part of my life.

So when I lost my scarf, I felt like my good week was over. Running away was my first instinct. When I locked myself in that bathroom stall, I was already preparing for an awkward, silent car ride back to Savannah. I was ready to never speak to Gemma again. Because why would she want to speak to me?

I was shocked when she came into the bathroom after Amry. She smiled and gave me a can of Coke. It was so nice.

We walked outside and sat on the bumper of Jace's car

for a while. She admitted she's heard the rumors around school. But then she did something that no one else ever has–she asked me to tell her about trich. She said my story is the only one that matters and no one else should be able to change that. Especially not my classmates.

The truth is, others do define how I feel about myself. If someone says I'm the weird girl who pulls her hair out for fun, then I believe that. At least for a while, until I calm down and work through it. But then another person will say something different, and the cycle restarts.

If I knew someone else who had trich like me, would I let them think such horrible things about themself? No way. I would want them to know they're strong, and awesome, and deserving of everything they want.

I only wish I knew why I can't believe the same. It makes things harder.

Gemma has been so kind to me this week that I assumed she must not actually know why I wear a scarf. I've tried to keep it a secret from friends in the past. Anyone who found out slowly pulled away. The friends that have stuck around pretend like it doesn't exist. Maybe that's my own fault. I wish I had owned it from day one and said "Hey world, my dad is gone, and this is a thing I have, and that's ok because I'm still going to try to be me."

I guess it's still not too late for that. Maybe this week is a step in the right direction. Maybe I'll leave here with a new lifelong friend, too.

Or…more than a friend? Gemma held my hand in the car on the way home. I'm glad it was dark. It made it easier to hide my face as I worked through whether she was just being nice, or whether it could possibly be something more. She's a touchy person. She loves to hug, and be close to people. I could be looking at it wrong. I wouldn't know what someone having a crush on me looked like if it slapped me across the face.

Do I even *want* it to be something more? I literally just blogged about not feeling strong enough. Not to mention, Gemma is out of my league in every way.

Amry would freak out on me if she ever saw that last sentence. It's a perfect example of the things I say about myself and shouldn't. Old habits will have a hard time dying. My entire brain is going to have to be re-wired. Most of the time, my thoughts are negative even when I want to be positive. But working through it at my own pace is better than not trying at all.

Wow, look at that...I'm already changing.

Amry is on the phone with Mom right now, who is asking thousands of questions about our week. Amry is doing most of the talking, but I'm trying to chime in every minute or two with an "mm-hmm" or short answer. I'm enjoying the space from Mom. It makes me selfish, I know. But Amry hasn't said anything else to me about being nicer. I'm re-paying her by not asking why she came back into the room freshly showered earlier.

I'm positive Jace and Am are, you know...doing IT. (I'm allowed to say stuff like that here, this is my blog.) I wish she thought I was more mature. I wish she would talk to me more about her love life. Or even just her sex life. It is 2019 after all–I know more about it than her and Mom could even imagine. I just haven't experienced any of it yet.

One day. And one day Amry will want to talk to me.

For now, I have a tattoo to pick out.

CHAPTER 13

"Can I at least choose *where* to get it?" My legs may as well be filled with lead. Ada skips along next to me, exuding a level of excitement that seems a bit excessive for someone who is about to watch their sister become permanently marked as a result of a lost bet. We pass the usual signs advertising to-go alcoholic beverages. I wish I could chug one of each.

Don't forget Amry…you did volunteer for this.

But that was yesterday. Today is today, and I'm feeling argumentative.

Ada looks down at Google Maps. "It should be just around the corner. And yes, but it has to be one of three places that I think will look the best."

"Fine," I sigh and try to look as pathetic as possible. "What if they're too busy to take me today?"

"Don't worry about that, I made you an appointment!" she gloats, eyes extra proud beneath her blue-shadowed lids.

"How did you have time to make an appointment for something that was just decided last night?" I ask.

"Well, they have this thing called a website. And you can make appointments there." She speaks to me like I'm five-years-old.

Which is relatable, considering I want nothing more than to fall to the ground and roll around in a fit until she agrees to choose another option for her victory. Instead, I work on convincing myself that this is exciting. Tattoos are bad ass, right? It's only the *tiniest* clump of needles jamming ink into your skin. It's only permanent. It's art, isn't it? Just look at Jace's tattoos—they're stunning.

Jace. Jace's tattoos. Which are attached to the rest of his body. My heart flutters faster and faster as I replay our shower, replay his chest touching mine, replay his hips grinding against my own. It helps ease my nervousness, but also makes me anxious–the good kind of anxious–in other ways. I grin and take another peek at the "good luck" text he sent this morning.

When I returned to our room last night, Ada hadn't asked what took so long. I don't think she even noticed my freshly wet hair or sand-free body. If so, she didn't say anything. She had been on her computer, typing away. Maybe I'm lucky that she seems to be more naive to these things than the average teenager.

"Here we are!" We stop in front of a brick building. The windows are tinted, making it impossible to see inside. The shop name takes up the entire front window in a swirly, artistic font.

"*Haunted Tattoo*?" Scrunching my nose, I look down at Ada. "Did you do this on purpose?"

"No!" She laughs, holding the door open for me. "They were my favorite of all the shops I researched. The name is just an added bonus."

"Right, because you're such an expert on tattoo shops," I whisper to her as I step cautiously inside. The white-walled interior encases a minimalistic lobby; a few plants and hand-drawn art pieces add just the right amount of character. The smell is sterile, reminding me of a doctor's office. Everything seems perfectly clean and inviting. Some of my nervousness is replaced with a tiny bit of unexpected excitement–the kind you get just before a new experience.

I only wish I knew what the tattoo was going to look like. Knowing Ada, I'll either walk out of here with something that I love, or with something she thinks is hysterical. If it's the latter, hopefully my sense of humor is working properly.

"Amry? Ada?" A woman around my age appears from the connecting room. She's tall and thin, wearing a pair of vintage-looking overalls over a black satin tank top. Her straight, silky hair is dyed a shade of deep green. Every inch of her exposed, light brown skin is covered in tattoos.

She's both the coolest and most intimidating person I've ever seen. Ada is ogling her like she's a goddess. Trusting her by appearance alone, I cross my fingers and hope she's the one who will be doing my tattoo.

"Yeah, that's us, I'm Amry." We meet in the middle of the room. "I think I have an appointment?"

"You think, or you know?" she jokes, arching an eyebrow at me. "I'm Brynn, you'll be with me today. Nice to meet you."

She shakes our hands and motions for us to follow her.

In the next room, clients sit and lie on chairs in a variety of positions. Some have their faces scrunched in discomfort, others are chatting with their artists like they're in a therapy session. The buzzing of tattoo guns echoes off of the walls, rhythmically stopping and starting as each artist works their way through their prospective pieces. I try not to stare at each tattoo as we walk by.

I feel less out of place than I thought I would.

"This is us." Brynn motions to the last chair on the right. I settle in while she fetches a folding chair for Ada. It only takes a minute for my skin to begin sweating against the leather. Ada rescues my purse from the tense, vice-like squeeze of my arms and gives me an encouraging wink.

"So you lost a bet, huh?" Brynn plops onto a stool beside me and tugs on a pair of plastic gloves. "I think it's cool you're holding your end of the bargain, but as an artist I also have to ask if you're absolutely certain you want to."

"How'd you know about the bet?" I ask, assessing my current level of fight or flight. Surprisingly, I don't want to leave. Curiosity and impending adrenaline have taken over.

"The online appointment form," Ada and Brynn say at the same time. Of course, modern technology is making this as easy and embarrassment free as possible.

"I want to do it. I just don't want to hate whatever it is," I say truthfully.

"I *have* been playing this whole thing up, but you don't really think I'd pick something bad, do you?" Ada looks slightly hurt.

Brynn tentatively looks back and forth between us, probably trying to determine if she's going to have to intervene in a sister argument.

"Well, deep down, no," I confess. "But you have to admit, getting your first tattoo is even scarier when you're not the one who picked it out."

Ada shrugs, as if she's considering the scenario for the first time. Brynn turns on her stool, shielding a smirk as she ties her impossibly shiny hair into a ponytail. I lean my head against the chair.

"I have the stencil ready, based on the picture Ada sent

me. Do you want to see it?" Brynn asks, swiveling back around.

"Yes!" I say a little too loudly.

"Me first!" Ada pronounces.

We stare each other down. Brynn pauses to wait for clarified instructions. Bless this girl's patience.

"How about this? I look at it first. Then you can see it after Brynn puts the stencil on, before she starts tattooing?" Ada suggests.

I huff dramatically, but nod in agreement. Ada and Brynn meet behind my chair to discuss line thickness, shading, and other verbiage I don't understand, but assume I will learn in the next hour. Ada lets out a happy little squeal, which better be a good sign. She sits back down, cheeks flushed and grinning as she reaches beneath her hair to tighten her scarf.

"You're going to love it!" she begins. "I think it would look best on your inner forearm, collarbone, or upper back."

Brynn has a small sheet of paper in her hand. I can't see what's on it, but the size alone is enough to reassure me I'm not about to walk out of here with a full sleeve. Not that you can do a full sleeve in a day, I guess. But what do I know?

I consider the three places Ada suggested. Since I'm ticklish, my collarbone sounds like torture. I don't like the idea of my back because I want to be able to see what's happening. With those two rejected, there's only one more option.

"Let's do my forearm—the left one," I declare, glancing down at the empty, nearly-translucent space just below the fold of my elbow. Would it be weird if I gave it a little pat and wished it farewell?

Brynn sets her station up, then props my arm into

place and gently stretches it into position. She shaves the area with a disposable razor and runs a gloved hand over it to check for smoothness. "Close your eyes and hold super still for me. I'll let you know when the stencil is on."

Following her instructions, I try to relax my shoulders. She rubs something cool and silky over my arm. Her fingers whisper softly against my skin as she carefully places the stencil and peels the thin layer of paper away. To my right, Ada makes another enthusiastic noise.

"You can look now," Brynn says quietly, trying not to startle me.

"Yes, look!" Ada grips my other arm, her exclamation anything but quiet.

Ada's eyes, hopeful and crinkled at the corners, are the first sight I see when I open my own. My neck seems to swivel in slow motion as I turn to check out my new, soon-to-be permanent souvenir. A mini illustration of a vintage quill lying next to an ink pot, exactly like the ones on Dad's bookshelf at home, is on my arm. Tears blur my vision and I fight to contain the sob that swims up my throat.

Was it just yesterday I told Jace there's nothing I can imagine having tattooed on my body forever? Less than twenty-four hours later, I'm eating my own words. The mark isn't even permanent yet, but I already have no doubt that I will cherish this for as long as said body lives.

"Do you like it?" Ada asks eagerly, not giving me a chance to respond. "I thought it would be perfect for you because I know how much you love Dad's collection, but it also makes sense for your job and how important books are t—"

"I love it," I interrupt, blinking the tears away before they can fall. "It's perfect."

Brynn gives us a moment. She looks just as pleased with my reaction as Ada.

"Let's make it last forever then, shall we?" She squeezes black ink into one of the tiny cups on her table and presses the button of the tattoo gun to test it. "Let me know if you need to stop for any reason. This will be a pretty quick job. Just breathe."

She places the tip of the needle to my arm. Instinctively, I hold my breath, then let it whoosh out as my skin adapts to the sharp sting. She completes a couple of lines then glances up to make sure I'm ok. Nodding, I relax into the chair to watch as she creates an entirely new part of me.

Ada never lets go of my other hand.

———

"I'm going to get like a hundred tattoos someday," Ada announces as we leave the shop and step back into the ever-moving crowd of tourists. "I'm living vicariously through you right now."

"Well, don't," I say, admiring my tattoo through the clear, plastic bandage Brynn stuck over it. "Sure, it looks cool, but my arm feels like it was attacked by multiple cats."

Gingerly, I hold it away from my body. I can't help but peer down at it every couple of minutes as we walk along. I'm proud of it, which isn't a feeling I was expecting to have.

There's something enthralling about knowing that a small space on my arm—on my body—is changed forever. Sitting in Brynn's chair for forty-five minutes left me with an everlasting reminder of Dad, of Ada...of this trip. Maybe Savannah is only the beginning of a series of new experiences for me.

"Can we get some ice cream?" Ada's question brings me back to the present.

"Hell yeah!" I grab her shirt sleeve and maneuver us around a crowd of people stopped in the middle of the sidewalk. "I'll never say no to ice cream."

Clouds from last night's storm still linger, offering welcome shade from the relentless temperatures of the past few days. The breeze is almost free of its usual humidity. I welcome its touch against my face and neck as we make the ten minute walk to Savannah's best-known ice cream parlor. A line of people spills out of the open door and onto the sidewalk. We take our place behind a young couple who are wrapped around each other, not an inch of space between any part of their bodies. It annoys me much less than it would have forty-eight hours ago.

Ada's face flushes and she turns to me in an attempt not to intrude on their publicly private moment. "Look, I found the menu online." She angles the phone so we can inspect the list of flavors.

While we wait, I perform my daily checkup on the Google review. This week has allowed me to forget about it for the most part, but every once in a while it shoots through my mind like a rogue firework. I've given up on trying to figure out who's responsible for it. But if I did know, at least I could reach out to them to apologize and ask if there's anything I can do. It's messing with my confidence as an editor.

Why can't it just disappear?

The line moves quickly. I'm about to step inside the shop when I feel someone close, too close, behind me. A pair of hands cover my eyes.

"Guess who?!" A female voice yells into my ear, doing little to ease my already rapidly beating heart.

I pull the hands from my eyes and whip around.

Gemma's freckled cheeks are level with mine. She hugs me before moving to wrap her arms around Ada. A shorter, curvy woman with the same blonde bob stands just behind Gemma.

"Mama, you remember Casey's friend, Amry. And this is her sister, Ada!" Gemma introduces us.

"Of course! Amry, you haven't changed a bit since high school! Ada, Gemma has told me all about you. It's so nice to see y'all," Gemma's mom replies in a Southern accent. She pulls Ada and I into a group hug.

So this is where Gemma inherited her love language of physical touch.

"You too, Mrs. Adams," Ada and I respond, almost in unison.

"Oh, please call me Trish. It makes me feel younger." She giggles. Gemma rolls her eyes, but doesn't look embarrassed. For a brief moment, I wish Mom was with us. I also wish Ada wanted Mom to be here.

"Looks like you had the same midday ice cream craving as us," I joke, reaching up to tuck a flyaway behind my ear. "Have you been here bef—"

"Ahh!" Gemma gently grabs my wrist and pulls me closer to her, eyes locked on my forearm. "You really did it! It's so pretty! Did you just do it? Did it hurt? Will you do it again? How did you decide what to get?"

I don't know which question to answer first.

Ada pipes in. "We just left the tattoo parlor. I picked it out. Brynn, the artist, was so awesome! Am handled it like a pro."

She smiles at me like I'm the bravest person on the planet. My heart melts a little.

"It's frieken' sweet." Gemma releases my wrist.

"Gemma," Trish reprimands her. "How many times have we talked about that word?"

"It's not even the *real* word, Mama…" Gemma mutters under her breath.

I give Ada a "see, every mother on the planet does this stuff" look. She sticks her tongue out at me. The line moves and the four of us gladly step into the air-conditioned parlor. Smells of chocolate and caramel swirl through the air. The couple in front of us orders a double scoop on a waffle cone. I stare at the case full of ice cream, debating between butter pecan, cookie dough, or both.

Dad used to say that butter pecan is an ice cream flavor for old people. His teasing never stopped me from loving it. It also never stopped him from digging into a fresh carton alongside me.

"What are you guys doing tonight?" Gemma asks, hopping from foot to foot to release some of her never ending energy. Ada looks at me expectantly and I freeze. I haven't told her about my impending "non-date" plans with Jace yet.

Mainly because I don't want to leave her alone for that long, and haven't been able to come up with an alternative plan.

"Ummmmm." I give myself a few seconds to think before deciding that honesty is the best policy. "I'm not sure yet. Jace asked me to go for a drink later, but I probably won't because then Ada would be bore—"

"Don't use me as an excuse, you're definitely going to hang out with Jace," Ada chastises. "I can hang at the hotel. I'll keep the door locked. It will be fine."

Her safety isn't the only reason I don't want her to be alone, but there's no good way to broach that subject at the moment. Or, ever really. If she knows I'm concerned about leaving her by herself, a good chunk of the trust she has in me would be erased. I would no longer be the "good cop." Mom and I can't both be on her shit list.

Ada may not realize it, but she's still a kid. She needs our help. She needs our love. Even when it's tough.

Trish sees the hesitation on my face—it's a look that only a mom could recognize. "Maybe Gemma can hang out with Ada in your room. Have a little movie night or something? I could check on them every hour or so."

Both girls' faces light up. They start chattering excitedly about snacks and what movie to watch. I consider giving Trish another hug, but settle for a moment of appreciative eye contact instead. She winks at me and herds us forward to order.

"That was a great idea, thank you," I tell her quietly as the girls place their orders.

"Not a problem." She gives me a little pat on the back. "I know Gemma will love it. And I'd do anything to help my Jace out, too."

She steps up to the counter, leaving me to decipher her statement and the knowing look on her face.

June 12, 20194:04 PM
From: ellie_p1971@tmail.com
To: ada-potata@tmail.com
Subject: You're amazing

Ada,
I'm not sure how often you check your email, so it could be a while before you see this. But that's ok. I've just been thinking about a few things and want to tell you while the thoughts are fresh.
I know you're having the best time with Amry this week. She's been sending me pictures. You're both so beautiful and you look so happy. I was worried about you leaving this week. The two of us have been together every single day since Dad passed.

Now that you've been gone a few days, I'm realizing that is a big reason our relationship isn't the
healthiest lately.

I can be controlling, and you need your space. We
both do. I need to learn to trust you more. I need to
let you make your own mistakes and learn from
them. It's my job to protect you, but it isn't my job
to oppress you. I have to let you be your own
person.

And the person you currently are is perfect. My
actions may often make you think the opposite, but
please know, I wouldn't want you to be anyone else.
I promise you'll see a change in me when you're
back home. It's time for us to start working on this
together, because it isn't Amry's responsibility to
constantly pull us back together when we're falling
apart. We have to stop letting her babysit us.

Anyway, I know this email is just full of jumbled
thoughts, but I promise they're all true. I'll see you
in a few days. I can't wait to hear about everything.

I love you so, so much.

Mom

CHAPTER 14

"First, I let you talk me into a tattoo. Now I'm letting you give me a makeover. What kind of power do you have over me?" I try to sneak a look in the mirror. Ada grabs my chin and forces my face back to her.

She rolls her eyes and pulls an orangey-red lipstick out of her makeup bag. Before I can protest, she swipes it onto my lips and cleans up the edges. "I can't help that I have good taste. You can look now, by the way."

I rise from my spot on the closed toilet lid and look eagerly in the bathroom mirror. My mouth falls open. Even in the fluorescent lighting of the bathroom, I look better than I have in ages. The lipstick provides a pop of color in the otherwise neutral makeup. The bottom half of my hair is curled, falling loosely around my shoulders. The top half is swept into a miniature version of my usual bun.

"Damn." I push my hair behind my shoulders. "This is...thank you."

"Yeah, yeah, yeah." She grins proudly, then smacks me on the butt. "Now go put on the outfit I picked out!"

My clothes are laid out on the bed. Ada lingers as I

remove my pajamas to put on ripped jeans and a summery, red blouse. My tattoo stings slightly with each movement. I'll get to show it to Jace soon, and that makes me smile through the small amount of pain.

"What do you think?" I slip my sandals on and twirl over to the mirror, where I inspect everything again. I can't remember when I last spent this much time checking myself out, but I have to say...I feel good.

Ada looks me up and down, eyes narrowed in thought as she taps her upper lip. "It's good, but I feel like you're missing something."

A lightbulb goes off in her brain and she dashes back to the bathroom. I follow her.

"This should do it!" she proclaims, pulling a floral-patterned scarf from the counter top. "Bend down."

I crouch to her level and she ties the scarf around my bun. The ends hang loosely with the rest of my hair. I have to agree—it completes the look.

"I love it!" I say, fingering the scarf gently and returning to the bedroom to gather my things. "Hey, do you remember how you started wearing a scarf?"

"Yeah." Ada perches on the edge of the bed. Her face relaxes as the memory falls over her. "It was Mom's idea. She first used the scarf she kept tied on her purse strap. That one was so small, and tight around my head, but it worked."

I wasn't there the night Mom saved Ada from having a melt-down over the homecoming dance. But I did get a phone call the second after she dropped Ada off at the school. Mom had been so proud of the scarf idea. It made Ada happy, for once. The next day they went scarf shopping and sent me fashion show-style pictures of Ada in all of the ones she chose. I still have the photos saved on my phone.

"And now you're a fashion icon because of it." I use my hands to do the Vogue frame around my face.

Ada wrinkles her nose, but I can tell she's actually pleased with the compliment. I seize the opportunity to continue on the subject of Mom. "Would you mind texting her to check in for us? I haven't talked to her today. Jace will be here any second and I don't want to forget."

"I'll try," she responds shortly.

She flings herself backwards onto the bed and stares up at the ceiling. I can feel the sudden change in her mood. Mine plummets right along with it. It's the first real twinge of frustration I've felt with her all week—at possibly the worst point in time.

"Okayyy?" I say, trying to prompt another response. She says nothing. "I'm not asking you to call and have a two hour phone conversation with her. It will take ten seconds to send a quick text."

"So why can't you do it?" She continues to stare at the ceiling. My face continues to heat.

I snatch my bag from the top of the dresser and check to make sure my wallet is inside. I sling the bag over my shoulder and turn away from her. Being the neutral party between her and Mom is exhausting sometimes. *How did Dad always do it?*

"Forget it. Sometimes I forget you're still a self-absorbed teenager." I regret the words as soon as they're out of my mouth. But they can't be taken back.

Right now, I don't want to take them back. Ada rolls onto her side and continues to ignore me. An apology rolls around on my tongue but I swallow it. Don't I deserve to speak my feelings sometimes, too?

A knock on the door makes me jump. Ada shoots up from the bed. We both look everywhere but each other.

I walk to the door and open it, finding Jace and

Gemma on the other side. Gemma is holding a pizza and a bag of Oreos. Jace is wearing jeans and a black t-shirt. The sight of him is almost enough to make me forget that Ada and I are in the middle of an escalating argument.

An argument that now ceases to exist because there's no time to finish it.

"Amry!" Gemma stares wide-eyed, skirting around me to put the pizza on top of the dresser. "You look frieken' hot. Doesn't she look hot, Jace?"

"She does." Jace's eyes roam over my face and hair. "Are you ready to go?"

"Yeah…" I turn to Ada and stare at her forehead to avoid eye contact. "Call or text me if you need anything."

"Have fun!" Gemma pipes in, oblivious to the energy in the room. "My mom said not to worry, she'll keep track of us."

Thank goodness for that.

Fighting the urge to slam the door behind me, I force a smile and join Jace in the hall. *Come on, Ada. Why did you have to do this right now?*

He excitedly stoops to kiss me, cupping my chin and pushing me gently against the wall. Adrenaline floods my veins, lifting my mood to a lighter state. I thread my fingers into his curls, which are still slightly damp from the shower.

"Oh, shit," I say, pulling away. "You have lipstick all over your face. Sorry, I forgot I had it on!"

He laughs and swipes at his mouth with the back of his hand. "It was worth it."

We move to the elevator and join the crowd inside when it arrives. Everyone is dressed to go out for the night. The smells of perfume and already-consumed alcohol intermingle in the air. Jace grabs my hand as we descend and keeps a tight grip on it when we exit.

"Wait!" He halts halfway down the walkway to the river taxi. "I almost forgot. Let me see the tattoo!"

I'd forgotten about it too, in the wake of Hurricane Ada. I hold my forearm out proudly. He carefully takes my elbow in his hands to get a closer look through the clear bandage.

"This is sick," he says. "Very Edgar Allan Poe."

"You think so?" I inspect the tattoo for the millionth time. Jace's comment makes me love it even more.

"I think it's great." He recollects my hand and we join the growing taxi queue. "Why did Ada choose that?"

I tell him all about the experience of my appointment and the inspiration for the tattoo as we board the boat and ride over to River Street. The taxi is the most crowded I've seen. As we grow closer to the shore, I can see that downtown Savannah is equally packed. We perch on the edge of our seats, glued together in an attempt to not bump into anyone else. The evening is balmy and my upper arm sweats against his, but neither of us make any effort to readjust.

"So, where are we going on this non-date?" I ask after we have successfully disembarked. The last rays of sun are gone, leaving Savannah bathed in yellow street lights.

"Non-date, huh? Ouch!" He lays a hand over his heart as if he's been stabbed. The lipstick he wiped off of his face is still there, orange against his brown skin. "Anway, it's a surprise."

"What if I don't like surprises?" I ask, looking at him sideways.

"Who doesn't like surprises?" The innocent look on his face is so endearing I can hardly stand it. Should a friend I'm only having a week of vacation fun with pull at my heartstrings like this? Because every second I've spent with him has wound them tighter.

"Don't worry, *I* do." I laugh and he looks relieved. "But I'm sure someone out there hates them."

"Now I'm definitely not telling you where we're going. Not that I was going to anyway." Jace pokes me in the side, studying my face so intently that he collides with a man on the sidewalk. They mumble apologies to each other and his face flushes.

"Smooth." I suppress a giggle. He puts an arm around my shoulders and pulls me closer to plant a kiss on my temple.

We pass the restaurant where Ada and I ate our first night. Is she having fun with Gemma? Is she still mad at me? I've moved past the anger brought on by our disagreement, and settled heavily into guilt. A quick check of my phone shows no calls or texts from her.

But I do have a missed call from Sloan.

Oh, shit. Her text from yesterday still sits unanswered.

AMRY

> I'm so sorry, I forgot to respond! Are you ok? Can I call you later tonight?

My phone doesn't even make it to my pocket before she responds.

ADA

> Yeah, I'm fine! Just checking in. I'll look for your call this evening.

"We're taking the next left." Jace points ahead and I nod, still staring down at my phone. "Is everything ok?"

"Yeah," I sigh and lock the screen. "For the most part. Ada and I were two steps from being in a full-blown fight when you and Gemma showed up."

"I thought I sensed some tension." We veer left, finding ourselves at the bottom of a steep street. "I was under the assumption though, that you two are perfect sisters who never argue."

"We don't argue much." My calves burn as we climb the incline. "But we're not perfect by any means. Especially since Dad died. I mainly spend my time being the go-between for her and Mom."

"Do they not get along?" Jace asks. "Sorry if I'm being too nosey."

"No, you're not at all." It feels nice to get this off my chest. "They butt heads. Ada is stubborn, as most teenagers are. And Mom can be insensitive towards Ada's trich. Not on purpose, but it doesn't help an already strained mother-daughter relationship."

"It certainly sounds exhausting for all three of you." We reach the top of the hill and Jace leads us to the right. "I don't remember you being a very stubborn teenager though."

He winks at me, tightening those heartstrings again. It's nice to chat with a third party—a third party who actually seems to care. Why is he so...good?

We come to a stop and I turn to face him. "To be fair, you weren't my mom or dad. They got to see all of the true teen angst. You were just some kid who had a secret crush on me, and probably only saw the best in me."

Jace smirks and confirms my theory with a quick peck on my cheek. I take a good look at him through the darkness. He's new, yet familiar. He's a stranger, but also pure nostalgia. Not the kind of nostalgia best left in the past, but rather the kind you want to bottle up and carry with you into the future.

Right now I would settle for carrying him back to his hotel room.

"We're here, by the way." Jace has brought us to a white building. He places his hand on the small of my back and ushers me to the entrance. A bouncer sits on a stool outside. Music pours from the open doors. The mural on the side of the building confirms where we are.

Savannah's famous piano bar.

"I've heard this place is fun!" I dig for my I.D. to show the bouncer. "Have you been here before?"

"I haven't." Jace puts his own I.D. back in his wallet. "And I didn't think I'd have anyone to go with this week. Don't you love when things work out?" He kisses my hand and pulls me inside.

Jace pays our cover and I tuck away a reminder to force him to take ten dollars from me later. The bar is dimly lit. Two pianos sit atop a small stage. The floor below is packed with tables. The show hasn't started yet so filler music blares from unseen speakers. Patrons flow inside, claiming tables and making trips to the bar. Servers squeeze through the crowd to assist with drink orders.

"Should we snag that?" I nod towards a two-person table that appears to be the last one. Jace leads the way, checking to make sure I'm behind him as we squeeze through the maze. I breathe a sigh of relief as my butt hits the chair. Bars have always given me minor anxiety, and the current weight of my argument with Ada still sits heavy on my chest.

I don't want to ruin my time with Jace though.

"Are you okay?" He looks me dead in the eye.

"Oh, yeah." I push my hair behind my shoulders and beg myself to relax. "Crowds, ya know? Hey, what exactly happens at a piano bar anyway?"

When I think of piano music, I think of classical music. And I highly doubt that's what all of these people are here to get drunk and listen to. But, stranger things have happened.

"They'll play anything you want—any type of music—

but you have to tip." There's a stack of paper in the center of the table and he reaches to grab a slip. "You write your name and song on this, then take it up with some cash."

People around us already have their cash and requests ready to go. Jace snags a pen and begins to fill out his own. When I try to see what he's writing he blocks my view and jokingly narrows his eyes at me.

Fine, I don't need his help. I brainstorm, rejecting several options before finally jotting down "Anything Spice Girls" in the title line. Boom. Perfect.

Jace stares at my request with a judgemental expression. "God, I don't think I've heard anything by the Spice Girls since you and Casey used to listen to them nonstop. I still hear them in my dreams. Or, maybe 'nightmares' would be the better word."

"You don't have any taste." I grasp his hand and pull it closer to me. He holds still while I use my pen to draw a tiny smiley face on his palm. "A new tattoo—to remember this week—and remind you of the Spice Girls."

"Wow, so detailed!" He scrutinizes it with a grin on his face. "I think you've missed your calling in life as a tattoo art—"

"Hey y'all!" A woman around our age appears at our table. "Can I get you two some drinks?"

Jace orders a Corona and I order the same. The server leaves to get our drinks. Two men climb onto the stage and settle onto the piano benches. The taller of the two is a young Black man with gold-rimmed glasses; the shorter a stout white man wearing a beanie in the middle of June. I just know his head is going to get warm under the stage lighting.

The show is about to start.

I do a final check for a text from Ada. Still nothing.

Our beers are plunked onto the table in front of us.

Jace grabs one and holds it up. "To an unexpectedly good week in Savannah."

I clink mine to his. "Cheers!"

Notes pour from one of the pianos; a jaunty little background song for the pianists to introduce themselves to. People start taking their requests to the stage. Jace collects ours and joins them. I keep my eyes glued to his back as he walks away. In one way, I have encountered a ghost in Savannah—a ghost of my childhood past, who has haunted his way right back into my life.

It's going to suck saying goodbye in a few days.

The thought is unwelcome—going against every rule I've set in place to have a no-strings-attached fling. How do I admit that I've already crossed the "casual summer romance" line? And it's not difficult to see that he has as well.

He returns and scoots his chair closer to mine, putting an arm around me. Then he kisses me, slowly, unbothered, unrushed. The music continues. The crowd is singing. But all I see, all I feel, is him. He allows me to forget about Ada, about Sloan, about Matt, about Dad.

Jace Adams makes me feel alive. And that's how I know this has gone too far.

I'll work through it later. There is still time to get my brain on track. At the end of the week, I'll go back to Orlando and start my new life. Jace and I will be friends, and it will all be as it's meant to be.

Five drinks later, we've vacated our chairs to stand with the rest of the crowd. Who knew piano music could create such a party? Everyone sings along to "Bennie and the Jets." We all tipsily bump into each other, but no one cares. Jace alternates between swaying with his arms in the air and grabbing my hand to twirl me in a circle. I revel in the carefree feeling that comes with being the right amount of drunk.

Matt would have made us leave three beers ago. For the first time, the thought of Matt makes me...happy. Happy that I'm not here with him. *Thrilled*—that's more like it. Jace twirls me again. I can't stop laughing.

My request gets chosen and they play "Wannabe" by the Spice Girls. Every woman in the room between the ages of twenty and forty goes wild. A lady at the table next to ours dances on her chair. She pulls me up onto the seat next to her.

Jace takes photos of me with his phone. I throw him a couple of peace signs and sing into my half-empty beer bottle. He shakes his head at me and places a hand on my hip to keep me from falling. The song ends and my new friend hugs me before I hop down from the chair.

I've officially reached the "hugging strangers" part of the night.

"Let's take this next one a bit slower," the man in the beanie says. People drop into their seats, gulping water and wiping sweat from their brows. "This was requested by Jace, and he wants to dedicate it to his blast from the past."

I give Jace a questioning look and he shrugs. He's turned into Shy Jace, who I haven't seen much of in his adult form. Maybe it's the alcohol. Maybe it's because he just dedicated a song to me like we're back in middle school. Regardless, I'm warm inside.

A version of "Open Arms" by Journey begins. People clap and make sounds of appreciation. It's an 80's throwback I'm familiar with—I have memories of my parents listening to it in the car, and even dancing to it in our living room. I think about Dad spinning Mom around our old, floral-patterned couch, laughing at how thoroughly grossed out the child version of me was by their display of affection.

But Jace couldn't have possibly known about that. This is about him and I. He chose this song to create a new memory, for *us*.

He gives me a sweet, closed-lipped smile and wraps an arm around me. Is this his way of telling me he wants more than what we've agreed to? Can I allow myself to hope something is still in store for us when this week ends?

Maybe it's not too soon.

The crowd sways around us, singing and humming along. I rest my head on Jace's shoulder. Alcohol courses through my veins but my mind feels clear—like I'm seeing possibility in my future for the first time in a long time.

CASEY ADAMS

Amry! I get to see you so soon! I'm getting married so soon! AHHH!

Anyway, just a quick note to let you know I ran into your mom at Michael's today. I invited her to the wedding and she said she'd think about it. I'm sure she's already told you though! We have extra spaces and your mom is awesome so I figured why not?

CHAPTER 15

It's after midnight, and Telfair Square is quiet for the most part. Every so often, a group of loud, tipsy tourists passes through. To be fair, Jace and I *are* two of those tipsy tourists, sitting on a secluded bench and happily munching on our late-night pizza slices. A cool night breeze whispers through the surrounding oak trees, blowing the wispy hairs around my face into my eyes.

"That was the best piece of pizza I've ever had." Jace wads his empty paper plate up and lays it on the bench beside him. "Or maybe food just tastes better at the end of a long night."

"I think it's the second option. But it is pretty damn good." I offer him the last few bites of mine and he accepts.

My phone lays silent on the bench beside me. Trish texted around 10:30 to let me know the girls were okay, which was nice of her. But what I really want is some form of communication with Ada herself. Impending conflict is one of my least favorite things on the planet. I'm ready to apologize.

Jace notices me staring at the phone. "I'm sorry you're worried. I'm sure she'll be ready to talk in the morning. We weren't teenagers so long ago...you know how it goes."

"Yeah." I sigh. "She's just the one person I always want to keep happy."

"It's because you're a good sister." He takes our plates to a nearby trash can.

Is there ever a time where he doesn't say the right thing? Maybe it's because Matt was always so particular, or maybe I have secret self-destructive tendencies, but part of me wishes he would show a side of him that isn't so...perfect. I yawn, evolving from tipsy to tired as the pizza soaks up the remaining Corona in my stomach.

"Can I ask you a question?" Jace sits back down. "It's kind of personal, just a forewarning."

"Sure. As long as it isn't another Spice Girls rebuttal."

"Nah, we're past that," he says, laughing. "I was just wondering...do you ever get tired of being the backbone of your family? You seem to be the go-to for your mom and sister all the time. That's a lot of pressure. Who do you go to when you need reassurance?"

I was anticipating a question about Matt. Or my job. Or sex. But not this.

"I've never really thought about it," I say truthfully. "They're there for me too. Have I made it seem like they're not?"

"No, not necessarily. But sometimes you seem...sad. I know from experience that sadness is easy to ignore. All you have to do is pretend to be happy, or distract yourself with issues you feel are more important. What I'm trying to say is, *you're* important too."

Ouch.

How did he do that? Am I okay that he just evaluated me? More importantly, do I admit that he's right? Sure,

I'm sad. Everyone gets sad, though. Life has to go on. I have it under control.

"It feels normal at this point," I say, honestly. "I thought I was doing a pretty okay job of dealing with it."

"Don't get me wrong, it seems like you are. I just had to ask..." he trails off before continuing. "Have you ever thought about seeing someone?"

"Like a therapist?"

"Yeah." He scoots closer and takes my hand. "I've been going since Mom and Dad died. It helps, Amry."

I tried therapy once, two months after Dad's funeral. I cried so much during the session that I spent three days in bed after. I felt *terrible*. So I didn't go back. Healing only happens after you've faced yourself and done the work–I know that. I've just never been willing to put myself through that first step again though.

Plus, like I said, I have it under control.

"Actually, I—" My phone lights up in the darkness. *Ada???*

I snatch it up, squinting at the bright screen. It's not a text from Ada. It's an incoming call from Sloan.

"Sorry," I say to Jace as I stand. "Do you mind if I take this? I've been accidentally ignoring my friend Sloan and I think she's worried about me."

"No problem," he says. "Take your time, I'll be here."

"Sloan? Sorry I haven't called yet. The night has flown by." I answer, walking away, putting distance between Jace and I. No response comes, just the unintelligible sound of two people arguing on the other end of the line. "Sloan? Are you okay?"

"Amry!" Sloan's hysterical voice pierces my eardrum. "You answered! I'm so sorry, I know you're on vacation but I really need to talk to you."

My pulse quickens with worry. Red flags may as well be

shooting up from the ground, trapping me in the square. "Sloan, are you safe? Do you need help?"

"Safe? Yes, I'm fine—physically, anyway. Do you have a few minutes?" She's nearly out of breath.

"Yes, what's goin—?"

"Wait, she answered?" A second voice—a male voice—comes through the speaker. "Sloan, I told you this could wait. Let her go. Hang up the phone."

My blood runs cold. I could identify that voice blindfolded in a crowded room. It's a voice high school me fell asleep listening to during late night phone calls. It's a voice that professed love to me. It's a voice that often criticized what I was wearing, or how I was acting. It's a voice I've recently been avoiding at all costs.

Why is that voice with Sloan in the early hours of the morning?

"Is that Matt?" The question falls out of my gaping mouth.

"Yes, yes it's Matt!" Sloan's footsteps fall heavy on the floor and a door slams. There's a brief moment of silence before the line erupts with the sound of two fists knocking.

"Sloan, what is—"

"Amry, I need to tell you something."

The pit in my stomach doubles in size. I have no idea what she's about to say, yet I know exactly what she's about to say. At least I've already unwillingly guessed some version of it. My sandals smack aggressively on the brick path as I pace nervously around a tree in the center of the square. I consider dropping my phone to the ground and stomping on it before she can say whatever it is she wants to tell me.

"I can't keep this in any longer!" Sloan is speaking so quickly I can barely understand her. "Matt said to wait until you're back from Savannah, but I can't! Normally stuff like this doesn't bother me, but you're the best friend I have and I've been going insane and—"

"Are you two dating or something?" I interrupt.

Matt continues to pound on some unknown door. Are they at his apartment? Her townhouse? What the *fuck* is happening?

"It's worse than that." Sloan starts to sob.

Oh my god, she's crying. Stone Cold Sloan is crying. Any hope I had of this being news that won't upset me goes out the window.

"Sloan, *please* just wait!" Matt's voice is muffled.

My brain digs through potential scenarios.

So, Sloan wants to date Matt? That's not so bad, right?

No, Amry, this is bad. This is betrayal!

Have they been crushing on each other all this time?

What happened to the barista?

Was I too stupid to see this happening right in front of my face?

At least Matt and I are over.

But she's one of your best friends!

Am I selfish to be angry?

Chill out, you don't even know what's happening yet.

"Am, there was no barista. It was me," She spits it out. "It was my bra you found. We hooked up a few times while the two of you were still together."

My knees buckle. I fall backwards, wincing as my butt makes contact with a brick wall behind me. My shoulders cave in. I should double check my hearing. They wouldn't actually do this to me. It's only a sick joke.

But even a joke like this couldn't possibly be crueler than the reality of the situation. Matt's pounding ceases. Sloan continues to sob violently. Shouldn't *I* be the one crying?

Instead, I only feel numb. How could I have missed the signs?

"Please say something," Sloan begs through the phone. "I'm so sorry! I love you, but I think I love him too!"

I try to formulate a response, but nothing feels right. I'm tired of being the understanding one. I want to be the selfish one for a change. I refuse to say anything to make her—make them—feel better about themselves.

"Thanks for ruining my vacation." My voice is so low I don't even recognize it.

I end the call. Sloan's name immediately pops back up on the caller I.D. I ignore it and block her number. Then I go re-block Matt's for good measure.

My body feels like it's on fire, but I'm shivering uncontrollably. A bead of sweat runs down my back. I want nothing more than to be in bed with the covers over my head. I've been so close to accepting Matt and I's situation; to being ready to move on with my life. How am I supposed to face him, or Sloan, ever again? How is it fair that I now have to deal with not only the loss of my dad and my boyfriend, but now one of my best friends?

Stop feeling sorry for yourself.

I swat the voice away. I'm sick of listening to it. I'm ready to let myself be angry, just this *once*. Don't I deserve that?

Jace appears from the darkness and hovers for a moment before sitting next to me. I feel his eyes on my face, but won't allow myself to look at him. I stare ahead, wishing he wasn't here. I wish he would just be quiet. But of course, neither of those wishes come true.

"Is everything okay?" He puts a hand on my arm and I snatch it away.

"Yep, all good. Just found out it was one of my best friends that Matt cheated on me with, but I'm perfect. I'm great." I stuff my phone in my pocket.

"That's—"

"I'm calling an Uber so we can go back to the hotel. It's too late to catch the water taxi."

"Okay…" He sullenly follows me out of the square.

The Uber ride is painfully silent. Normally I would feel awkward in these situations and try to force conversation, but I can't bring myself to care. I sit tight to the door to avoid any physical contact with Jace. I know he hasn't done anything wrong. I shouldn't be taking my hurt out on him.

Maybe this is just a flashing sign that I shouldn't be allowing myself to have the feelings I've been having. I was stupid to believe it was okay to fall for someone else so quickly. I won't put myself in another position to be a second choice when Jace goes back to Nashville. When I go back to Orlando.

The Uber has barely come to a stop before I get out of the car. Jace tentatively trails behind me to the elevator. He moves his weight from foot to foot as we wait for it to come. I keep my arms crossed so he can't try to take my hand. The goal is making it to my room—that's all I want.

We're rising past the third floor before he speaks. "I'm sorry, Am. Can I make you some tea or something? We can talk about it if you're comfortable."

"No, thank you."

"Ok. Well, I'm here if—"

"Jace, what the hell are we even doing?" I hate myself for causing the pained look on his face, but there's no stopping my tirade. "This is so stupid! I'm fresh out of a breakup. You're using me as a rebound from *your* breakup. All of this has been a terrible decision."

"What?" He slumps against the elevator wall. "I'm sorry if I made you feel like a rebound. That's not the case at all. I promi—"

The doors open onto our floor and we awkwardly step around each other to exit. He takes a step toward me, palms facing up as if to surrender to the fight I'm not-so-subtly picking. The face I drew on his hand smiles up at me, mockingly. My arms stay firmly crossed. If I let him touch me, I'll fold.

I'm not going to fold.

"You simply seized the opportunity to have a movie moment with your childhood crush, Jace. You said it yourself yesterday–you're just living your teenage dream." I step back to maintain my forcefield. "We've made this more than it needs to be."

"This is far from a rebound situation, Amry." For the first time, there's a slight edge to his voice. "If either of us have been using the other for *that*, no offense, but it's you."

He should have just punched me in the stomach. That would have hurt less. The hallway seems to lengthen before my eyes, doubling the distance between us even though we're rooted in place. Tears prick the corners of my eyes. I'm officially overwhelmed; being pulled in too many different directions.

I need to apologize to Ada. I need to drink a gallon of water to fight off the dryness in my mouth and the impending headache that the beer will bring in the morning. I need to work through the bomb Sloan just dropped on me. I need to drown myself in a hot shower and go to bed.

I need to get away from Jace.

"You know what?" I look past him, keeping the tears at bay. "You're right. That's why I suggested we just 'have fun with it' in the first place."

It's the biggest lie I've ever told. Panic intermingles with my anger. It's too late though–my words have struck too deep.

"Perfect. Wonderful." Jace reaches in his pocket for his room key. "Goodnight, Amry."

He leaves without a second look in my direction.

I want to do the same, so badly. Two seconds ago I was prepared to storm off in a rage and never give Jace a second look. Now I'm cemented to the spot with...guilt? Alarm? Sensory overload?

In every relationship–romantic, family, friendship–I'm the relaxed one. Even through stress and discomfort, I know how to reel myself in and handle things with grace. Someone has to keep everything running smoothly, and that someone is always me. It's the natural role the universe has chosen for me. Now look where I am. I've exploded.

Maybe I was never keeping things together as well as I thought.

I consider curling up in the middle of the hallway. But if a guest caught me sleeping outside their door, on top of the 1:00 AM argument they've just overheard, Ada and I would probably be escorted from the hotel. That's an additional problem I'm not willing to add to my list right now.

My hands are shaking so hard it takes a solid three minutes to dig through my bag and find the key. Our room is silent. The girls must already be asleep.

I enter as quietly as possible, noticing all of the lights are still on. A shuffling sound comes from the corner. I tiptoe in further to find Ada curled up in one of the chairs by the window. She's gazing out at the river, re-tying her scarf onto her head. Her face is puffy and wet with fresh tears.

Several strands of auburn hair sit neatly piled on the arm of Ada's chair. Gemma is nowhere in sight.

MATT GERALDS

Am, I'm so, so sorry. I told Sloan to wait until you're home, but you know how she can be. She's been worrying herself sick. She cares about you. Please say you will meet up to talk about this when you're back next week?

ADA'S PRIVATE ANXIETY THOUGHTS

(SERIOUSLY...NO ONE WILL EVER SEE THESE.)

June 13, 2019

Why am I the way that I am?

I have a friend who often asks that as a joke, when they do something embarrassing or silly. Lately, I've been asking that question myself. At first it was in that joking way, but it's more and more serious every day. And right now, it's the only question that seems to fit the current state of things.

WHY AM I THE WAY THAT I AM?

Gemma and I had so much fun for the first couple of hours she was here. She had gotten me out of the grumpy mood I was in after Amry and I's fight. We ate pizza. We had a lame pillow fight that wasn't actually lame. We talked about school, and how our lives there are so different. Her mom came by to bring us some popcorn and candy. It was great.

Then Gemma kissed me and ruined everything.

"Ada, did you not just admit to your crush on Gemma

in your last post? Why would that ruin everything?" you may be asking.

You must have missed the part in that same post where I said I'm not ready to drag someone else into my issues. I think Gemma is...so awesome. She's nice, and talented, and beautiful in every way. I have the biggest, fattest crush on her. But how could she ever feel the same about me? *Why* does she have to feel the same about me?

Us being together would come with too many problems. We would have to come out to our friends, to our families, to everyone at school! Neither of us knows anything about being in a relationship. We're going to be Seniors, with so much to worry about. College admissions, test prep, extracurriculars, **GRADUATION**.

When I say it like that, it almost sounds like the perfect year to fall in love for the first time. But how can it be? I'm scared. There...I said it.

I want her, but I'm scared. Scared she'll hate me after she learns what it's like to actually be with me. Scared that she'll get tired of me and my anxiety. She's an optimist. I'm a pessimist. There's so much about us that doesn't line up.

She left crying and when she was gone I cried my own tears...and started pulling. It's the first time this week that I've really, really pulled. I did a good bit of damage to the right side of my scalp. Of course Amry walked in at the worst possible time.

I was ready for that to continue *our* argument, but it didn't. Instead she calmly picked up the strands of hair, threw them away, then sat down in the opposite chair and burst into tears with me. We must have cried together for a solid five minutes. Then she hugged me, and everything both of us were feeling just kind of fell out of our mouths.

She talked to me. She really, openly talked to me. She

trusted her teenage sister with her burdens. So I trusted her with mine.

I told her about Gemma and I's fight. I told her about my *feelings* for Gemma. When I admitted my sexuality to her, she started crying again. They weren't sad tears though—she was happy for me. She was excited for me. That alone makes my concerns feel a bit smaller.

It's 4:30am and she just fell asleep. I'm not sure if I'll get any sleep tonight, but we're going shopping downtown tomorrow to find dresses for the wedding so I guess I should try. Do I text Gemma? Do I sleep on it?

I think I'll sleep on it.

Side note: if you're wondering what the kiss was like— it was life changing.

CHAPTER 16

Casey's text about inviting Mom to the wedding was the first thing I noticed this morning.

I'm excited she might come, but for selfish reasons. I currently can't stand the idea of having to avoid Jace at the upcoming festivities. With Mom and Ada I'll have two people to focus my attention on instead of one.

The existing awkwardness between Ada and Mom may cause a different type of discomfort, but it will be easier to navigate. I'm a professional at that.

Just to be safe, I haven't mentioned anything to Ada yet. Mom is going to call later to confirm whether or not she's driving up this evening. If she does she'll be at the hotel when we return from the rehearsal dinner. After my chat with Ada last night, I feel better about her attitude towards Mom. She seems ready to accept that she needs support right now—for both exciting and difficult reasons.

When I spoke to Mom this morning, I really wanted to tell her about Ada's week. She's discovered so much about herself in just a few short days. She's found the zest for living that she'd lost for so long. But, I kept my mouth shut.

It's not my place to tell Mom. It's Ada's. I don't *have* to be in the middle of them all of the time. I'm going to work on that moving forward. It'll probably take a lot of constant reminders to mind my own business. Hopefully I'm up for the challenge.

Mom and Ada are the only part of my life that I woke up feeling semi-positive about. The conversation with Sloan, and I guess technically Matt, in some capacity, feels like something that would only happen in a book or movie. When I first discovered Matt was cheating on me, I was distraught. Just like any heartbreak, it's gotten easier every day, and I've held strong to knowing the worst was behind me. Until last night happened.

Betrayal is the word that keeps coming to mind. Will I eventually find it in my heart to forgive them? Possibly. Do I plan to keep either of them in my life *after* I forgive them?

Absolutely not. And even though she has just re-broken my heart, I already miss Sloan.

Then there's Jace. How I treated him is what really makes my guts twist into knots.

I'm not sure I've ever caved to emotion like that in front of anyone. I was rude and dismissive in a way I didn't know I could be. The pain on his face is all I could see behind my eyelids as I tossed through a few hours of sleep. I had a dream that I went to his room and apologized. It would have been so easy to actually do that.

He was only twelve steps away. Not that I've counted, or anything.

It seems this all played out because I shouldn't have gotten involved with Jace in the first place. Stupid, tiny doubts have been fighting their way to the forefront of my brain all week but before Sloan called I was ready to let myself fall. I needed something to wake me up and put me on track, no matter how amazing Jace is.

There was no text from him this morning. Why would there have been? He'll probably go out of his way to avoid me until the wedding is over and he can hightail it far, far away from me and Savannah, Georgia.

Fighting the urge to beat my head into it, I slump against the dressing room wall. Ada is looking for a dress to wear to the wedding and will want my full attention. Despite both of our moods today, I know she'll want my honest opinion. She's never too grumpy to talk about clothes.

"Does this look like one of those hospital gowns that you can see your ass in?" Ada flings the curtain open and stalks out with intentionally bad posture. Her shoulders are slumped forward, giving the shapeless black shift dress even less shape on her short frame.

"Well, I can't see your ass, if that's what you're asking." I circle her. "But it is kind of...plain and potato sack-esque?"

"I frieken' knew it!" She throws her hands up and barricades herself back into the room. "I wish I had my sewing machine. I could find a way to fix all of these lame dresses."

The hovering employee looks slightly offended and I silently mouth an apology to her. She shakes her head, mouthing "no worries." She must have a younger, angsty sister too. Bonus points if her sister is also in the .01% that knows how to sew her own clothes and thinks shopping in stores is too "mainstream."

"I'm only trying this one because you asked me to." Ada re-emerges, this time in a strapless, burgundy maxi dress that has a slit to her mid-thigh. She isn't slumping this time, and I'm suspicious that the look of disdain on her face is forced.

"I LOVE it!" I exclaim before I can help myself.

Play it cool, Amry. She's not going to give it any consideration at all if your level of excitement is too high.

"I mean," I reel myself in to try again. "That one is...cool. Very mature."

Nailed it. She'll like it if she thinks it makes her look older.

"I agree!" the employee pipes in, giving me a wink.

Ada walks to the mirror at the end of the hallway and does a slow turn, inspecting herself while she plays with the movement of the dress. The confidence in her stance is a clue that she likes it more than she's letting on. I saw the hint of a smile that lingered on her face for roughly half a second.

"Meh." She speedwalks back to her room, dress billowing in her wake. The curtain closes and the spell is broken.

At least I can give myself credit for trying.

"I suppose this one will work." Two minutes later she's back in a knee-length black fit-and-flare. It's simple. Cute. I give a nod of approval. Satisfied, she retreats for the last time.

"Give it to me and I'll go pay while you change," I say. "Then we can move on to the next store."

"That's okay, I'll pay." She peeks her head out. "Do you want to head to Banana Republic and I'll meet you there?"

"Are you sure?"

"Yes, it's basically right next door. I'm a big girl, Am." It's more of a statement than a snarky reply.

"You're right, you're right..." I concede, backing down the hallway. "See you there. Call if you need anything."

The day is sticky; sweltering. Retail therapy seekers swarm around me on the sidewalk, entering and exiting store after store along Broughton Street. I cross over to

Banana Republic. An employee greets me and shows me to the dresses.

There are too many options—different styles, colors, textures. Only a few are stocked in my size, cutting the variety in half by no choice of my own. Each time the door opens I glance up to check for Ada, desperate for her opinion.

If last night had turned out differently, I might have a brighter outlook on shopping. Perhaps I'd be searching for what I think Jace would like best. Maybe a nice green, similar to the shade of the flecks in his hazel eyes. Maybe something form fitting, because he wouldn't be able to get enough. He'd only be thinking about getting me back to the hotel after the wedding…

Stop it, Amry.

As it stands, this will be strictly an Amry (and Ada) decision.

"That's already a no from me." Ada appears beside me and takes the purple dress I have draped over my arm. "You need something hotter."

"Sometimes what it looks like on the hanger is totally different than what it looks like on a body." I reach for the dress. She snatches it out of my grasp and hangs it on a nearby rack.

"You learned that from Mom, didn't you?" She grins and hooks her shopping bag over her shoulder. "Hey, why aren't you a bridesmaid, by the way?"

"Oh, Casey and Ed aren't having a wedding party," I say. "They didn't want to place an extra financial burden on anyone since it's technically a destination wedding."

"Makes sense. Bridesmaid dresses suck anyway."

"Mmhmm."

Formal dresses are one of my irrational fears. I still have flashbacks to shopping for my senior prom. I'm lucky

Mom didn't kill me during the first round. She made Dad take me the second time. I knew I'd finally found the right one when he cried.

He won't be there to do the same for my wedding dress one day.

One hour later, I have a dress and we're sitting down for coffee and lunch. I watch Ada scroll through her phone, chin resting in her palm. She's been quiet today. Outside of shopping, anyway. We're both swimming in our own thoughts—thinking through our issues but mutually enjoying each other's company.

We sit on the second-floor patio. I watch the tops of people's heads as they walk by on the sidewalk below. Trolley bells trill nearby. There's a clear view of Madison Square ahead, its trees creating a perfect frame around it. Savannah is our little historic bubble. I don't want to go home in a couple of days, even after last night.

There's still no word from Jace. My single, remaining shred of pride is all that keeps me from reaching out to him. I've typed and deleted five different texts. He would probably erase any message from me without reading it, then block my number. I deserve it.

Is Ada speaking to Gemma yet? I lean forward discretely and try to peek at her phone.

"It's just Instagram." She catches on immediately and shows me the screen.

"Oh, I, I was only—" I stammer.

"Mmm-hmmmm." She smirks, locking the phone and sitting it on the table.

The natural lighting makes her glow. Her floral scarf stands out against her black tank top. Her skin has a slight tan from all of the time spent in the sun.

I want to tell her how beautiful and strong she is. I want to convince her that she deserves the excitement of first love just like every other teenager on the planet. I want to talk to her more—really talk to her—like we did last night. Or rather, early this morning.

"I want to apologize to Gemma." The statement comes from Ada's mouth so unexpectedly I wonder if she was reading my mind.

"Yeah?"

Don't be too eager, Amry.

"Yeah…" She pauses as the server brings our lattes and sandwiches. "My anxiety is the only excuse I have. But if we're both hurting, maybe not being together is the wrong decision. I always imagined I would be better before I found someone who liked me. I imagined I wouldn't have…this."

She points to her head. I take a bite of my grilled cheese and chew slowly, considering my response. I understand where she's coming from. When you daydream about being in love, you're always the best version of yourself. You want to have your own shit together so you can enjoy it.

You don't want to give them a reason to leave.

"That's a brave thing to admit," I tell her. "Coming from someone who loves you more than anything, no one expects you to be perfect."

"I know. I just want to be."

"Any relationship is two-sided. Believe it or not, if you're in a relationship with Gemma, she's going to do wrong sometimes too."

"Yeah, she might hug me too much or something. Or be too cheerful," Ada jokes.

I roll my eyes at her. "Your anxiety may make things a *little* more difficult. But it's not a dealbreaker, Ada."

"So…I might just have to work slightly harder every now and then?"

"Is Gemma someone worth working harder for?" I ask.

She runs a palm over her scarf then brings her hand to her mouth, holding it there as a memory softens her face. "She is. How I've decided this in three days, I don't know. But, she is."

"I know she is too."

I'm surprised to find a couple of tears running down my face and I wipe them away, laughing.

Ada stands and walks to my side of the table. Then she hugs me. In the middle of a crowded restaurant at lunch time. For the moment, I'm full of nothing but a grilled cheese sandwich and excitement for my baby sister.

———

WHEN THE DAY STARTED, it seemed like there were infinite hours until the rehearsal dinner. Now, as we dash into the hotel room at 5:45, everything feels rushed. Having less than two hours for Ada and I to both shower, get ready, and make our way back across the river seems like a daunting task. We were too absorbed in another Savannah afternoon and lost track of time.

I notice the envelope on the entryway floor just before I stomp it to death. Ada runs straight into my butt as I bend over to pick it up. I catch myself with my free hand to avoid toppling completely over. She mumbles an annoyed apology and squeezes around me.

Ada's name is scrawled across the envelope in attractive cursive handwriting. I hold the letter out. "You have a delivery."

"Huh?" She stops rummaging through her clothes. Her eyes dart between me and the envelope. A grin creeps across her face, as if she already knows who it's from. She snatches it from my hand and collapses onto the edge of the bed, ripping it open.

"It's from Gemma!" she yells, extracting a letter and unfolding it.

"Oh, is it?"

I feign nonchalance, secretly dying inside to know what it says. Pretending not to care, I dig through my suitcase to find an outfit. Every few seconds, I glance at Ada. Her smile grows larger and larger as she reads. She lets out an ecstatic squeal and I jump. I've never heard her make a noise like that before.

"She beat me to the apology! And there's more...look!"

She places the letter on the bed and reaches into the envelope to remove a dainty, gold necklace. It twinkles in the light filtering through the window. A tiny gold ghost charm dangles from the end, spinning in the air between us.

"To remind us of the ghost tour. That's the first night she wanted to hold my hand. She has a matching one!"

If we were cartoons, little hearts would be circling her head like birds. A rain cloud would be hanging over mine. I would need to hit myself with a hammer to snap out of my mood.

The ghost tour feels like weeks ago. I'm thrilled for Ada, but my own memories from that night overshadow hers and bring my spirits (no pun intended) down again. Ada and Gemma developed their bond that night. Jace and I rekindled ours.

Then we sealed our fate with a kiss.

When did I become so dramatic? I edit romantic comedies, not live in them. I need to suck it up and be a good sister.

"That's awesome, Ada. I love seeing you like this."

"Yeah, yeah, love you too." She gingerly folds the letter

and tucks it into her suitcase. The necklace gets laid out with the rest of her outfit.

"We should probably hurry!" My sense of urgency returns.

"Are you excited to see Casey?"

"So, so excited." I peel my t-shirt off and head to the bathroom. "It's going to be a good night. And tomorrow night will be even better."

Again, it's not a lie. I want Casey and Ed to have the wedding of their dreams. I want Ada and Gemma to experience teenage summer love and everything that comes along with it. I want Mom to come up and enjoy the remaining vacation with us.

I only wish I hadn't gone and ruined the occasion for Jace and I.

My phone pings on the bathroom counter and I look down to see yet another email from Google. I consider ignoring it–it's probably just the same "we're looking into this" message I've received ten times before. The subject line looks different though, so I slide it open.

The review has been removed.

My hand shakes as I go to my business page and refresh it three times just to be sure. It's really gone. *Amry Edits* is back to its five-star rating. Half-dressed, I run out of the bathroom and wrap my arms around Ada's waist, spinning her around the room.

"Am, what the hell?!" She kicks her feet in the air.

Finally. Some good news.

MOM

I'm coming! I'll go straight to the hotel and be there when you get back. I know it's only been a few days, but I'm ready to see my girls.

AMRY

Yay! Can't wait to see you too. The front desk will have a key for you. You'll just need to show them your I.D. See you in a few hours. Drive safe!

CHAPTER 17

The rehearsal dinner restaurant could be a stop on Jefferson's ghost tour. It's part pink Colonial home, part pink haunted mansion. I can hear the clink of silverware and intermingling conversations coming from within, but I still feel like I'm about to walk into a dark room full of cobwebs and old furniture covered in sheets.

And ghosts, obviously. But I should be used to that by now.

"Are you coming?"

Ada pauses on the second step, turning to face me. I've stopped to stare at the giant lantern hanging from the front porch. In the dim lighting, her black cocktail dress and dark, smokey makeup match the gothic, yet elegant vibe of the restaurant. She's been impatient all evening, and I know it's because Gemma is waiting for her inside.

"Savannah, Savannah," I mutter. My lace skirt scratches my legs as I climb the stairs. "Alluring, yet haunted. Pretty as a picture, yet haunted. I should contact their tourism board and offer my assistance with writing a new slogan."

"Hilarious. But I think people already know it's haunted. That's half the fun of coming here." There's not even a hint of a smile on her face. She opens the front door and pushes me inside.

Fair point.

A hostess greets us and I tell her we're with the Adams-Suarez party. She politely points us in the direction of a private room. Ada grabs my hand to lead the way. We pass through the main dining room and every suspicion of the creepy house I was imagining slowly disappears. Glittering chandeliers hang from the ceiling, illuminating elegantly set tables filled with guests. Servers run around, refilling wine glasses and placing plates of gourmet food on the white table cloths. I once again feel like I've stepped back in time. It's cozy. My mouth waters over the smells of seafood and perfectly cooked steaks.

Our party has a private room, with a single large chandelier hanging over a long, rectangular table. Classical music is played from a shiny piano near the door. The pianist nods at Ada and I as we enter. The deep teal wallpaper serves as the perfect backdrop for a few people who are already taking photos. I recognize Casey's parents as two of them.

Jace is acting as their photographer.

He doesn't see me. I'd rather him not catch me staring when he does, so I turn in Ada's direction, grasping for a distraction. Too bad she has already disappeared from my side.

"Amry!" A high-pitched scream comes from somewhere across the room. I turn to spot Casey running at me full speed—at least as quickly as she can in her heels. We collide. Her long blonde hair swishes around us. She smells like a combination of floral shampoo and vanilla lotion; a smell that hasn't changed since the day we met.

She clings to me, like we haven't seen each other in years.

"If it isn't the soon-to-be Mrs. Suarez." I pull away to take her hands and look her up and down. "At least I assume you're the bride, considering you're wearing white at the rehearsal dinner and all."

"Nope, you have me confused with someone else."

"My bad. Wrong rehearsal dinner."

She releases my hands and pushes her hair behind her ears. "You look wonderful! Did Ada style you? I follow her on Insta. She's talented!"

"I'll pretend not to be offended that me looking wonderful must mean my younger sister dressed me," I joke, fingering the strap of my satin, champagne-colored top. "But yes, she did."

"I've missed you! Also, don't think that I've forgotten you have some Matt-splaining to do," she whispers menacingly as she squeezes me one more time.

"Matt-splaining? Did you spend your whole drive up creating that phrase?"

"You'll never know. Now, spill."

"I'll give you a quick recap at some point, but the full story will have to wait until after your honeymoon. This is your time, Case."

"You're no fun!" She pretends to pout.

"How did the rehearsal at the hotel go?" I ask, changing the subject.

"Oh, it was good. Quick and easy!" She takes me by the hand. "Come make rounds with me!"

Casey's family makes up most of the guests in the room. I recognize them all. Her aunts and uncles raise their hands to wave at me as we meander by. It's almost like being at a family reunion. My own family was small, but being best friends with someone from a giant family

213

provided me with all of the experiences I didn't get other-wise while growing up.

"Amry, look at you!" A frail hand lands lightly on my forearm, stopping Casey and I in our tracks. Her Grandma's eyes stare up at me, less vibrant in her old age, but still the same blue as Casey's and so many other Adams. "Honey, I haven't seen you in years. You look exactly the same."

I bend down to give her a gentle hug, secretly preening at the compliment. "Gram, you don't have to lie to me like that."

"I would never lie to you, you're basically my grand-child too! Only I like you better than this one, who never brings you around to see me anymore." She gives Casey a playful slap on the wrist.

Casey rolls her eyes. "Amry doesn't live in Jacksonville, Gram. She's in Orlando now."

"Oh, I know that, I'm just messing with you. Though I do miss the days of you two running around my house, wreaking havoc with Jace."

His name is a trigger. I find him across the room. This time, he's staring straight at me. He looks away, pretending to focus on his glass of red wine.

"That boy is around here somewhere," Gram contin-ues. "I know he will be happy to see you too."

Oh, Gram. If you only knew *how much* Jace and I have already seen each other this week—in more than one way.

"It's so good to see you." I distract her with another hug. "Being with the Adams fam always feels like home."

Gram lights up at the compliment. Casey takes the opportunity to yank me away and we continue on our route around the room. I say hello to Casey's parents, who also bring up Jace after a few moments. Then I'm intro-duced to Ed's dad, who, lucky for me, *doesn't* know Jace.

Maybe I should just hang out with him all night.

With Casey's latch on me, I don't stay in any particular spot for too long. After we've spoken with roughly seventy-percent of the guests, I find the opportunity to escape, seizing a glass of wine from a nearby tray. I gulp it down and use the moment of alone time to lower my adrenaline levels, which have spiked in the social setting.

We're calm, Amry. We're cool. Now DON'T look for Jace.

"Hello again!" Gemma's mom joins me, grabbing her own wine from the tray. "Fancy seeing you here."

"Trish, hi! How are you?"

"I'm just fine darlin', thanks for asking." She steps closer to me. "This is lovely, isn't it?"

"It is! I'm looking forward to dinner. I can't get enough of the food in this city."

"You're telling me. I've gained five pounds this week." She pats her stomach. "But I don't care, because I've enjoyed every second of it."

I like her. And I like her daughter, too.

Speaking of her daughter…

"This is going to make me sound like an awful sister, but I have no idea where Ada is. Have you seen her?" I ask.

She grins, nodding to the far corner of the room. Ada and Gemma sit on the floor next to each other, squeezed together. Gemma whispers something in Ada's ear and she slumps forward, shoulders shaking with laughter. Their joined hands rest on the floor between their thighs. The matching necklaces shine around their necks.

I scrutinize Trish's face from the corner of my eye. She seems like a perfect Mom, but I'm not sure how much she knows about the girls' relationship. It's not my place to accidentally tell her if Gemma hasn't.

"Oh, good," I say, relaxing my shoulders. "I've gone

almost this entire vacation without losing my teenage sister. I'm going to add this to my resume."

She guffaws, like I'm the funniest person on the planet. Maybe I should start hanging around Casey's family more often again. They think I'm funny and they tell me I'm pretty. It's really good for one's self-esteem.

"I see she got the necklace." Trish leans to me, lowering her voice. "And hopefully the letter too?"

I continue to analyze whether or not she's in the loop. *Come on Trish, give me something.* Across the room, the pianist begins a new song.

"She did. That was very thoughtful."

"I've always worried Gemma bein' true to herself would make for a difficult road." Trish looks lovingly in her daughter's direction. "I was lucky enough to marry my first love. This sounds bad, but I've dreaded the day that Gemma would potentially find hers. Mainly because I don't know if I'll be able to handle the heartbreak that will eventually come with it."

I listen intently, looking from the girls in the corner to Trish's tear-filled eyes. I want to tell her that heartbreak isn't always a bad thing. Often, it's necessary. Plus, not *all* relationships end in heartbreak.

It's not the right thing to add to the conversation though. This moment is about Ada and Gemma, and the support they need.

"I accepted Gemma's sexuality the moment she came out. It's only been a couple of years, but I feel like I've been waiting forever for her to come home excited about a girl."

"She seems like she knows how to wait for what she really wants. She's amazing. I've loved getting to know her this week."

Trish places her free hand on my shoulder. "She definitely isn't a fly-by-the-seat-of-her-pants girl. She does take her time, with all things in life. Her feelings for Ada came on so fast, I was worried at first. But I've decided Amry, that if Ada has made Gemma feel this way in three days, it must be right."

I place my hand on top of hers and squeeze. "I agree. And I hope you'll find comfort in knowing that Ada is also the type to think things through. She's tough on herself, and she has things she needs to work on, but knowing when to follow her heart comes easily."

Fighting the urge to cry has been an everyday occurrence on this trip. I'm so happy for my sister. I'm happy Gemma has an awesome mom. I'm happy *my* mom will be here soon.

I still haven't told Ada, but I think surprise is the best tactic at this point.

Trish goes to find her husband, leaving me with my thoughts—one of them a recurring realization that won't leave me alone.

I *need* to talk to Jace—and it won't be a fun chat. Until just now, I wasn't sure what to say to him. Gemma and Ada have been lucky enough to fall for each other this week. It was the right time for both of them. But it's not the right time for me, and Jace deserves to know that.

————

"WE CAN'T THANK all of you enough for being here over these next couple of days," Ed says, wrapping an arm around Casey at the head of the table. "We've been planning this for a long time, and look forward to partying with you more tomorrow!"

He wraps up their thank-you speeches and everyone turns to toast each other. Ada taps her millionth mocktail of the week to my wine glass. I stare at the final bites of my uneaten dinner, foregoing the asparagus and hoping that will leave enough room in my stomach to finish off the exquisitely seared scallops.

"Ugh," I mutter to myself as the server brings around a dessert menu. "I have no room, but how am I supposed to say no?"

Ada shrugs and steals a scallop from my plate.

"I was going to eat that!" I hiss at her.

"Hey I'm only trying to help you make room for dessert." She pops the buttery delicacy into her mouth and turns back to Gemma.

Jace makes eye contact with me from across the table. He puts a hand to his mouth in an attempt to hide his smile. "I'll share a dessert with you. If you want?"

His position across the table has made things tricky. Throughout dinner, we made awkward eye contact. That led to polite smiles. We then jumped into shared conversations with those around us. Now, apparently, it's time to share dessert.

"Do I get to pick?" I ask skeptically, leaning forward to grab the menu from his outstretched hand.

"As long as it involves chocolate in some capacity," he bargains.

"I can live with that."

Our fingers brush as he hands over the dessert list. Those same fingers once brushed over less public parts of my body. How is it fair that can never happen again? I wish I had more of those instances to turn into memories.

A few minutes later, the server sits a substantial slice of cheesecake with chocolate sauce between us. Jace passes a fork to me. We dig in, our faces drawing nearer in the process. We're still surrounded by people, but sharing dessert makes everything feel more intimate. The volume of the conversations around us seems to lower, but it doesn't really. The room seems emptier, but there are no less people.

"God, that's good." Jace swallows a large bite.

We carve our way through the slice, making occasional small talk about the wedding and his family. Does he wonder what it would feel like for his parents to be here? An event like this would feel strange for me, knowing there's no possible way my dad could attend. If we were still—whatever we were doing—maybe I'd ask him. Where it stands, the question feels too personal.

We find ourselves at the final bite and Jace gives me a competitive look.

"I'll rock, paper, scissors you for it," he says, grinning.

"You're on! Two out of three?"

Jace is declared the winner after two rounds. I watch enviously as he scoops up the last of the cheesecake, doing a victory fist pump with his other hand. He brings the fork to his mouth then stops.

"You know what? I'm suddenly too full for this. It's all yours." He holds the cheesecake out to me and I narrow my eyes at him.

But I'm not about to say no to the bite. I hold my hand out for the fork. He ignores me and guides it to my mouth with an expectant look, then holds my stare as I purse my lips around the dessert.

"You really missed out," I say after I swallow. "The last bite was the best one."

I feel eyes on the side of my face. Turning, I see Casey at the end of the table. Her and Ed study Jace and I intently. The blush that floods my face can't be prevented, and Casey's expression is one that I know all too well. Her wheels are turning. She's figured out my secret, no hints from me (or Jace) required. Simultaneous grins spread across the couple's faces.

God. I'm going to be questioned to death at some point in the not-too-distant future.

Jace holds his middle finger up to Casey and Ed, blocking the gesture from his grandparents with his other hand. The grins on their faces grow even wider. They return the sentiment, raising their fingers at the exact same time.

The two of them really are made for each other.

With dinner and dessert finished, guests stand to move about the room. Jace pushes his chair away from the table, looking down at me as he rises. "Do you have a few minutes? Can we go somewhere and talk?"

"Sure." The light-heartedness of the last few minutes evaporates.

It's time. This has to happen.

"Where are you going?" Ada asks as I stand.

"Outside with Jace," I tell her. "Meet me there in ten?"

She nods and I straighten my skirt. Jace waits at the end of the table and I follow him out of the room. The restaurant is preparing for closing and everything looks much different going out than it did coming in. Staff members bustle around, sweeping and mopping and stripping table cloths. The hostess holds the door open for us and wishes us a good night.

We cross the street and step into Reynold's Square.

Great. Another chat in another Savannah square. If I get any unexpected phone calls I'm jumping in the river.

Fairy lights illuminate the trees. I wish I could appreciate the peacefulness. Jace leads us to a bench, but I don't sit.

"Actually, I'm going to stand. I'm tired of sitting and also super full." I *am* so full all I can think about is unzipping my skirt. But the truth is, I need an exit strategy. Sitting will make this last longer.

"I feel that." Jace climbs to sit on the back of the bench. He rests his elbows on his knees, clasping his hands. There are a few beats of silence as both of us try to muster the courage to speak first.

"Dinner was good," I say awkwardly."Thanks for the last bite of cheesecake."

"No worries, it's only a favor I'll hold over your head forever," he jokes. "Or maybe it was my way of offering an apology for last night."

This would be so much easier if Jace had turned out to be an asshole. But he's far from one, always saying and doing the right thing. Always being more considerate towards people than they probably deserve.

"You're not the one who should be saying sorry. We both know that should be me. I was upset about something that had nothing to do with you and I still chose to take it out on you." I stare down at my healing tattoo.

A group of Casey's family members exits the restaurant. They're all tipsy, laughing and hugging each other, enjoying the pleasant summer evening. Trish is amongst the crowd, with Ada and Gemma following behind. I know I don't have much time.

"It's okay," Jace says, noting my distraction and reeling my attention back to him. "We all get angry sometimes. It's part of being human."

"The past few weeks have just been...a lot." I flop down onto the bench and look up at him. "The past couple of years, actually. Dad, then Matt, now Sloan. It's all made me realize, I don't think I even know who I am as a person. Like, what do I want? Where am I going?"

Jace slides down the back of the bench until he's sitting next to me. He holds one of my hands between both of his. My shoulders relax immediately just feeling his touch. It's frustrating; it makes me feel wobbly and unsure again. Jace makes everything feel...right. I need him to feel wrong.

"It's hard to look inwardly—to see what those who love you see. You have to give yourself permission to see those things, too. Then everything else will fall into place," Jace says.

Gemma sees us and waves. She begins walking in our direction but Ada grabs her arm to pull her back and whisper something to her. They turn their backs and continue to wait on the other side of the street.

"You're right...I know you're right." I return to the discussion. "I just need to be patient with myself. But how I do that is an entirely new mystery."

"I can help." Jace pushes my hair behind my shoulder. "I can help you see the you that I know—the present you. And also help you remember the great things about the past you."

He tries to kiss me.

I turn my head and his lips fall on my cheek. He lingers for a moment before pulling away. Not wanting to prolong the discomfort, I pull my hands from his and wipe my palm on my skirt. It isn't sweaty. I just can't handle the lingering sensation of his skin on mine, no matter how badly I may want it there.

I feel ashamed.

"That's not where I thought this was going." He scoots a couple of inches away from me and sits up straighter. "I'm just another line on your list of current problems, huh?"

There's an element of truth to his statement. Even though, "problem" is the last thing I view him as. He's more of a badly-timed opportunity, standing right in front of me, and I can't reach out to grab him because my brain won't allow me to.

"Jace, no. *You're* not the problem. It's just the wrong time. I wish this was all happening a year, or even a month from now."

"But it's the right place, Amry," he argues. "It may be the wrong time, but it's the right place. Look around you. Look at Savannah. Look at the week we've had. Look how we've reconnected, in *this* place. Sometimes that outweighs timing."

Damn you, Jace. That was beautiful.

I push his sentiment away. I've made up my mind, but my decision is still too shaky and prone to outside influence. I need to sit on it—to fully accept it. This is the only way I'm going to be able to move forward in my life.

"I'm sorry Jace, I just can't commit to this right now." I shoot to my feet with the intention of looking him confidently in the eye. I can only focus on the space above his head. "Ada is waiting for me. We'll see you at the wedding tomorrow."

A couple of years ago, I edited a self-help book that discussed how important it is to walk away from your decisions with confidence. When I was practicing this conversation in my head, I envisioned myself strolling away, strong and pleased with my choice. I had been ready to appreciate Jace and I's week for what it was, and move forward in friendship.

Now that I'm in the actual moment, I feel more confused than ever. To make things worse, I stumble over an uneven spot in the bricks when walking away. Can I do anything right?

We're getting off the water taxi before I remember Mom is waiting for us in the room and Ada still has no idea.

I'm exhausted. It's late, my conversation with Jace sucked, and I'm not sure I'm up for dealing with an angry Ada combined with an overzealous mom. Why didn't I tell Ada sooner? Why didn't I tell Mom to come in the morning instead of tonight?

Trish and I lead the way up the path to the hotel. Ada and Gemma follow several feet behind, holding hands and singing some song I'm probably too old to know. I wish Ada could share some of her newly acquired carefree energy. I wish I wasn't so unsure about *everything*.

If I could go back in time, I would choose a different hotel. I would avoid the coffee shop and churro muffin on the day Jace was out and about in the area. Tonight would be the new first moment I reconnected with him, and that would be too late in the game to start falling for him, right?

Or would we still find a way? And what would those changes mean for Ada's week? She wouldn't have Gemma and that would be all my fault.

Shut up, Amry. Go to bed.

"Goodnight! See y'all tomorrow," Trish tells us when we reach their floor. Gemma steps out behind her after hugging Ada and I, one of us a bit tighter than the other. The doors have almost closed again when a hand shoots in to stop them and Gemma pops back inside.

"I forgot something!" She looks at me shyly then turns to give Ada a peck on the lips before rushing out of the elevator for a second time.

Ada's fingertips float to her lips. She looks like she could melt into the floor and float through the ceiling at the same time. I link my arm through hers and tickle her ribs. "I'm happy for ya, kid."

My legs feel heavier with each step to our room. I make as much noise rummaging for my key as possible. Hopefully Mom is still awake, and if she is, I want her to know we're here. I enter first, immediately locking eyes with her where she sits in one of the chairs by the window. I give her a little wave.

"You're going so slow! I'm ready for my pajamas!" Hurricane Ada pushes by me and abruptly freezes at the foot of the bed. She stares at Mom, her expression indecipherable.

"Surprise!" Mom says, doing a little dance that is somewhere between a jazz hand and the YMCA. "Did y'all know there's a T.V. in the bathroom, by the way?"

It's indeed a surprise, when instead of saying something smart-alecky, or turning to smite me on the spot, Ada jogs to Mom and steps forcefully into her arms. Mom looks at me over the top of her head and gives a thumbs up. She smooths her hand over Ada's scarf and kisses her forehead.

"I got your email," Ada mumbles into Mom's chest. "I have so much to tell you."

CASEY ADAMS

You disappeared so quickly tonight! Please tell me you're coming to get ready with me in the morning. We have a suite at the hotel, where the wedding is.

Bring your mom and sister! Mama will meet you in the lobby.

AMRY

Of course. We will be there! Get some rest, Mrs. Suarez.

ADA'S PRIVATE ANXIETY THOUGHTS

(SERIOUSLY...NO ONE WILL EVER SEE THESE.)

June 14, 2019

I should be upset with Amry and Mom for ambushing me.

Then why does it feel like a nice surprise instead? It's confusing–I was so upset with Mom two days ago, then excited to see her sitting in our hotel room last night. How have I changed so much this week? Maybe all I needed was a vacation.

Grumpy Ada has left the building. Hopefully I have a while before she returns.

Dr. Reilly *has* told me before that I'm more likely to take my anger out on others when I'm feeling stressed. Unfortunately, the ones that I explode on are usually the ones I love most. Time away is the real therapy I've been needing.

Let's hope I can remember this for—let's see—the rest of my life. Ugh, why am I only 17?

My young blogging career has gone completely down-hill this week. I've had to make some schedule adjustments.

Since Amry sniffed my secret out very quickly, I've had to save writing for the earliest hours of the morning, while she sleeps. Now that Mom's here, I'm doing it in the bathroom at 3:00 A.M. I've turned the tv on to block out any sounds of typing. Turning on the shower is my backup plan, although the water waste wouldn't be very eco-friendly of me.

Enough rambling. Let's get into the good stuff.

Gemma and I made up. I won't go into detail, because some things in my life deserve privacy. Yes, I KNOW that makes no sense because this blog is literally just me talking to myself. STILL, typing thoughts makes them feel more public. And what if this is—potentially, super potentially—a public space one day?

All you need to know is I have a gold ghost necklace I plan to never remove, memories of a vacation I'm never going to forget, and a girlfriend.

Just call us Geda, or Amma, or any other celebrity couple name that may come to mind. Amry prefers Amma. I prefer Geda. I'll consult Gemma later today.

Mom is undecided. On both the couple name and the relationship, but not for the reasons you may think. I have a mom who believes that love is love, and everyone deserves to be with the person they want to be with. THANK GOD. She couldn't have been any happier when I told her. I know it's because I was honest with her, rather than trying to keep it a secret like I normally would.

She's only worried because Gemma happened so quickly. When she started telling me how she feels, I was annoyed and wanted to leave the room and sit in the hallway until Amry forced me to come back. Instead, even though I didn't want to, I took a deep breath and listened to Mom. And she made sense—who knew *that* was possible?

Her sixteen-year-old daughter left for a week-long

vacation and got a girlfriend five days into it. It's kinda crazy.

"You just have to meet her." That was my response. No arguing, no crying, just a mature (hopefully) reply.

Lately, all I've wanted from Mom and Amry is to be treated, and spoken to, like I'm not in the third grade. I was fifteen when Dad died. I know that life without him, combined with my trich, have affected some parts of my teenage years. They have also played a huge role in Mom's need to baby me, and Amry's need to help Mom baby me.

Tonight they didn't baby me. We laid around in our pajamas and talked about everything. We talked about Gemma and I. (And that I'm considering applying to the Savannah College of Art and Design!) We talked about Dad. We talked about Amry and her mess of a life with Matt and Sloan and Jace. (No offense, Am.) I've never felt so close to my mom and sister. This is a new chapter for us. I know it.

It was the same comfort I used to feel when the three of us would watch movies and eat popcorn in Mom's bed.

Amry just knocked on the bathroom door and it scared the shit out of me. (Don't worry, not literally.) I'm only sitting on the toilet, not actually using it. She's now threatening to punch me because it's 3:30 A.M. and in her words, she's "about to piss on herself."

I need a couple more hours of sleep anyway. I can't have bags under my eyes for my first full, official day as someone's girlfriend! I'm secretly excited about the wedding itself, too. I've never been to one! Maybe I'll get to slow dance with Gemma. Maybe Amry will slip me a sip of her champagne during the toast…

Don't tell her I said this, but I hope her and Jace will make up. I like him. I like THEM together. I know Amry wants time to herself, and I admire that, but I don't want

229

her to miss out on something, someone, she really wants because she feels like she has to stick to a certain timeline. I want her to make the right decision for herself.

Sorry, I had to sneak that last thought in. She's trying to unlock the door with a bobby pin. Sweet dreams!

CHAPTER 18

"Good morning, Phillips family!" Casey's mom greets us in the deliciously cool lobby. We're late. We thought it would be no issue to take the water taxi across the river and walk to the hotel where the wedding is taking place, but with our dresses, shoes, makeup, and toiletries, it had been easier said than done.

"We should have taken an Uber," Ada mutters, reading my mind.

Mom wipes a few beads of sweat from her upper lip and pulls her hair off of her neck. "You two have been traipsing around in this heat all week?" she asks. "It's hotter here than it is at home!"

"I mean, we're still in the South, Mom..." Ada points out.

"It's absolutely SWELTERING out!" Casey's mom notes our overheated appearances and fans us with her hands. "If anyone needs to shower off we have two bathrooms in the suite!"

"I will probably take you up on that," Mom says. "Katrina, how are you? I feel like I haven't seen you in ten years."

Katrina takes a bag from Mom's hand and hugs her around the shoulders. "Not much less than that, I'm sure! Gosh, how old are we?"

"Old," Ada whispers to me as we follow them to the elevator. I snicker under my breath. Mom gives us a scathing look over her shoulder.

Her hearing isn't old. I'll give her that.

This hotel is more modern than ours. The lobby is filled with minimalistic clean lines and art-deco inspired fixtures; a big change from the majority of Savannah. Our hotel is nice, but still has the type of environment that makes you comfortable going for complimentary coffee in your pajamas. I can't say the same for our current surroundings.

We pile into the elevator and Katrina hits the button for the fourth floor. Though a good five inches shorter, she looks exactly like Casey. Today especially, her blue eyes beam with the type of happiness that's only possible on your only daughter's wedding day. She doesn't even have makeup on yet and her skin is glowing.

"How is Casey feeling?" I ask. "I've never seen the girl get nervous, but if there's any time she would start, today would be the day."

"Oh, she's been perfectly fine so far," Katrina replies. "Even more talkative than usual, if you can believe that. Poor Ed is so quiet, I have to wonder if he really knows what he's in for!"

Everyone is familiar with "dad jokes," but over the years of being around various parents I've learned that there is a completely separate, yet similar, category that can only be classified as "mom jokes." And Casey's mom Katrina has always been the master of them. I don't think she ever expects anyone to laugh—she just enjoys telling them. I'll always laugh regardless.

We file out of the elevator and Katrina leads us to the very end of the hall. A fusion of women's voices circulates behind the last door on the right. The door is propped open and Katrina bumps it with her hip. "Look who I found!"

Casey looks up from shoveling a bagel with cream cheese (honestly, it's more like cream cheese with a side of bagel) into her mouth and jumps to her feet. Gram, Trish, Gemma, and a couple of other women I don't recognize smile in our direction. Gemma waves enthusiastically. Casey immediately begins taking stuff from our hands and laying it on the bed. "Come! Have some breakfast. There's plenty...more than plenty!"

"Hey, hey, hey." I take our stuff back and discard it myself. "No manual labor on your wedding day. Get back to your bagel, we'll be right there."

Ada heads straight to Gemma. Mom falls into conversation with Gram and Trish, her eyes darting over to Gemma every few seconds. I can tell she's holding herself back from immediately ambushing the girl.

The suite is bright and open, every space cluttered with makeup bags and shoe boxes. Casey's wedding dress hangs from one of the bathroom doors. The sight of the garment bag brings the familiar tears rushing. Again.

Great, another day of crying. I'm a human fountain this week.

"Amry," Casey says as I approach the breakfast table where she's sitting with the two unfamiliar women. "These are Ed's sisters, Mia and Isabella. They just got in this morning."

They're around our age, maybe slightly older. They could pass for twins, one thinner with a dark bob, the other curvier with vibrant red waves. I've heard a lot about them, but they're more beautiful than I ever imagined. How did Casey get so lucky to land two cool sister-in-laws in addition to Ed?

"It's great to finally have the chance to meet you!" I shake their hands. "Where did you travel from?"

"I flew in from Houston," Isabella, the one with the short hair, says. "I was supposed to get here yesterday but my flight was canceled."

"Ugh, that's always terrible," I sympathize.

"I actually drove from South Carolina," Mia chimes in. "I live just a few hours away, in Charleston."

"Charleston looks so fun, I've always wanted to visit!" I tell her.

"Oh, you would love it. It's similar to Savannah in a lot of ways."

"Future girls' trip, maybe?" Casey grins. "No significant others allowed, of course."

"That won't be a problem for me," Isabella swears. "Brian always loves a good weekend home alone."

"So does Sierra," Mia laughs. "We both believe in healthy boundaries."

I like them already, which makes today look even better. Despite Matt and Sloan. Despite Jace. Despite the fact that I'm secretly dreading this vacation coming to an end, because I only have a faint idea of what my life may look like in the coming months.

Today is going to be good.

"I think everyone is here now," Casey says, holding up a bottle of champagne. "Should we start the day with a toast?"

Isabella and Mia pour flutes full of champagne and orange juice. I take the glasses and pass them around.

Gemma and Ada's hopeful faces fall when I give them plain orange juice instead of a mimosa. "Sorry you two."

We all gather in a circle around Casey. Gram holds her glass up. "Casey, your Papa and your parents and everyone else in the family have been looking forward to this day ever since you introduced us to Ed. The two of you make each other better. It's a pleasure to spend time with all of the women in this room today because they are dear to you, which means they are dear to me. I know Ed and Mia and Isabella wish their mom could be here with us, but trust that she will be carried with us as we celebrate. To a beautiful day!"

Gram raises her glass to take a sip and we all follow suit. Mia, Isabella, and Casey all have tears in their eyes, which they blink away with their first sips of mimosa. Casey never had the opportunity to meet her mother-in-law, but from what I can see of the rest of Ed's family, she must have been awesome.

Casey finishes her drinks and walks to her bag to rummage around for something. A few seconds later, she pulls out a white silk robe with the word "Bride" bedazzled across the back. She pulls it on and ties it securely around her t-shirt dress.

"You look adorable, truly," I joke. "But I thought you hated rhinestones?"

"Oh, shut it." She pokes me in the shoulder. "I knew you were going to say something, which makes this even sweeter."

She pulls out a second robe, this one a deep shade of purple, and passes it to me with a smug, tight-lipped smile. "For you."

I unfold the robe, reading the bedazzled word I already expected to be there: Bridesmaid. "You think you're funny, huh? I'm not even a bridesmaid!"

"Well, yes, and I know," she says sarcastically. "But Gram bought them for us. You know we can't say no to that lady."

Gram wanders up as I secure my own robe and clasps her hands together. "Just perfection! I saw them and immediately knew they were made for the two of you."

For the next hour, everyone enjoys mingling and reminiscing over mimosas and bagels. I get to know Mia and Isabella, and help Casey run through the final checklist for her wedding coordinator. Matt and Jace only pop into my mind a few different times, and I'm able to easily push them away with another drink or a new conversation.

"Nice robe," Ada says as I meander over to the window with her, Mom, and Gemma. They're pointing out different Savannah sights and discussing whether or not they're haunted.

"Thank you." I grab the bottom of the robe, flaring it out and giving her a curtsy.

Gemma and Mom are oblivious to my presence, still lost in their own conversation. I raise my eyebrows at Ada as if to ask, "How is it going?" She winks at me and smiles so big her cheeks reach her forehead. I take that to mean, "Even better than I hoped."

"Oh, shit!" Casey suddenly yells from across the suite. "Oh no. Oh no, no, no, no, no!"

Everyone rushes to her. She's kneeling beside her things again, frantically digging through her bags of toiletries and clothes. We all flood her with questions at the same time, trying to determine what is wrong, immediately thinking the worst.

Makeup spilled on her veil? She lost Ed's ring? She forgot to bring the marriage license?

"I think I forgot my shoes!" She crumples backwards onto the floor, looking defeated.

The rest of us look relieved, which seems to further exacerbate her. "Do you know how long it took me to find those shoes? They checked all of the boxes! And now they're sitting two hours away in Florida."

We all exchange glances, searching each other's eyes for possible solutions.

"I could go to Jacksonville and get them…" Trish says, checking her watch. "We have plenty of time."

"Thank you, Aunt Trish," Casey says, standing. "But there's no way I'm going to let you do that. It would take at least four hours of your day and I'd rather you be here."

"Maybe one of us has a pair you could borrow?" Katrina gestures around the room, a defeated look on her face.

"The only person with a foot as big as mine is Amry, and I doubt she has spare formal shoes with her." Casey looks down at her size ten feet. I nod to confirm her assumption. Being two of the tallest girls in our grade was eighty-percent of the reason we became friends in the first place.

"We could go find a new pair?" Mia offers. "There are plenty of shops and boutiques around. A few of us could split up to cover more ground."

Casey fans herself with a nearby napkin, pacing back and forth to consider. She checks her Apple watch. "Okay, yes. Let's see, hair and makeup will be here in just over an hour. Maybe whoever goes can text me pictures and I'll let you know which ones I like? I'll Venmo whoever buys them!"

"Perfect." Isabella searches for her purse. "Mia and I can go!"

"I'll come too!" I run to find my wallet.

"I'm so sorry about this!" Casey follows us to the door

and wraps us all in a giant hug. "I don't deserve any of you —thank you, thank you!"

"You're going to have to let us go if you want us to hurry," Mia laughs into Casey's armpit.

The three of us enter the crowded elevator, squeezing together in the back corner. "I *thought* everything was running just a bit too smoothly so far," Isabella admits. "Even with Casey's superb organizational skills."

We're almost to the exit before I realize I'm still in my bridesmaid robe. But I've already committed to the task, and carrying it will be more of a nuisance than keeping it on. I tie it a bit tighter and reach for the front door.

"WAIT!" An out-of-place yell echoes through the lobby. "Wait for me! I'm coming too!"

Casey sprints toward us, tying her hair into a ponytail as she runs. She's also still wearing her robe over her dress. At first glance she looks like someone who just rolled out of bed. She comes to a halt, looking confused at our rightfully-befuddled faces.

"You can't come with us," I tell her. "Hair and makeup will be here soon. They'll need a bride to beautify."

"Oh, there's plenty of time to get back." She pushes through us and opens the door, waiting for us to follow. "We just have to make sure I have time for another shower, because I'm a mess."

No one argues with her. Isabella and Mia look as if they're waiting for me to make the final call. "Okay, fine. But we have to *hurry*."

"Isa and I will go one way, and you two can go the other?" Mia asks. "We'll text pics to Casey. Amry, what's your number? Just in case."

I put my number into her phone and the four of us part ways. Casey hooks her arm through mine as we cross the street. A few people pause to tell her congratulations when we pass, and she thanks them with an unsure look on her face.

"How do they know I'm getting married?" she whispers.

"Are you serious?" I ask her, stopping to make a show of straightening my robe collar and then hers. The realization hits her, a deep shade of scarlet creeping into her cheeks. She walks faster, a smirk decorating her face.

"One second." She pulls me under the awning of a restaurant. We're standing in front of an ivy covered wall and she holds her phone up to take our photo. "This will definitely be one of my new favorite memories of us."

That's Casey. Always finding a way to live in the moment. I wrap my arm around her shoulders and we continue on our way, bypassing coffee shops and bars, keeping our eyes peeled for any hint of a store that may have a shoe selection. Casey's phone pings with a text from Mia and she shows me the photo before declining their first option.

"I've figured out your secret, by the way," she tells me as we power walk. "Or should I say, your secretssss."

"What are you talking about?" I ask, even though I already know.

"I know you and Matt must have split," she says, pulling me to the side of the sidewalk to avoid an oncoming family. "And I also suspect that you and my dear cousin Jace have had something going on this week."

"Casey, we are not talking about this on your wedding day!" I say, laughing nervously.

She makes a sound between a growl and a sigh. "Can you please, *please* just confirm whether I'm right or wrong?"

I stare at the cobblestones beneath my feet, taking note of Casey and I's synchronized gait. "You're not wrong. But that's all I'm saying today! And for the next week, until you're back from your honeymoon."

"I KNEW it!" She does a little skip and then falls back into step with me. "Amry, we could be related by marriage! Then you'll be like my sister and my...cousin-in-law?"

"STOP!" I yell, jokingly, but seriously enough for her to back off. "There's a lot to unpack there. I swear, we will discuss later."

"You're no fun," Casey says as her phone pings with a second photo from Isabella and Mia. "But we seriously do need to find some shoes. I love those two, but they're not quite aware of the pains of wide feet."

"Wait…" I halt, taking a serious look at our surroundings. "If we are where I think we are, there's a great little accessories shop just around the corner. Ada bought some scarves there earlier in the week!"

I take her by the wrist and pull her along behind me. The boutique sits right where I thought it was. "Yes, let's go in!"

A bell over the door announces our arrival. A few customers look up from their browsing and a muffled "Be with you in just a sec!" comes from the back room. Our silk robes are thoroughly soaked with sweat and we take a moment to bask in the air-conditioning. Casey makes a break for the shoes in the front corner and starts digging for the largest sizes.

"How are y'all today?" A voice appears behind us. I turn to see the owner's familiar face. "You visited just the other day, didn't you? Thanks for coming back! I'm Cheryl, by the way."

"Yes, with my sister! This is my best friend." Casey stands from her crouching position on the floor and Cheryl looks back and forth between our robes. "As you may be able to tell, she's getting married today. But we've run into a slight problem."

Casey explains her predicament. Cheryl listens like an investigator gathering information on a crime. Once Casey finishes her monologue, Cheryl holds up a finger and disappears into the stockroom and returns with three shoe boxes in her arms.

"I didn't ask your size, but I guessed a ten or eleven?" Casey nods. Sitting the boxes down, Cheryl removes the lids. "We *just* got these in. I haven't even put them on the floor yet. Maybe one pair will work?"

Casey bends to lift the tissue paper covering the shoes. She passively inspects the first two pairs, but jumps nearly three feet into the air when she sees the third. "These are almost exactly like the ones I bought!"

Cheryl looks elated as Casey lifts a strappy, black velvet heel from the box. She plops down onto the floor and removes her dingy Vans to put the shoe on. It fits perfectly. She slides the second one on and takes a lap around the store to test them out.

"You're having a real Cinderella moment right now," I joke.

"And Cheryl is my shoe genius fairy godmother!" She spins back to her Vans. "I'll say this now though, I refuse to be home by midnight."

I send a "mission accomplished" text to Mia and Isabella while Casey pays for her shoes. She asks Cheryl to take a picture with her for the wedding scrapbook. I snap one with my phone and rush her outside. The sun is higher in the sky when we step back onto the street and I check my phone.

"We have about seven minutes to beat hair and makeup to the suite," I tell her.

"Challenge accepted." Casey takes off down the sidewalk, robe billowing out behind her. "The only problem is I could use a snack!" She yells over her shoulder.

Why am I friends with athletic people? I suck in a deep breath and run as fast as I can to catch up to her. "I know a place we can get a good muffin!"

JACE ADAMS

I can't see you tonight without telling you that I'm not upset with you. I'm disappointed, but could never be upset with you for being honest. I need you to know that, and want us to both have a great time celebrating Casey and Ed.

CHAPTER 19

"And nowwww!" the DJ yells into the microphone. "The moment you've all been waiting for! Introducing...Mrs. and Mr. Casey and Eduardo Suarez!"

I thought Casey had been joking when she told me she threatened the DJ to say her name first in their announcement. She was obviously serious though. Good for her.

Loud electronic dance music blasts from the speakers. Casey enters the ballroom first, heading straight to the center of the dance floor where she squats down into a crouching position. Two seconds later, Ed runs in and jumps over Casey, a la elementary school leapfrog. All of the guests give a standing ovation as the couple goes straight into their first dance.

Casey's off-the-shoulder lace gown has been bustled up for the reception. I catch glimpses of her emergency wedding shoes as she and Ed twirl across the floor. Everyone in the room watches with smiles on their faces. A few intermittently reach up to dab tears from their eyes. I myself have indeed been crying since Casey emerged from her dressing room in the suite two hours ago.

The flow had then increased when Ada walked out of the bathroom twenty minutes later, adorned in the strapless burgundy dress with the slit. I was able to blame the sobs on the occasion, but those specific tears were over the shock at seeing Ada in a color other than black. A color on a dress that, combined with her elegantly-styled scarf and dramatic makeup, made her look five years older. Mom cried too.

And Gemma is still trying to pick her jaw up off of the floor.

"It's not a big deal," Ada had said, smoothing the floral scarf. "I mean, Amry got a frieken tattoo this week. She inspired me."

Mom and Ada sit to my right. Ada is watching Casey and Ed dance, her head on Mom's shoulder. Mom is running her hand over Ada's scarf, slowly and carefully so as not to pull it loose. Ada probably hasn't willingly let Mom get that close to her head in over a year. Mom catches me staring and blows me an air kiss. I catch it and pretend to eat it. She rolls her eyes at me.

Casey doesn't know it, but inviting Mom to the wedding wasn't just a polite gesture. It was the turning point for a good portion of this week's healing. For Ada and myself. As much as I love them, Jace was right when he observed that I don't give the same energy to myself that I give to them. Helping them learn to communicate without my added two cents will benefit all of us. Our relationship can be stronger than ever. It already is, and Mom has been here for less than twenty-four hours.

The first dance ends, and the newlyweds pull apart with a final kiss. Casey's dad Martin comes to the floor and makes a show of bowing to her before taking her hand for the parent dance. Isabella and Mia both come to join Ed, standing where their mother isn't able to. The three of them sway together, singing along to the song and offering each other a tissue to dab their eyes every now and then.

In a way, the three siblings remind me of Mom, Ada, and I. They are missing someone dear to them—perhaps the person that each of their hearts loved the most. But they all know that they still have the gift of each other. Ed's dad eventually comes out to join them and several wedding guests clap. I glance at Mom and Ada again, and though Dad is heavy on my mind, I'm not sad because I see him through them. He's still here in that way, and always will be.

The parent dance ends and a peppier song comes over the speakers. The DJ invites guests to treat themselves to the open bar while last-minute dinner touches are being made. Seeing as it's been a few too many hours since my last mimosa, I cross the room to join the others waiting in line beside the large ballroom windows that provide a panoramic view of Savannah sitting several stories below. Evening is setting in, bathing the distant bridge in various shades of pinks and oranges.

"Nice wedding, huh?"

I turn from the window to find Jace behind me. He's dressed in a khaki suit, his button down shirt a deep, rusty orange. His curls look different than usual, most likely held into place by some type of gel. A simple gold chain shines around his neck. I saw him across the room at the ceremony earlier, but seeing him up close is an entirely different experience. He looks like he belongs in a boy band. Scratch that, he looks like he owns the boy band. My breath catches in my throat at the mere sight of him.

I never responded to his text because I don't know what I'm doing anymore.

"Yes," I reply, finally finding my voice. "Yes, it's perfect. You look nice."

The line moves and we follow. "You...also look nice," he tells me. "Nicer than the wedding, in my opinion. I hope that's not too weird to say."

I look down at my blue wrap dress and the only pair of heels I own. I want to tell him that he can say things like that to me anytime, and I'll return the favor. Instead, I settle for a simple, "Thank you. So do you."

"When do you head home?" he asks. He hasn't looked me in the eye a single time, focusing instead on the window just past the right side of my face. His expression is dull, his eyes not quite as bright and inquisitive as they usually are. How much of that is my fault?

"Tomorrow afternoon," I say. "We'll spend the day here with Mom then drive back to Jacksonville."

There's always that moment at the end of vacation where you feel nauseous at the idea of going back to your normal life. It's crazy how a week of a new bed and a new routine can make you feel like an entirely new person. Even more crazy when you actually *are* in the process of becoming an entirely new person.

The dread of leaving weighs heavy on my shoulders. Knowing I have to pack my bags and get back on I-95 makes me feel unsettled. Knowing I have to go back to my apartment in Orlando makes me feel panicky.

Not having Southern cuisine and endless drinks at my fingertips makes me feel bored and hungry.

The thought of saying goodbye to Jace makes me want to tumble to the floor on the spot.

But none of this matters. When you're an adult you can't always live the way you want to live in the moment. You can't make the wrong timing the right timing. You have to move forward, pushing every obstacle out of the way as you go.

And in two weeks, life will be so back to normal that everything will be nothing but a memory anyway.

"How about you? When are you going back to Nashville?" I ask.

"Sunday," he says. "I extended my trip by a day. Trying to suck every last drop out of Savannah, ya know?"

Boy, do I know. It's our turn to order and I request a vodka Sprite from the bartender.

"Will you get a Savannah tattoo added to your sleeve?" I look at Jace's arm. It's covered by his suit, but I've reached the point where my memory will never forget what it looks like.

"Planning to. I just don't know exactly what I want yet." He runs a hand down his arm. The smiley I drew on his palm is still there, faded but not gone. He reaches for my wrist and pulls my arm to him. "It looks like yours is healing nicely."

A shiver runs through me at the contact. Perfectly timed, the bartender sets the drink in front of me and I use it as an excuse to pull away. My wrist buzzes with the memory of his fingers. I have far too many areas on my body that will light up with anticipation each time he comes to mind—each time I hear his name.

My drink is strong. Just strong enough to wrangle the emotions that are washing through me. The vodka beats them back down again. I should go back to my table, but as usual, something invisible is holding me next to Jace. He's been so kind to me, even after I've now verbally dismissed and walked away from him twice.

I can see in his face that he wants this—him and I. His feelings were never going to be casual. It's painfully obvious mine weren't either.

I just wish I had a substantial amount of time to figure this out.

"It looks like they're starting to serve dinner," Jace observes. "I'll talk to you later, Amry."

And then he's gone, back to his table. I watch as he takes a seat next to his grandparents—his mom's parents. They've obviously been watching us, because they wave at me as I stare in their direction. I force myself to smile and wave back.

Soon, the distance between Jace and I will be much larger than a 2,000 square foot ballroom. My chest caves in on itself. I refocus, standing up taller to confidently walk to my own seat. Casey is chatting with guests at one of the tables, and she lovingly gives me a smack on the butt as I pass by. It helpfully pulls me out of my spiral.

"Did you go to the bar for a glass of water?" Ada eyes my drink as I set it down.

"It's a vodka sprite, you child." I take another sip, peering around the floral centerpiece to look her in the eye. "Tastes like being over twenty-one."

She tries to kick me under the table but catches Mom's calf instead and begins apologizing profusely. Mom waves her off as our food arrives. Everyone at the table eyes each other's dishes, oohing and aahing over the variety of surf and turf, shrimp and grits, and vegetarian pasta. Ten minutes ago I was starving. Now I taste nothing as I fork the first bite of mashed potatoes into my mouth.

After dinner, the dance floor fills quickly. Discarded heels and suit jackets are scattered throughout the ballroom. The elegant environment is slowly dying, replaced by more alcohol, mood lighting, and nostalgic music. Mom is one of the first people on the floor, her navy blue dress flaring around her as does the electric slide with Trish and some of the other middle-aged women in the crowd.

"I'm not sure whether I should be embarrassed," Gemma says as we stand at the edge of the scene, unable to look away. "Or if I should record this and put it on YouTube."

"Same," Ada says. But she continues to grin as she watches Mom cut loose.

Mia catches my eye from her spot on the floor and spins her way over to me. "You should come dance with us!" she yells over the pounding speakers. She grabs my hand and pulls me out behind her before I can think about declining the invitation. Isabella welcomes me into their circle with a hug, and before I know it I'm matching their energy—singing and whirling and jumping like we're the only ones in the room.

"You're all having way too much fun without me!" Casey squeezes her way into the middle of us, doing a sexy move that causes Ed's eyes to go wide as he stumbles up behind her. We cheer her on, and the magnetism of the bride brings more and more people out to join us, creating a sweaty mosh of accidental bumping and toe-stomping that I'm somehow delighted to be a part of.

After a while, the 2000's throwbacks come to a halt and the DJ announces a slow dance. The change in energy leaves me disoriented and disappointed. I meander off of the floor to search for a much-needed glass of water. Gulping it down, I sit and watch couples leisurely spin around the floor. Casey and Ed stand at the center, bathed in the continuously moving colorful lights above. Off to the side, Ada and Gemma shyly clutch each other, chattering away and leaning in for a couple of innocent kisses. Ghosts glint around their necks. A younger boy runs by them and pulls Gemma's hair. She yells at him as he scurries away.

The infamous younger brother.

I look across the floor. On the other side, Jace is doing the same thing I am—sitting and watching. He feels my eyes and meets my stare. Through the constantly changing lighting and dancing couples that disturb our lines of vision, we never look away.

Then he's moving, weaving in and out of the dancers, coming to a halt in front of me.

"Can I at least have one dance?" he asks, holding out a hand.

I filter through all of the pros and cons within seconds. "I don't see why not."

He leads me to the floor and drops his palms to my waist. I wrap my fingers around his shoulders, trying to stay close enough for comfort, but not so close that we're pressed against each other. I wish I could be closer.

"I don't think I've slow danced with anyone since high school," he jokes.

"Hm," I say, thinking. "I don't think I have either."

His sleeves are rolled up, revealing the tattoos and smooth, brown skin of his forearms. Without the suit jacket, his shirt is slightly damp beneath my palms. I know I've sweat through my dress as well. Even air-conditioning can't combat dancing at a summer wedding in the South.

"Gemma and Ada look happy," he says, smiling in their direction. "They're cute together."

"The cutest," I confirm. "I'm just glad Ada fell for someone who also happens to live in Jacksonville. Otherwise, that would be a pretty doomed first relationship."

"It would be depressing, to say the least."

His Ivory soap smell floats between us. Our combined body heat is distracting. His neck is right directly in my line of vision and I want to bury my face in it. I want to hold him. I want to kiss him. I also want to run away.

"Jace, I'm sorry that we couldn't figure this out," I say, staring at the floor beneath our moving feet. "I am glad that we got to reconnect though."

He breathes deeply through his nose and for a

moment, I don't think he's going to respond. Then, finally, "Me too, Am. You made this vacation...sweeter than anyone else could have."

We finish the dance in silence. Our hands linger on each other for a moment after the song ends, then fall away. There isn't much more time left in the night, and we both know it. The cake will be cut, Casey and Ed will leave, and this Savannah, wedding-vacation bubble will officially burst.

"Thanks..." It's not what I want to say, but it's all I can formulate.

"Anytime." Jace wraps the curl hanging next to my face around his finger. "You have my number. Keep in touch. I'm always available if you need to talk. About anything."

"Same for you," I tell him. "Have a safe trip home. Don't drive too fast."

"Never," he replies, face coming closer to mine. His lips brush my forehead, and then I'm standing alone in the center of an empty, silent dance floor. The overhead lights flick back on as he walks away to join the crowd around the wedding cake.

The rest of the evening is a blur. I go back and forth between truly enjoying my time celebrating Casey and Ed, and dissociating and questioning every decision I have made with Jace—every decision I have made in life that brought me to this moment. This moment where I can't stop questioning the path for my future. This moment where I'm stuck between doing what I think is the best for myself, and wondering why I'm not more sure of my decision to let Jace go.

I eat cake. I take photos with Mia and Isabella and Casey. I chat with almost every member of the Adams family, and learn the names of the younger kids I've never met. I hug Casey and Ed goodbye before we send them on their married way. I cry—a lot, for both happy and sad reasons.

I don't let myself search the room for Jace.

"What a lovely night," Mom says as we exit the hotel after collecting our things from the suite. "I'm so glad I was able to come."

"It was perfect. Everything Casey and Ed wanted." I force a smile at Mom. I'm parched, and my feet hurt so badly I couldn't stand to put my shoes back on. I carry my heels in my free hand, the sidewalk warm and rough against my bare feet. I'm too tired to be embarrassed about it.

Ada and Gemma join us, followed by Trish. "I guess we should make a run for the water taxi," she jokes.

"Yeah, I'm going to settle for a walk," Gemma says, leading the way up Bull Street.

"Are you okay, honey?" Mom asks quietly as the other three walk ahead. "I saw you dancing with Jace. If you're not ready to talk about it, I understand. But as your mom, I have to ask."

She knows me well. I'm not ready to talk about it. But I *need* to. She didn't push me when I gave her the brief summary of Jace and I's week, so I don't expect her to do it now. And who better to give advice than the woman who knows me best?

"I don't know where my head is at right now," I tell her, truthfully. "I'm torn between giving myself the alone time I need, and taking the chance on a connection I didn't even know was possible until a few days ago."

"Why can't you have both?" Her question is a blunt one; one that I haven't allowed myself to ask.

"How would that even be possible?" I heave my bag up further onto my shoulder. My feet are starting to feel sensitive against the jagged sidewalk, matching the rawness of my attitude. "I don't want to be that girl who is in a new relationship a month after she split with her boyfriend of ten years. Especially when that relationship ended partly because I've been a real loser since Dad died."

Mom stops dead in her tracks, grabbing my arm to hold me there with her. Her expression is steely. "Amry Jane Phillips, why would you say something like that about yourself? You have been *grieving*. Maybe you could have controlled some of the controversy with Matt, but it is NOT your fault that he has the emotional span of a brick."

Snorting, I clap a hand to my mouth, causing my bag to fall back down to my elbow. I don't think she meant to be funny, but her speech at least jarred me out of my self-pity. Her stern face slowly disappears as she bursts into laughter with me, then pulls me into a hug right in the middle of the street.

"What are you two doing back there?!" Ada yells from ahead. "We are trying to catch a boat, you know!"

Mom releases me and we continue our march towards the river. "I honestly don't know where she gets her sassi-ness from," Mom says. She can't see the "Seriously?" face I make at her.

"Okay, so maybe I'm not a loser," I continue, taking a deep breath as we reach the top of the Death Stairs. "But shouldn't I still give myself a period of alone time? I can't pull a new man into the mess that is currently me."

"You're viewing this as an all-or-nothing decision," Mom retorts, her legs shaking as she focuses on the climb down. "God, this is frightening...Um, but what I mean is, you can get to know Jace without making a serious commitment to him right away. He doesn't even live in the same state. Wouldn't that be a positive if you wanted to take things slow?"

The soles of my feet are officially irritated. I swear

under my breath that I will never use these stupid stairs again. "I don't know, Mom. No solution seems like the correct one."

We join the others at the base, relief washing over me as my feet meet the coolness of River Street's smooth stones. Trish pulls a bottle of water from her bag and offers some to the rest of us. "This is better than a gym membership, I swear!"

The taxi dock is close, and I can't wait for a cool shower and a night with one of my books. That's the one type of romance that never lets me down. Maybe written romance will be enough to last me for the rest of my life? I'll make it a challenge.

"Well, Am," Mom picks up where we left off. "I guess you're just truly in the middle of one of those 'wrong time, right place' scenarios. They're never any fun but—"

"What did you just say?" My legs stop working.

Mom looks back at me, confused. "I said it's a 'wrong time, right place' conundrum?"

My heart is beating in my ears. I'm thrown back into a memory of Jace and I after the rehearsal dinner. *It may be the wrong time, but it's the right place. Look around you, Amry…*

It's a sign.

I drop my things to the ground, shoving my shoes at Mom. "Can you please take my stuff back to the hotel?"

"What?" She's looking at me like I've just sprouted horns. "I don't know if I can carry all of—"

"ADA!" I yell, attracting stares from some of the late-night tourists on River Street. "Come here! I need you to help Mom carry my stuff."

She trots back to us, also looking at me like I've lost my mind. "Carry your own shi—"

"Please!" I say to them. "I'll meet you back in the room, but I have to go do something. NOW."

I don't wait for an answer. For the second time today, I'm sprinting down an uneven cobblestone street. Somehow, my feet no longer hurt. I only hesitate for a second before I begin running up the Death Stairs, causing a young couple to press against the railing to avoid colliding with me.

"Am, you may want your shoes!" Mom yells. I wave her off without looking back.

It's the right place. It's the right place! I don't have to say no to this feeling. It's the right place!

I'm out of breath by the time I reach the first crosswalk. The "don't walk" symbol glows bold and red. "Watch it!" someone yells at me as I push through the group on the corner and dash in front of oncoming traffic. A horn beeps and I know it's directed at me, but I don't slow down. Jace is my destination, and I can only hope he's still there.

If not, I'll have to grovel at his hotel room door, and all of this uncharacteristic running will have been for nothing.

I want Jace in my life.

The thought comes clearly, no strings or rebuttals attached. I repeat the phrase in my mind, ignoring every opportunity to find an if, and, or but about it. Right now, as I run barefoot through the streets of one of the country's oldest cities, I know what I want. I refuse to talk myself out of it.

I want Jace in my life!

Restaurant servers fill the sidewalk, pulling patio furniture inside for closing. A couple of them stop to stare at me, whispering to each other. Normally this would make me self-conscious, but I have no time to devote to that. They shrug at each other as I run around them, then go back to their tasks.

The hotel is in my line of vision. My breath comes in

short, desperate bursts. I beg my lungs to please get me a bit closer. Patrons on bar balconies pause their conversations and stop to point at me. Some of them laugh, but most just look behind me to see if I'm running from anything in particular. "Run, Forrest, run!" a random guy yells, and it feels appropriate, because now I know that famous movie was actually filmed right here in Savannah.

The doors are just a few yards away. *I'm going to make it!*

"Amry?!" A surprised voice floats to me from the opposite side of the street. "Amry, what's wrong?"

I look over, and there he is. Jace is at the edge of the sidewalk, looking both ways before he crosses the street to meet me. Reassurance floods my brain as I stop, putting my hands on my knees to take the most satisfying breath I have ever breathed. Adrenaline courses through me, and for a brief second I think I understand why there is such a thing as a runner's high.

Jace reaches me, placing his hands on my shoulders to steady me. He searches my face, looking concerned. "What are you doing?" He notices my bare feet. "And where the hell are your shoes?"

"You were right!" I spit out between breaths, reaching up to wipe my brow and tuck my windblown hair behind my ears. "You're right. I had to come tell you."

"Tell me what?" He maneuvers us out of the center of the sidewalk and I collapse against an iron fence.

"Our timing is wrong. But the place is right!" I stare him dead in the eyes. "It took me a bit to realize that, but I know it's true. There's a reason we came together this week."

Jace says nothing. His expression is somewhere between worry and a smile. My bravery is fading fast, and I wonder if I've pushed him away one too many times. I can't say I would blame him if he rejected me and sent me back on my barefoot way right now.

"Do you mean that?" he finally asks.

"Yes!" Feeling hopeful, I reach up to place my hands on either side of his face. "I'm not saying that I want to start planning *our* wedding tomorrow, but I won't be able to live with myself if we both go home and do nothing but send each other friendly, sporadic texts."

He's silent again, returning my stare as people skirt around us on the sidewalk, whispering. I can't believe that I'm involved in such a dramatic display. But I've never felt this desperate for someone to hear me.

After what seems like an eternity, he places his hands on top of mine, dragging them down my arms and sides until he reaches my waist. A welcome shudder takes over my drenched body. I may die if he doesn't say something, or at least pull me closer.

"That's all I've wanted to hear you say for the past two days," he admits.

Relieved, I fall forward onto his chest.

"Amry," he says into my hair. "I promise I won't pressure you to rush this. I won't pressure *us* to rush this. I just want us to try, and if I'm correct, trying will get us to where we need to be."

Unable to live any longer without his mouth on mine, I make the first move. He kisses me back with an urgency that I haven't yet felt from him. He pushes me harder against the fence, covering every inch of my mouth and neck with his lips. I run my fingers through his hair (confirmed, gelled), then drop my hands to rest on his lower back. My emotional balance feels restored, the regret I thought I may feel from admitting my feelings for Jace nowhere in sight.

After a few minutes of making out, and a few whistles

from passerby, Jace pulls away and checks his watch. "We've missed the last taxi. Not that I think you could make it back there in your condition, anyway," he jokes, glancing at my feet.

"Uber it is?" I suggest, and he requests a car.

This Uber ride is the complete opposite of our previous one. Instead of distance, we're pressed together in the middle of the back seat. Instead of silence, we are both asking a million questions about the upcoming months. Will I stay in Orlando or move back to Jacksonville? How often should we visit each other? How much do we share with other people about our developing relationship?

Our driver dumps us out without saying a single word, most likely annoyed by our cheerful new romance. But I don't care, and Jace gives him a good tip anyway. I add the ride to my list of things I already plan to Venmo him money for. That is one thing I will still continue to insist upon.

We climb into the elevator together for what will most likely be the last time. No one joins us on the trip up, and honestly, we prefer it that way. Last time I made out in an elevator, I was unknowingly only minutes away from the blow that would change the path of my life. Now, I'm amidst the journey, hopeful and full of positive anticipation for the future.

I stop by my room to catch Mom and Ada up (and wash my feet) before making a final walk down to Jace's room. He greets me with a plastic cup of hotel wine, and we toast to the week that I secretly already know Casey will take credit for for the rest of our lives. Jace discards our empty cups and heads to the bathroom to start us a shower.

When he returns, he finds me on my hands and knees, looking underneath the bed.

"What are you doing?" he asks, dropping to the floor beside me. "Did you lose an earring or something?"

"Oh, no," I say, sitting back onto my heels. "I was just checking for any bras that may not be mine."

We burst into laughter at the same time. He takes me by the waist, pulling us both up to our feet. "You're funny. And that's only one of the things I like about you."

"I'm glad you appreciate my sense of humor." I press my lips to his bare chest.

He makes a show of untying my wrap dress, sliding it down my arms and tossing it onto the bed. "Let me show you exactly how much I appreciate that, and every other part of you."

Then he takes me by the hand and leads me to the bathroom, where a steamy shower is waiting to wash our perfect Savannah evening away.

CASEY ADAMS

Amry and Jace, sitting in a tree. K-I-S-S-I-N-G.

Or should I say kissing in the street? Mama saw you guys and all I have to say is I KNEW IT!

AMRY

Shut up and go on your honeymoon!

CHAPTER 20

"Keep, toss, or donate?" Mom holds up one of my many ratty white t-shirts and looks at me expectantly.

"Keep," I confirm. "That's one of my faves."

"Are you serious?" Ada looks up from her spot on my apartment floor, where she's elbow deep in sorting through my sock drawer. "That thing looks like you bought it in 2005."

"I would say it was more like 2012." I choose to ignore the sarcastic undertone of her statement. Mom folds the shirt and tosses it into the already overflowing "casual clothing" box. Ada returns to her routine of matching socks, pitching the occasional stray spares into a garbage bag next to her.

I've been home from Savannah for three weeks. The first few days back in Orlando weren't so bad. I had been distracted by diving back into my work routine, and dreamily reliving every cherished vacation memory. Especially the Jace-filled ones. But by the beginning of week two, I was antsy. And a few days after that, impossibly lonely. My normal options of meeting Matt for dinner or spending hours in TJ Maxx with Sloan were no longer possibilities.

That's why, three days ago, I called Mom and admitted that I'm finished with Orlando. Then I contacted the apartment office to break my lease. There's nothing here for me anymore, and I want to go home. I don't think Jacksonville will be forever, but I know it's where I belong at this point in time. It's where I've belonged since we lost Dad.

"You have so much more stuff than I thought!" Mom pulls the final item of clothing from my closet and shuts the doors before moving on to help Ada sort through my dresser. "We'll have to get you a storage unit until your apartment is ready. That won't be a problem though."

"Yeah, it's definitely not going to fit at home with all of Mom's junk," Ada comments. Mom grabs a pair of socks from Ada's pile and tosses them back at her. They bounce off of Ada's shoulder and she retaliates by throwing them in my direction. I'm focused on sorting through a stack of old magazines and the socks hit me right between the eyes.

"Hey now!" I retrieve the socks, standing to walk them back to their pile. "You two are supposed to be helping me pack, not inciting violence."

I gaze around the bedroom, taking in the newly blank walls and empty surfaces. I've accepted that this place can no longer be my home, but I'm still going to miss it. There are lots of memories here; visits from Mom and Ada, Dad helping me map out my gallery wall on move-in day, occasional sleepovers with Matt, binge reading in bed while the breeze flows in through the open balcony door. It will be difficult, but I really want to avoid bitterness towards any of those moments. I want to tuck them into a back corner of my brain and remember them fondly for what they were.

"Should we take a snack break?" I bring myself back to the present and meander over to the bedroom door. Mom and Ada follow me to the kitchen where I pour us all a glass of water and prepare a plate of cheese and crackers. We eat standing around the island, elbows propped comfortably on the counter.

"What time are you meeting with Matt and Sloan?" Mom adds a second cracker to the top of her cheddar, creating a tiny sandwich.

"I wish never," I say with a sigh, checking the time on the microwave. "3:30 though. I need to leave soon."

The uncomfortable feeling of panic creeps over me. Seeing Sloan and Matt is the last thing I want to do. But sometimes what you want to do and what you need to do are two different things. Do I think they deserve closure? No, not really. But I do think *I* deserve closure. That's why I've agreed to meet them for coffee before the moving truck comes tomorrow and I officially put my time here behind me.

"Remember my advice." Mom chases her cracker with a sip of water. "Don't let them run the conversation. You're the one in charge here."

Yes. I'm the one in charge. I'm capable of saying goodbye to these relationships in style. I won't let them turn the tables and place blame on me. I won't leave feeling guilt that shouldn't exist.

God, I hope I'm able to actually pull this off.

"Are you going to confront Sloan about the Google review?" Mom pushes further.

"I haven't decided yet."

It hasn't been proven, but ever since the possibility popped into my head that Sloan was responsible for the review, I haven't been able to let the idea go. It makes sense—the timing of it all. It appeared just a few weeks before Matt and I's anniversary. Perhaps it was an act of jealousy?

Then, it disappeared shortly after the phone call in Savannah. The email from Google said it was removed by the reviewer. Maybe at that point, she was looking to relieve some of the guilt. It would also explain why there were no added details; why I wasn't able to trace it back to any of my clients.

It's a painful thought. How much of our friendship was a sham? As gross as it is, I miss her. I wish it *had* been a barista.

"Can I *please* come?" Ada leans further across the island, a pleading look in her eyes. "I'll sit at a different table! I'll be your spy and make sure they don't try any funny business." She makes a fist and smashes it into her other palm.

"If you were slightly more intimidating I'd consider it," I joke. "I'll be ok by myself. Honestly, I don't plan to stay for more than twenty minutes."

The clock moves too quickly and it's time to leave before I know it. Ada clears our dishes and moves to the living room. She flops down onto the couch, absorbed in responding to texts that I know are from Gemma based on the smile on her face. Mom passes my keys and purse to me before wrapping me in a hug.

"Once this is over you'll feel so much lighter," she says into my ear.

It's been raining off and on all day, but my car's interior is still roughly 3,000 degrees. I opt to roll the windows down, enjoying the feeling of the light mist on my face and arms. It will surely make my hair a frizzy mess, but I don't care. Matt and Sloan are two people I'm no longer trying to impress. Moving forward, I'm focusing more on my wants and needs. And what I currently want is to feel the afternoon Florida shower on my skin.

We've agreed to meet at my favorite coffee shop. Having the comfort of my favorite latte will make things the slightest bit more enjoyable and easy to manage. I also secretly love that they both have to come to my side of town. Normally I would agree to go out of my way for them. The final traffic light turns red, catching me just before my turn. I take the opportunity to text Jace.

AMRY

I'm almost there. Wish me luck!

The light changes to green and I turn into the busy parking lot, claiming the first available spot. Matt's white Acura is parked closer to the front. I wonder if Sloan rode with him, and realize that I have no idea if they're officially a couple or not. Her car doesn't seem to be in any of the other spaces. My phone buzzes as I reach for the door handle with a shaking hand.

JACE ADAMS

You've got this! I'm proud of you. Call me when you're finished! Tell Matt I say hi. ;)

Maybe I'll do just that if the occasion arises. I make my way to the entrance, legs quaking beneath me. Remembering Mom's words, I hold my head a little higher and feel immediately more confident. This is for me. After this I can move on without feeling burdened.

One of the usual baristas greets me as I enter and I smile back at him. Scanning the cafe for Matt and Sloan, I spot them at a table in the front corner. Their hands are joined on top of the table and Sloan pulls hers into her lap when she sees me. I order my latte, not caring that I'm making them wait, then head in their direction. Sloan stands as I approach, nervous energy that I didn't know was possible for her radiating from every pore.

"Amry, hey!" She lowers back into her chair as I take my seat across from them. "How are you?"

Matt stays silent, piercing me with a neutral gaze. I force myself to hold eye contact with him as I respond. "I'm pretty great, actually. How are y'all?"

"We're good," Sloan answers for both of them, toying with the buttons on her navy polo shirt. Matt's Ralph Lauren t-shirt is also navy and I can't help but wonder if they matched intentionally. The choice wouldn't be out of character for either of them.

Awkward silence takes over but I refuse to break it. I sip my latte, looking at Sloan, then Matt, then the ceiling. Matt speaks for the first time. "This is...weird. But I knew it would be."

"I won't argue with that," I agree. "So, you two are together then? Like in a real relationship?"

"Yeah," they say at the same time, Sloan's voice full of hidden happiness where Matt's is less enthusiastic. I sense trouble in paradise already, and part of me feels sorry for Sloan. At least until she opens her mouth again.

"It's almost like it was meant to be!" She links her arm through his, grin disappearing from her face when she meets my eyes and remembers the full history of their doomed love affair.

"Yeah!" I say with fake excitement. "More meant to be than our friendship!"

Hurt creeps over her face and I almost feel bad. But I'm done with the small talk.

"How long?" I ask.

"What?" Matt responds.

"How long were you together behind my back?"

My question grabs the attention of a few nearby customers. I can tell they're trying to secretly eavesdrop but I don't mind. I need to know the answer so I can accept it. Then I need an apology. Then I can wish them the best, and leave.

They exchange a worried glance. "It started at last year's office holiday party," Sloan says.

"The hooking up, or the flirting?" I prod.

Another look passes between them. "The hooking up," Matt confesses. "But flirting had been happening for a while before that at work."

My partially digested cheese and cracker snack sits heavy in my stomach. It's almost August, which means Matt and Sloan have most likely been crushing on each other without me knowing for almost a year now. And having sex for not much less than that. It would still hurt even if it had only been for a couple of months before we broke up, but the longer time period makes me feel stupid. It makes me feel like *they* thought I was stupid, laughing behind my back as they ripped each other's clothes off.

I had been at that holiday party with the two of them. When could they have possibly found the chance? Where had I been? It would have had to happen *at* the party, because I stayed the night at Matt's after. I suppose it doesn't really matter now, but it would have also been nice if one of them had the conscience to be honest with me about it sooner.

"That's a long time." I fiddle with my straw, slumping further back into my chair.

"Please know it was an accident." Matt pulls his arm from Sloan's grip. "We didn't plan for everything to happen like this."

"No, Matt." My gaze snaps back to his. "It would have been an accident if you'd stopped after the first time you flirted, or if you'd come to me after your first kiss. I would have been upset, pissed even, to learn that my boyfriend was in love with one of my best friends. But at least I wouldn't have felt like an idiot."

"You're not an idiot," Sloan says softly. "We tried to stop."

"Oh, come off it, Sloan. You both think everyone is an idiot." I try to keep my voice down but it's easier said than done. "You have a lot to learn about dealing with people's emotions. Because unlike the two of you, most of us feel things!"

They're silent. I'm breathing heavier than usual, gazing around the room to calm myself down. I make accidental eye contact with the girl at the next table, and it may be a figment of my imagination, but I swear she winks at me encouragingly. It gives me the boldness to continue.

"Look, I don't want this to be some drawn out, dramatic ordeal," I tell them. "I've had several weeks to work through this, and I'm fine. I'm going to be okay. More than okay."

Jace's face enters my mind and the pain in my stomach eases.

"So, what now?" Sloan asks. Matt's green eyes are filled with the same question.

"I'm moving back to Jacksonville," I announce. "I leave tomorrow. And I'll be honest with the both of you, this is probably the last time we'll speak."

"Are you sure?" Matt looks taken aback, like he's just now accepting I'm not going to be in his life in any capacity.

"Positive."

"I am sorry, Amry." Sloan looks like she might cry. The shine in her eyes, though authentic, seems out of place.

"I'm sorry too." Matt presses his hands into the table so hard that his knuckles turn white. "For everything."

"Is there anything *else* you'd like to apologize for?" I pry, staring directly at Sloan.

She looks genuinely confused. "I don't think so?"

Something in her expression makes me back off. *Maybe she didn't write the review.*

Oh well, that's no longer a problem on my list anyway.

The apologies have been secured, and with them, I'm ready to move forward. I take a final look at two of them. They've played very different roles in my life, but I'll always remember them the same way—successful, orderly, and serious—yet also dear to me for a large portion of my past. I stand, collecting my purse and remaining coffee.

"I have to go," I tell them. "But thank you for the apology. And good luck with work and everything, seriously."

I turn away before either of them can reply, feeling freshly invigorated as I float out of the coffee shop. Jogging to my car, I fumble for my keys, excited to get inside and call Jace. I open the door and freeze with one foot in the floorboard. Matt is running through the parking lot toward me. He stops at my window and I raise my eyebrows at him.

"Are you really moving?" He dabs at the sweat forming on his upper lip. "Is this really it?"

"Why wouldn't it be?" I ask. He balks at my question.

"Well, I don't know. It just feels weird to think about you not being here."

"I guess you're gonna have to get used to it." The statement is so direct I can't believe I've said it. I go to lower myself into the driver's seat. Matt grabs my hand, staring down at my arm.

"Is that a *tattoo*?" He squints, looking back and forth between the ink pot and my face.

"Mmm-hmmm." I pull my hand away from him. "Cool, huh?"

"I guess…" He can't hide the judgmental look on his face though. I wave at him and try to close the car door.

"Amry, wait!" He holds on to the outside handle. "Surely we will see each other again? Who knows, maybe our paths will cross and there will still be a future for us at the end of all of this."

"Yeah, I don't think so." It takes everything in me not to laugh in his face. "Jace Adams said to tell you hello, by the way."

He blocks me from closing the door a second time. "There's one more thing I have to tell you, Am."

"Did you find more of my stuff at your apartment or something?"

"No…" He keeps a firm grip on the door. "But I did write that review."

It's the first part of the whole interaction that I haven't been prepared for. I feel the confident look slip off of my face. The corners of my mouth turn down. My shoulders slump towards the steering wheel. The nasty words of the review—*his* review—come back to haunt me once more.

"How could you do that?" My voice breaks. "It was so…mean! You watched me go crazy for weeks!"

"I just needed to know you could still feel something. I needed to know you could still be passionate about something," Matt says. "You lost *you* when your Dad died. It was just an experiment. To see how you would react. I'm sorry."

"That's the dumbest fucking thing I've ever heard. But hey, if that's the best way to comfort your next grieving girlfriend in the future, go for it. Relationships aren't experiments, Matt! Have a nice life."

I slam the door, jamming the key into the ignition and

starting the car. Matt lingers outside of my window, finally moving out of the way as I begin to reverse. I take one last look at him in my rearview mirror before exiting the parking lot. He's still staring in my direction, looking away only when Sloan walks up beside him.

My first instinct is to cry. But the tears refuse to come. After a few deep breaths, I find a smile creeping its way onto my face instead.

It's all over.

I have closure. The answer about the review is not what I expected, but I still have it. I can move on with absolutely no qualms.

I connect to bluetooth, tapping Jace's contact as I merge onto the highway. He answers on the first ring. "Hey!" His voice sends shivers down my spine. "You did it! How did it go?"

"You may not believe this, but I was kind of a badass…" I say excitedly.

"I completely believe it because you *are* a badass." He listens as I tell him about the interaction, interjecting only with sounds of approval to hype me up.

"How's your day?" I ask after I finish my story. "What are you up to?"

"Now that you ask, I was kind of hoping you could come pick me up?" There's a playful edge to his question.

"Huh?"

"I'm at Orlando International," he says. "I thought you and your family could use a hand moving your things tomorrow."

"Don't mess with me, Jace!" I tune in, paying closer attention to the background noise on his end. The unmistakable sound of a plane taking off fills the speaker. My already heightened mood ascends with it.

"I'm outside of terminal B. Hurry, I can't wait to kiss you!"

"Were you in cahoots with Mom and Ada on this?" I ask even though I already know the answer.

"You'll never know." He fakes an evil laugh. "Drive safe. I'll see you soon."

The call ends and I flip a u-turn, trying my best not to drive full speed in the direction of the airport. Traffic grows thicker and thicker. I tap my fingers on the steering wheel to keep myself from exploding out of excitement. Miraculously, I find the correct terminal without getting lost. I drive slowly along the pickup area, searching the crowd for the only face I want to see.

His curls catch my eye first. I slam into park, bolting out of the driver's seat. He meets me at the back of my car, all freckles and toothy grin and bouncy hair. His lips find mine, and it feels so good that I don't know how I survived the past three weeks without him. Let alone how I'm going to survive the foreseeable future of long-distance dating. But if this is how we get to greet each other every few weeks, I'll take it.

"Stay in your car! No parking!" A gruff security officer stalks toward us. We grab Jace's suitcase and scurry to our seats, laughing. Jace places his hand on my thigh as we drive, filling me in on the details of his surprise.

"How long will you be in Florida?" I ask.

"Just a few days," he replies. "I'll fly out of Jacksonville on Tuesday. That way you have the alone time you need for your therapy appointment on Wednesday."

"We have to do something fun tonight!" I tell him, thrilled that he remembered to take my new mental health endeavors into account. "Before Mom and Ada put you to work tomorrow."

"I have a few ideas." We catch a redlight. Jace leans

over to me with a mischievous look in his eyes. He brushes his lips against mine before trailing kisses down my neck, ending at my collar bone.

"Oh yeah?" I don't want him to pull away, but unfortunately I'm still operating a motor vehicle.

"Ada and I were thinking, maybe a ghost tour?" His eyes twinkle with pride at the joke.

"Screw you," I laugh, picking up speed in the direction of my apartment.

I don't say it out loud, but I think he already knows that I would do another ghost tour for him. I'm quickly learning that I would go anywhere for him. And when the time is right—when *my* time is right—I'll prove it.

ADA'S PRIVATE ANXIETY THOUGHTS

(SERIOUSLY...NO ONE WILL EVER SEE THESE.)

August 5, 2019

I can't believe school starts next Monday.

Last year, I spent the final week of summer feeling so anxious that I pulled almost nonstop. This year, I'm almost 100% sure that I'll be stepping into those hallways knowing that I haven't pulled since returning home from Savannah in June.

Well, I guess that's not completely true. I have pulled some, but if you could see the amount of new hair on my head, you would think otherwise! I've even started going scarf-less around the house sometimes. Mom says my new growth is as soft as a baby chick. I told her that's lame, but I do love the proud look in her eyes.

In our session the other day, I asked Dr. Reilly a question that has been bothering me. I wanted to know: Should I feel guilty that getting my first girlfriend seems to be the solution to all of my problems? Shouldn't I have been able to make this progress myself?

Because as much as I love (yes, love!) Gemma, I can't

help but think this. How am I supposed to be a proud, up-and-coming independent woman if I can't help myself?

Anyway, his answer was: She isn't the solution to all of your problems, and you have made this progress yourself.

I didn't believe him at first, but then he laid it out for me. He pointed out, Gemma's encouragement is part of the solution, but not THE solution. Gemma isn't physically following me around, pulling my hand away from my scalp. She may be the puzzle piece I needed to make progress, but I'm still the one who is making the decision to improve. I'm still the one in control.

That's the idea that I'm carrying with me into my senior year. Inspiration and encouragement may come from outside sources, but I'm still the one in control—of all areas of my life. I'm hopeful that this is the knowledge that will help me remove the negative stigma from old challenges, and face new challenges as they come.

And they will come. Gemma and I have been open about our relationship all summer, so a lot of kids already know. More are going to find out. Some will probably say ignorant things. Others will want to know why someone like Gemma is with the shy girl who wears scarves. But we both are who we are, and we're ready to own it.

Changing subjects, Amry moved back to Jacksonville. She's staying with Mom and I for a couple of more weeks, just until her new apartment is ready. I know she wants her own place for her independence, but I secretly wish she would stay here with us. Almost every night this summer has been a memorable one. We watch a lot of movies. We go to the arts market every weekend. Mom bakes so, so many cookies. Gemma comes over and we play Rummy, the only game that ever used to get Dad fired up.

I don't want it to end.

I know it has to, though. If not when Amry moves to

her apartment, then definitely in a year's time when she decides to move to Nashville to be closer to Jace. She won't say that option out loud yet because she's too private, but my room is right next to hers. I can't help but overhear some of their late-night Facetime conversations.

I wonder how this summer would have turned out if Matt hadn't cheated on Amry— if she had found someone else to go with her to Savannah. I'm not sure any other place would have made a lot of things clear for me. No other place would have led me to Gemma, or repaired Mom and I's relationship, or opened my eyes to my dream college. No other place would have opened my kickass sister's eyes to everything that she deserves— or made her get a frieken tattoo. (A paranormal influence, I'm sure of it.)

No other place is Savannah. Period.

ACKNOWLEDGMENTS

Phew. I'm allowing myself a moment to take a giant breath, because what a wonderful whirlwind this has been. You don't truly understand the amount of work that goes into publishing a debut novel until you're in the thick of it. Like any other writer, I've been dreaming of this moment for what feels like forever. The final product is only a reality because of the help I've had along the way.

First, a massive thanks to all the people in my life who have assisted in cultivating my love for books and story-telling over the years. To my parents and all of my grand-parents, thank you for encouraging my love for books. To my past teachers and educators, thank you for expanding my knowledge and pointing out my writing potential. To my friends who also love reading, thank you for being there to swap books and gush with me over *Twilight* and beyond.

My first draft would still be sitting half-finished without the love and patience of my husband. Slade, thank you for always telling me to keep going when I would write myself into a corner or jump too deep into the waters of compari-son. Thank you for listening to me ramble about plots and publishing and other things that probably felt like a foreign language to you. You've always been in my corner, and I know you'll continue to stay there for every book moving forward.

Mama, Aunt Nancy, Shelby, Taylor, Jess, and Anja—thank you for powering through my first draft and giving me the feedback it desperately needed. How lucky am I to have women in my life who I can trust so dearly with my work? Even after the first draft, you've all remained to provide honest advice, celebrate little milestones, and generally cheer me on as *Pulled to You* has transformed into its final form.

I can't continue without another special thank-you to my mom. Mama, your eyes are always the first on my projects. You're my sounding board, my biggest fan, and my best friend. You hype me up when I need it, and talk me down when I find myself in a spiral of negativity. There's no one else I would trust more with my creative ideas. I love you!

To Britt at Paperback Proofreader, thank you for doing such an excellent, thorough job of proofreading and beta reading. That was a step I was incredibly nervous for, but I couldn't have found a kinder, more knowledgeable person for the job. Not to mention, your Instagram feed is heaven, and sometimes I look at it just to feel a bit more relaxed.

Lorissa, thank you for giving Pulled to You new life with this amazing cover. I had no idea what direction I wanted to go, and it's like you read my mind! I'm in love.

Kristen, thank you for always taking the utmost care with formatting all of the new editions of my books. Forever thankful for your knowledge, advice, and attention to detail.

Finally, thank you to everyone else (in real life and online) who has shown support as I've shared more and more about this release. So many of you have shared my posts, waited patiently for pre-orders, and remained curious about the project. You've all had my back, and I feel incredibly lucky.

ABOUT THE AUTHOR

Miranda's earliest memory of writing goes back to a third-grade story competition, where she wrote about a cat and a horse who became best friends. Spoiler alert: it was bad and she didn't win. She's almost over it now.

These days, Miranda writes contemporary romance novels. She lives in Florida, where she works in the travel industry and dreams about living somewhere with seasons. She hates raisins, and would put her life on the line for a good chocolate chip cookie.

www.ingramcontent.com/pod-product-compliance
Lightning Source LLC
Chambersburg PA
CBHW030652260626
47157CB00007B/2608